THE END

P.A DOUGLAS & DANE HATCHELL

SEVERED PRESS
HOBART TASMANIA

THE END

Copyright © 2016 P.A Douglas & Dane Hatchell
Copyright © 2016 by Severed Press

WWW.SEVEREDPRESS.COM

ISBN: 978-1-925493-65-8

Author Note: This edition of The End is the extended preferred version. Although places and names in this story may depict real people and places, this book and the contents therein are fiction. Acknowledgements: I just wanted to thank everyone at Severed Press for the opportunity to give this book the due justice it truly deserves, and to Dane Hatchell for tackling it with me.

PROLOGUE

Systematically taking each step as if it might be her last if she let her guard down, Sergeant Ashley Fox moved forward through the large, abandoned Sears building. Aisle after aisle housed the latest of civilization's treasures. Ominous shadows grew and stretched out to reach her in the fading light attached to her M-4 rifle.

The moans and endless taunts of the undead lingering outside buzzed slightly above the eerie silence. Despite the seemingly countless numbers surrounding the building, they were the least of her concern. And though she had been trained to face the harshest conditions in a war situation, there was always the element of the unknown that worried her the most. The *unknown* presenting itself in this moment broke the paradigm of what humanity knew about death. And since death had violated its eons-old rules, she didn't know if she was capable of succeeding in her mission.

Behind her, Corporal Russell Chadwick limped along, doing his best to keep up. Only minutes after breaching the building, fate gave him the short draw of straws. Two ghouls had leaped out from around a corner, surprising both him and Ashley.

Not following protocol, she had stepped into the attackers' line of sight before clearing the area. Chadwick instinctively put himself between her and the nearest putrid pus-bag and knocked it to the ground.

Before she was able to get a clear headshot, the other zombie fell on top of Chadwick—biting off a solid chunk on the backside of the soldier's neck. He quickly turned with pistol in hand, shooting the zombie in the head as it chewed his flesh, lips flapping. He snuffed the other one out with a single shot before Ashley even had a chance to react.

"You're bleeding! Damn it. I shouldn't have been so careless. How bad is it?" she asked, a dull pain in her chest tightened around her heart.

He had dismissed her with a wave of his hand, and pointed for her to lead the way.

Chadwick now followed with one hand tightly covering the wound. This only added to the misery he suffered from a sprained ankle the day before, keeping him from taking the lead.

He couldn't have lost that much blood, but he was beginning to lose some color. Ashley didn't know what she should do as she played the predicament over in her head that led them to the store in the first place.

A shape barely recognizable against the darkness moved from an aisle a few rows ahead. She instantly froze and strained like hell to make out the figure. Sure, she could have squeezed off a few rounds and asked questions later. But she had already made that mistake two days before. An old woman had reached out in desperation from behind the safety of a dumpster. Ashley rewarded the surprise with a bullet between the old woman's eyes. Brains and blood splattered against the brick wall as a final memorial to someone not even undead. She had to be sure of her target or risk killing another innocent.

A moaning hiss uttered from the figure, echoing through the rest of the store. The zombie shuffled forward. Its neck bent at a painfully odd position. Dribble poured from its gaping mouth as it reared its head back, wide milky-white eyes glared down on her. Its clothes were torn to bits. Red coagulated blood and mutilated flesh covered the zombie's midsection.

In one hand, the zombie held a piece of its own entrails. The gore strung from his hand to the floor then back up and into the gaping hole that had once been the creature's stomach. A string of blood spread across the tile floor traced the zombie's steps.

The overwhelming odor of rotting flesh and its grotesque appearance acted like invisible ropes holding Ashley down. She grabbed the front neck of her T-shirt and stretched it up over her nose. The makeshift filter did little other than to mix the horrendous stench with her hot, bad breath.

The morbid love-cry of the hungry zombie was followed by rustling and clatter from an area to her right.

It was time to dance, and if she wanted to take the lead, she had to push out the fear and move. She brought the open sites of her rifle on the monster a short distance away. A squeeze of the trigger put a single round between its eyes.

Blood and gray slime sprayed out from the back of the creature's head as it fell limp to the floor. It lay there, one hand clutching the remains of its mostly devoured intestines. A cavern in the undead victim's forehead leaked blackish-red gunk.

There was no time to dwell on the latest kill. There were more of the undead heading her way, and for some ungodly reason, they had the need to announce their arrival with horrible moans that laced the air with fear.

"Chadwick, we gotta move faster. I don't know how many we're up against. You good?" After a heartbeat longer than what she thought it should take Chadwick to respond, she looked back and found him face first on the cold tile, his hand no longer applying pressure to his neck wound.

"Shit," she grumbled and backed up and dropped to a knee. With her gaze at full alert in front, she reached down and searched his neck for a pulse. Nothing.

Damnit.

She stood and looked around, trying to decide her next move, when she felt him brush against her leg. "Chadwick?" Ashley lowered her rifle and shined the light in his face. He certainly looked dead. Maybe some involuntary muscle had twitched? She had heard of things like that happening.

Before turning her attention away, Chadwick's eyes sprang open. Milky-white eyes within blank orbs gazed back. His hand came up and grabbed the barrel of her rifle.

Ashley gasped and jumped back, pulling the rifle free of her reanimated companion's hold.

The former corporal staggered to his feet, bringing up the ghastly song of the undead from his throat.

A hand touched Ashley's back. She frantically turned around as a zombie grabbed for her.

The creature's blood-stained teeth shone in the rifle's light.

It was too close for her to get off a shot. She brought the rifle up with both hands and put it crossways between them. A quick push aided by surging adrenaline had it staggering backward. Wanting this to end quickly, she grabbed onto the rifle's barrel, crouched and spun around, bringing the stock behind the knees of the approaching zombie, sending it to the ground. She put the barrel next to its head and pulled the trigger. Skull and brain splattered across the floor, the shot echoing throughout the store.

Chadwick lurched forward with a shaky hand reaching out for her. His face gaunt and his jaw hanging low enough for her to see his bottom teeth. The lifeless eyes threatened to steal her very soul.

More clatter and footsteps grew closer as she slowly backed away from what had once been her teammate and friend.

Ashley brought the M-4 to the ready and trained the sight on his forehead. A lump rose in her throat, she tried unsuccessfully to swallow it back down. Tears welled in her eyes blurring her vision. This was Chadwick… Russell. She couldn't find the nerve to kill someone she had been so close to. Not even as her very life was threatened.

He moved in, pushing against the gun's barrel, arms close enough that they touched her. She shoved him back with the rifle, dropping the weapon to her side in one hand. She couldn't bring herself to do it. A trained soldier and she couldn't bring herself to kill one of her own. The whole world had gone to shit and she was tired. Life wasn't worth living anymore. She began to weep uncontrollably, shaking in her boots. She winced as two hands went for her throat.

Chadwick opened his mouth to fill it with her flesh.

A gun blast rang out from over Ashley's shoulder that dropped Chadwick to the ground for good. Startled, she turned to face the shooter, weapon drawn. Her flashlight revealed a thin little man holding up a small handgun.

Civilian.

"We need to go," the man said. "This way!" He motioned with his pistol for her to follow.

She didn't obey. Her plans to leave this Earth suddenly snatched from her wanting grasp. Her weapon still drawn on the little man, she said, "You shot Chadwick!"

4

"Listen, lady, whoever that was, wasn't your friend. I did that guy a favor. I did you a favor. Now let's go!" He turned and bounded forward. "There are a lot more of those things in here. So if you want to live, I suggest you move!"

The survival instinct took over, and she chased after the man. There was no time to mourn for her lost friend.

The two made their way around the winding aisles, the man constantly slowing for her to keep pace. As they traveled, another zombie peered out from the corner of an aisle filled with large flat screen televisions.

Ashley stopped and took aim.

"No time, let's keep going!" warned the stranger. He put his hand on her elbow and led her across the store.

"Where are we going? Are you alone?"

The man didn't reply, obviously too focused on reaching safety to play a game of twenty questions.

They eventually came to a large door across from a section of refrigerators. The man stopped at the door and knocked twice in rapid succession. "Open up, it's me!"

Metal scraping concrete sounded on the other side, and then the door swung open. Ashley followed behind her rescuer and watched the man who had moved the refrigerator peer around it. Now that they were clear of the doorway, he shoved the refrigerator back in place.

Sergeant Ashley Fox found herself staring at four strangers. Two huddled around one another like mice in a corner. Flipping the safety lever on her rifle, she scanned it around the room to get a better look using the light attached to the barrel.

The man who had moved the refrigerator looked to be in his forties. Her rescuer was younger, maybe early twenties. A little girl who couldn't have been out of middle school and a somewhat older girl sat on the floor in the corner of the office space, with scared expressions looming over their faces.

The man who had led her through the store stepped forward with an outstretched hand. "Sorry, I didn't have time to introduce myself earlier. I'm Victor. I work here. Well, I used to work here, that is... until all this happened."

He stepped back after shaking hands and pointed to each of the survivors in his group. "That's Phillip... and Jenny. And this is Kieta, my girlfriend."

The older girl stood and stepped forward to introduce herself properly. As she came into the light, Ashley instantly saw she was *very* pregnant. Her belly poked out from under her shirt and was nicely tucked away under her stretchy cut jeans.

"Hi." The young woman reached out her hand. "Please tell me you are here to rescue us. We've been trapped in this hell-hole for the last three days with nothing to eat."

"I, uh, I'll do my best," Ashley said as she reached out to take Kieta's outstretched hand. "I'm Sergeant Ashley Fox." After a quick arm pump, she let go. "Is anyone here injured?" She heard their negative replies. "That's good. I can radio for a chopper. If we're lucky, we can get one here in a couple of hours."

Ashley reached for the radio attached to her belt. It was no longer there.

HIDE

1

Things are generally either really simple or really complicated, and this was... well, just simply complicated. If thinking to himself wasn't hard enough, the background noise from Cynthia Smith stressing over the current circumstances, the consistent banging of those undead things against the latch overhead, and static from the piece of junk they called a radio made it harder. Eric Micson sat wondering what had happened to his friend, Tyler Wellington, in the middle of this God-awful chaos—which was akin to living in a bad horror movie.

He and Tyler had been best friends going on four years now, and if Tyler would be anywhere in this mess, surely this would have been the place. Eric couldn't complain though, with what was going on outside and all around them. At least he was safe. But Tyler's fate wasn't the only concern he had. What about his parents? Eric had only been down in this prison for maybe two days now and yet it felt like weeks.

Eric knew that he wasn't the only one feeling this way because tensions were starting to stir between the other two ever since the radio station stopped broadcasting, and that was only forty-five minutes ago.

It's crazy how fast things can just fall apart, he thought.

"What, in the name of Christ, do you think is going on up there? We can't stay down here forever. It's starting to smell like piss. I just can't take it anymore. Is it just me or is it getting hotter in—?"

"Cynthia, would you please shut the hell up for just one second? You're stressing me out. Seems like you haven't shut that trap of yours since the broadcast stopped. It'll come back on. Just give it some time, for Christ sake," Kent Kingsly said, and rubbed his forehead with the top of his forearm.

"Well, Kent, what's worse? Listening to my *so-called trap* or sitting in silence with all the racket going on above us? It's driving me crazy," Cynthia said.

"Would you two just knock it off? I'm the youngest one here, and you two are the ones acting like children," Eric said. "If it wasn't for me, you two would still be stuck out there—probably dead, *or worse*. Based on what food and water we have in the pantry, we should be fine for days. And besides, you heard what the radio said before it cut off. The best thing we can do right now is just wait this thing out."

"Sure, that might be easy for you to say, but no one even knows we're down here. What are we supposed to do when we run out of food and water, huh? Go up there and face those rotting things? They're dead." Cynthia gritted her teeth.

Despite the fact that Cynthia was extremely pessimistic as well as stressed out of her ever-loving mind, she was right. Things were not looking good, not at all. At first, there must have been only three undead hovering over the latch to the shelter; a shelter that Tyler's dad had built in their backyard, less than two years prior. And now days later, there had to be at least thirty or more of those bastards trying to get in.

Ever since Tyler's mom passed away, Mr. Wellington kind of *lost it* with the paranoia thing. But you couldn't blame him. With all the talk of society collapsing from global warming, or sun flares destroying the electrical grid, or flu pandemics, or whatever; what else was he supposed to do now that he was alone?

In his spare time, he dug this huge hole in the back yard and turned it into this bunker. He did it all by hand, using just a regular garden shovel. The hole had to be at least twelve to fifteen feet deep. He called it a *bomb shelter* and swore up and down the Russians were planning an attack with some biohazard warfare or something, but Tyler and Eric both knew better than that. It was more like a *time waster*. A *let's do anything but think of my loss* kind of thing. Mrs. Wellington's death was hard on Mr. Wellington, but even harder on Tyler. Not only did his friend miss his mother, he had to deal with his delusional dad spending countless hours on things that might be hazardous for his emotional health. Three years had passed since the car crash. But the real question for Eric still remained the same: Where in the world could Tyler and his dad be? Where else would they have gone?

Realistically, there was no way of knowing how many of those things crowded around in the yard over them. Kent had simply guessed a number and started rounding it up over time to equally balance the level of noise that seemed to grow louder each couple of hours. It sounded at times like hundreds of feet stomping about, not to mention the scratching that took place at the door, and the ever-growing moaning. Moaning that seemed almost constant.

Kent was probably right, but they sure as hell hoped to God that he was wrong. How did the undead even know we were down here to begin with? The only logical answer was the generator. It had to be the generator that was attracting the attention.

The medium-sized gas generator set next to the pantry of food and supplies. Two ten-gallon gas barrels sat beside it, filled to the brim. An extension cord ran from the generator into the wall, powering the few wall outlets that existed along one side, as well as wall switches to the lights in the main room and in the bathroom. A makeshift ventilation system ran from the generator's exhaust. A small fan motor kicked on powered by the generator pulling carbon monoxide up a piping system into the wall. *Pretty crafty for an old man like Mr. Wellington.* Tyler's dad wasn't known for his handyman skills. Eric guessed the old man must have done a lot of research on the internet to get plans on how to build the shelter.

The exhaust released above ground somewhere in the back yard. The vent's pipe stuck out of the ground about a foot, and it lightly vibrated when the generator was running. There was no doubt the generator noise traveled through the ventilation system and echoed out into the street.

Come to think of it, those things out there could probably even hear us talking too when the generator is off, Eric thought. They turned the generator off while they slept. The things up there seemed to thin out and quite down after about an hour with it shut down.

Mr. Wellington definitely didn't have much money and it showed in the structural foundation of the shelter. At least it was cozy. The shelter was only built for two, seeing as to how it only had two twin size beds set to the side in one very tight corner. The shelter was basically just one big room. A small table between the beds had an alarm clock on it. The clock wasn't worth a damn because it didn't work when the generator was off. They had put a new battery in it, but that didn't help. So, they didn't bother to set the time. The clock continually blinked *12:00*. The flashing clock added to the dreariness of the situation; reminding them that the world no longer operated according to a schedule. They could have turned it off, but for some reason, didn't.

Some of the structure must have leaked. The walls on one side of the room were covered in rust from the roof to the floor. A large trail of water descended from the ceiling line to the floor, causing that corner of the room to have a faint odor of mold and mildew. If it wasn't for the toilet being backed up, the place wouldn't have smelled of piss. The first day into their hideaway, the toilet started overflowing and urine ended up all over the floor. The toilet pump stopped working. Kent got a good laugh out of it. Something about seeing Cynthia get all worked up seemed kind of funny to him. At least he still had a good sense of humor in the middle of all this. It was surprising, to say the least, that he still had one, but Eric was thankful for it.

There was a sink by one of the beds, but it didn't work. It was on the same side as the rust-stained wall. Probably where the rust had come from. There were some dry goods and canned food in the room, but not a lot. Eric didn't know what Mr. Wellington was thinking. Maybe he planned to buy some more and never got around to it. There was no way to warm any of the food, and of course, just like a bad movie, they had been unsuccessful at finding a can opener—another small detail that seemed to slip past Mr. Wellington.

The overhead latch leading to the outside was at the end of the room opposite the beds. A small ladder leaned against the wall to get to the door handle. The ladder looked as if it was supposed to be mounted to the wall, but Mr. Wellington had failed to do that too.

The shelter door had a small glass window about the size of a dollar bill, but it wasn't worth the trouble of trying to look out of.

All you could do was look straight up and right into the rot-festering mouths and hands of the dead. By this point, so many of them had gathered over it that you couldn't tell when it was day or night. The scratching and banging of their efforts to get in had Eric feeling like he was in a pot of water slowly heating up. He couldn't take much more.

"This is the last one. I can't believe I'm already down to the last smoke," Kent said.

Eric perched on the bed looked over at Kent, who was lying against the wall beside the ladder. Eric had only just met the man but liked his attitude right away. Kent came across cool and like he had his shit together. Like he didn't have a care in the world, which didn't make any bit of sense. Because the world as they had known it was turned upside down overnight—delivered over to rotting cannibals, and Kent was just... cool with it. Something Eric admired. Kent was lighting a cigarette no doubt. When did he ever not have one lit?

Cynthia obviously had worn herself out in the last hour from all that pacing and stressing. She sat across from him on the other bed, surprisingly silent. For an older woman, Eric couldn't place it, but he found something rather familiar about her, but decided it best to keep that to himself. It just didn't seem like the right time or place; not after just meeting her two days ago right before leading her and Kent to the underground safe haven.

He stared at Cynthia for a moment, taking to memory her supple form as she lay still on the bed. Her fiery red hair halfway down her back definitely shined true to her similar personality.

Surely she's a professional of some type. Maybe even a school principal.

Despite the bit of dirt on her face and the ragged *attacked by flesh eating zombies* look that she had going on, he imagined her cleaned up and in a feminine business suit, standing tall and thin. She had the legs for it if anything.

Eric briefly smiled to himself before looking back at Kent, who seemed to be enjoying that cigarette just a little too much. 12:00 flashed from behind the bed, and Kent sat with a red shadow of himself blinking against the floor from the clock.

"I'm surprised you have any cigarettes left. You've been chain smoking those things since the three of us arrived," Eric said.

"Man, what I wouldn't give for a tall glass of scotch right about now," Kent said. "It would help me catch some sleep. I just don't understand how she does it." Kent pointed to Cynthia lying on the bed. "The constant racket from up top is just too much, and she manages to get some shut eye. To tell you truthfully, I probably wouldn't be able to fall asleep even if I had an entire bottle of scotch. And yet, she is out like a light. But seriously... just a single glass, oh that would be sweet. Just enough maybe to knock the edge—"

"You know, I've pretty much decided that you talk as much as you do simply because you're in love with your own voice," Eric said. "Instead of thinking about what we don't have that we really need, like a can opener, we should decide what to do with what we have. Cynthia is right, man. We need to figure something out before we're totally out of food. We can't stay down here forever."

"Speaking of food, it's obvious why those things want to get in here. To fucking eat us!" Kent grumbled and puffed on his cigarette. Blowing the smoke up toward the overhead door in little *O* shapes, he flicked his cigarette ashes on the floor. "We're stuck in here like sardines in a can, just waiting to get plucked out and chewed up."

Kent cocked his head to the side and gazed out at Eric through narrow eyes. After pulling a drag off the smoke, he said, "Less than a few minutes before I ran into you on the street the other night, I watched three of those things take down an old man. He moved slow—slower than those things, even. They cornered him. Had him trapped. What was I supposed to do? Get attacked with him? They tore out his guts with their bare hands and ate that crap like it was spaghetti. That old man died before any of them even took the first bite, man. It was insane."

"Would you two please shut up? I'm trying to sleep over here."

"Yes, ma'am!" Kent said and shook his head. "Man, she gets bossy when she hasn't had her beauty sleep." He chuckled and blew smoke from his nose.

"That's right, and I'm trying to get it now. So turn off the generator, will ya? Let's lie down for a bit. It isn't like we have anything better to do, and I'm tired. Can't sleep with that generator running all night. It shakes the bed too much. How you two aren't tired is beyond me. We've been up forever, it seems." Cynthia lay with her back turned to the rest of the room. "What sleep I've had so far is mostly from my body shutting down on its own."

*

Cynthia laid there, thinking of life and how unexpected it could be. Less than a month prior, she lay in that same position in her apartment, an empty bottle of sleeping pills and over fourteen shots of Crown in her stomach. Her attempt at suicide only led to an embarrassing trip to the hospital, thanks to her roommate coming home from a trip one day early. What she found ironic in her current situation was how the tables had turned. There was surely nothing left to live for now. Everyone she knew had to be dying or dead and eating people, but now she somehow felt the need to survive. She found her second wind of purposeful hope. It made no sense.

If anyone was going to make it out of this alive and live to tell the tale, she wanted more than anything for it to be her. And on the plus side, being stranded in a locked-up shelter, at least she was with a halfway decent-looking man. She thought of Kent and that scruffy, unkempt beard, his *too cool for school* aviators and attitude. So what if he was probably close to thirty and still dressed like a teenager. On him, it worked.

He may not actually be a real rock star like he said he was, but he sure does play the part, Cynthia thought. And besides, she had been a girl long enough to tell when a man was hitting on you, even just a little.

Above them in the backyard as they prepped for yet another night tucked away in the underground bunker, things weren't getting any better. For the last two days, the number of living dead continued to increase. The constant moaning became louder and louder with each new member that joined the ranks, which brought others from even farther away.

2

"Can you guys make it around to the back? That's the only place safe enough to let you in," a man hollered from a building.

"How do we get there?" George craned his head out the window, staring up at maybe his last hope of salvation.

"The alley to the right—beside the building—it leads to the back. You're going to have to ditch the truck. It won't make it through there. I have most of the alley blocked off. You're gonna have to run like hell!"

The older gentleman flung the driver's side door open and leaped out of the truck, pulling a young boy across the passenger seat and along the driver's side, leading them both out of the vehicle's safety, and into the parking lot surrounded by the madness of an approaching blood-hungry mob. Turning to the rear of the cab in a spastic frenzy, the old man opened the back door and grabbed a bag from the seat. When he turned around, the man that had been yelling from the second-floor window only moments before had vanished. Without hesitation, he bounded forward—snatching the boy along with him.

There was no other choice than to chance this escape. The truck was practically out of gas, and George was getting worn down. Besides, this was the only radio station broadcasting he had been able to find in the last forty-eight hours, which meant that someone was alive, which meant that it was a safe place to be. George knew exactly where the WKBM radio station was located, because his nephew had interned with the station just this last summer. Unfortunately, this area seemed everything but safe, which was the last thing the old man had hoped to find as they had pulled up to the building.

As they had idled across the street a block away, he could tell right then that things were about to get ugly. The crazed mob was everywhere. The ones that didn't take immediate notice of the truck still lingered in the streets and at the entrance of the radio station, just banging away at the door, or what was left of it. George imagined it was boarded up pretty good. But how long would that last?

Even with a good dozen or so of the irrational maniacs completely oblivious to their new visitors, George still had his hands full. "Run, Billy! Run."

The little boy took off, disappearing around the side of the building and into the alley.

They had made their way across the parking lot and about fifty feet away from the side of the building leading into the ally. Those blood-covered cannibal freaks were right behind them. "There's just too many of them!"

At this point, it's not like there were any other options. At least fifteen crazies had made their way past the truck and were headed right for him. Him *and* Billy.

Time seemed to stop. For the first time in two days, his mind finally wrapped around the situation. His attackers were dead. All dead. From the time he was chased from that gas station and found Billy in the park all alone, he had thought something had caused the people to go insane. Perhaps by a disease or something terrorists put in the water supply. But no, these people, these things, were dead and yet continued to function.

The smell of scorching flesh in the heat of day created a potent odor. It was like leftover dead fish on the porch in summertime. Just gut wrenching. With more than a dozen of them closing in, he saw the closest one was a young male. He had to have been in his mid-twenties and was definitely anything but alive.

The young man walked right at George, arms raised, and a mouth wide open, dripping fresh blood. There was dried blood too, over its cheeks and neck. Some had run down its white shirt and formed a stain shaped like Lake Michigan. It was too hard to tell if the blood was from someone else or if it was the creature's. A huge chunk of its neck was completely torn open, but the blood in that area was all clotted up on the torn, puffy skin. One eye socket was caved in where an eye had once been. The ghoul had scratches going from the crushed socket up the side of its face to its forehead that looked like they had been made by a human hand. Large bits of flesh were missing, and parts of the skull showed beneath the deep cuts in its scalp.

George then noticed another one behind it, traveling with a slight limp. Part of the knee bone was visible. The tendons from the knee down to the ankle were showing. A large trail of blood followed behind on the pavement as it shuffled toward him.

It wasn't until one of the other zombies behind the small horde closing in on George let out a guttural moan that he realized he had been standing there for a moment totally dazed. He also hadn't noticed how much closer the mob had gotten and that their pace had increased as they neared him and the boy.

Snapping out of it, he finally realized that there were more walking in his direction from all over the parking lot, all with that same wide stare of sheer madness. The expressions marring their faces said *you have something I want and I'm coming to get it.* The ones that had been banging on the front of the building were no longer there. Instead, they had joined the ranks of those already in pursuit of the fresh meat. The moaning started to get out of control as each slowly joined in, one by one. The truck was blotted out by bodies closing in on George and the boy.

"Mr.! Hey, Mr.!" The voice came from directly overhead. "What are you doing? Get to the back! Get to the back of the alley!"

George shook himself back in control, turned, and made off toward the alley.

Jumping over a few small boxes and bumping into a trash can or two along the way didn't seem to slow him down at all. He could see the end of the alley just a few yards ahead.

Billy had managed to make his way back there, and stood at the end staring up at a huge gate, chain, and padlock that blocked them or anyone else from going any farther.

The fence had to have been at least eight or nine feet tall. The only thing it was missing was barbed wire at the top to give it that prison *look.* Even without the wire, there was no way they were going to make it over that.

In a state of total defeat, the harsh reality that *this was it* shown on their faces. *This was how it was going to end*, finally set in for George. Leaning as tightly against the fence as they could, George took Billy into his arms and squeezed him so hard he felt it cut off circulation.

The rotting things were making their way across the parking lot directly on their path. A path that led to a literal dead end.

"I'm glad I met you, Billy." Dropping to his knees against the fence as the alley began to fill with the undead, George closed his eyes, and almost began to faint. The smell of rot and decay intensified. "Close your eyes, Billy. Just close your eyes." Shuffling feet and wailing moans grew closer. The alley's tight walls echoed the dread as the seconds passed.

Wincing with one eye barely open, Billy wrapped tightly in the old man's embrace, he watched the creatures steadily closing in on them. The zombies shambled their way through the alley, some falling over boxes and crates, while others climbed over the fallen, taking the lead.

One zombie tripped over an empty broken pallet that leaned against the alley wall and fell head first toward the ground. Its head popped like a melon, blood spraying onto the ground around its head. It made no attempt to break its own fall.

Another zombie immediately climbed over the fallen creature, stepping on its neck, unconcerned for anything other than advancing on the two helpless souls trapped in their path. Then, blood shot from its mouth onto the ground, along with chunks of something red. A sea of the undead would soon fall upon them like a tidal wave and compressed them into the brick wall cage.

Something metallic rattled behind him. He let out a loud scream with his eyes still closed as a hand grabbed him by the shoulder and pulled him in toward it. Images of open mouths filled with festering teeth swarmed into George's head.

"Get in! Get in!" a tall man with long, dark hair shouted at them. He had unlocked the gate and held it open.

Billy darted through the opening and to an open door leading into the building.

Shock had George's feet cemented to the pavement. His body no longer responded to the command of his will.

The stranger grabbed George by the shirt and pulled him past the gate, snaked the chain through the fence, and then secured the lock. "Get in there!" He pushed George toward the open door.

George stumbled toward the open door and breached the opening. He fell to his knees and then crashed face down toward the tile floor, his bare hands cushioned the impact at the last second.

The door closed behind him, and vomit slowly made its way up his throat and into his mouth. Choking the emesis down, George feebly rose and looked around the room.

"Dude, your dumb ass almost got us killed. What were you thinking?" the stranger said.

The moaning grew louder, or was it all just in George's head? He struggled with the idea that what he had witnessed could easily have been something his subconscious created. They had been on the run for days without much rest. The amount of calories burned far exceeded the paltry amount of food they had scavenged along the way.

"Hey, you deaf? Acting like one of those things isn't going to make them ignore you. You got to stay ahead of them. If—"

"I'm sorry," George said in a soft, distant voice. He bit his lip and turned his gaze to the floor. "My son..." The bitter words hung in the air. For the first time in two days, he dropped the inner walls blocking his emotions. His incapacitation wasn't due to the lack of rest or food, not even the dead coming back to life. It was the stress of not knowing where his only child was in this hellish disaster. "We came here because we thought it would be safe since the—"

Bang! Bang! Bang!

The door started to rattle, and the tall man leaped over to it and shoved his shoulder against it.

The quick action of the man slapped George back into the moment. Basic survival instinct kicked in and he joined his newly unacquainted friend, pressing against the door.

Billy had his hands spread across his chest. His gaze darted from side to side. "What do I do?" Billy asked.

The stranger replied, "Grab that two-by-four over on the wall! Hurry!"

George watched the boy act without hesitation. Billy certainly functioned better under fire than he did. Despite the fact that George had all of his weight against the door, both he and the stranger bounced a bit off of it as the mob pounded to get in.

Billy pointed the board toward the stranger, who snatched it from his hand.

"Watch out," the stranger said.

There were metal brackets to each side of the doorway. George kept his hands tightly against the door as he shifted his body to allow the stranger to put the barricade in place. It slid in smoothly, and the two were able to step away from the door.

At first, the two only exchanged heavy breathing, and then the stranger broke the silence, "Yeah, the makeshift lock was built before I started working here and that's been ten years now. People used to come around at night. Mostly trying to get free shit—records and stuff. Sometimes girls smitten by the sexy voice of a DJ would come by," his gaze shifted over to Billy, "and they would try to *give* him something. Most of them were underage, so the rule was to leave the barricade in place until the morning shift arrived. But you don't care about any of that. And it really doesn't make a fucking bit of difference anyway... not anymore." He closed his eyes and leaned his head back. Shaking it off, he looked back at George, and said, "I'm Seth, but most people know me as the Spider from *The Midnight Madness Show*."

"Hey, I know that show," Billy said. "My older sister listens to you. She likes all of that scary music. My dad says *crap in a can* sounds better. Hah, but I don't know. I kind of like it."

"Well, that's cool, kid. Hey, you gotta name?" Seth asked.

"His name is Billy, and I'm George. George Wellington. Thanks for saving us. We would have been goners if it wasn't for you."

"Seems silly under the circumstances to say *nice to meet you*. But I'm glad I was able to get you two in here. I'd feel just awful if I would have watched those things get you," Seth said.

"Imagine how we'd feel," George said, feeling a little levity return in his spirit.

"I think the door's secure, but I'd rather hole up upstairs. Put another door between us and them," Seth said. He turned and headed for the stairs. "So you say this is the only station that has been broadcasting, huh? That doesn't sound good. It was smart of you to assume this place was safe since I'm alive, but we're basically trapped in here."

"I was listening to the radio, and your station has been the only one left broadcasting for the last two days. I figured... well, *we* figured there must be survivors and safety here. It was Billy's idea. I knew how to get here because my nephew used to intern here."

As they reached the top of the second flight of stairs, Seth reached for the single door at the top. "Well, this is it. A home away from home. It's not much to look at, but it beats being outside. Sorry about the mess. I wasn't expecting guests."

As Seth opened the door, a distinctive odor greeted George. He well remembered the herbal smell from his younger days. Inside, the room was larger than he had expected. One large window faced the street. A large desk with the electronic equipment set by one wall and a couple of couches staged across from one another offered a place to sit. A neon sign above the desk showed OFF AIR. Empty beer cans littered the floor along with a few inappropriate magazines for Billy's age.

"Wow, I've never seen so many CDs in my life," Billy said as he gazed at the rows of shelves above the desk.

George couldn't help but see a little bit of his own son in Billy despite the age difference, and that made him smile. Even with Billy's parents gone, he still looked happy and excited about new things.

The innocence of youth, George thought.

"This place is so cool. I want to be a DJ someday when I get big," Billy said, awe in his voice. "I think that would be the best."

Seth picked up a beer can on the desk and swirled it around. He brought the beer up to his lips and turned the bottom up, and then crushed the empty can. "Yeah, kid, if there is a *someday* ever again. You two sure did stir things up out there. There's twice as many of them out there now. All of the racket you two made must have gotten the attention of some from a few streets over, which means by tonight there'll be more. Probably a lot more."

"What does this button do?" Billy asked. He had taken a seat behind the desk and pointed, his mouth hung open.

"Which button, kid? There's got to be over a hundred buttons on that thing," Seth said, and then looked over at George who had already planted himself on one of the couches, claiming the entire thing for himself.

"Hey, you want a beer, old man? I've got a few," Seth said.

"Sure, why not. I need something to help me relax a little."

Seth reached into a small cooler beside the desk and tossed George a cold beer. "As long as we have power, this station is going to be airing twenty-four seven. Someone has got to keep the hope alive… someone."

"So can the people out there hear us talking now, Seth?" Billy asked.

"Not right now, but we can take care of that in a hurry. Move over, Billy-boy. Let me show you how to be a real DJ."

Billy hopped out the chair while Seth commanded the seat.

"I don't usually allow anyone behind the desk while I'm on air, but today I'm going to make an exception," Seth said.

"Thanks!" Billy said, delight in his voice.

3

As Eric became aware of his surroundings, he peered through strange shadows and darkness. Wherever he was, it was vaguely familiar.

He felt trapped. A dull pain in his head felt like it grew as each second ticked by.

It wasn't until he stood that he realized he was on the school bus. He had never been on a bus at night. What had happened? Was there a wreck and no one had come to rescue them? Did he fall asleep and the driver was too stupid to realize this and took him back to the parking garage? Mom and Dad were going to be so pissed.

The floor leaned at a strange angle. It took a little effort to maneuver to the aisle. One thing for sure, this was no parking garage. And as his mind sharpened, he remembered the crash. The bus driver had screamed, and then the bus turned abruptly to the right. He remembered bouncing in his seat a few times, and then seeing the ditch through the window. His head smashed into the window before the bus came to a stop. Everything had gone dark.

Squinting to see out of the side door by the driver's seat, he called out, "Hello… hello, is anyone there?"

Something rustled in the back of the bus. There was nothing there, though. Just empty seat after empty seat.

Less than a week earlier, he had gotten into trouble with his parents when they found out that he had been frequenting small get-togethers on the weekends that involved a lot of heavy drinking. Along with other punishments, his parents decided to take away the car. He wouldn't be in this predicament now if hadn't gotten caught.

Another noise startled him—this time from behind the bus. Something slapped the pavement, as if someone ran a slow moving wet mop back and forth. The surrounding darkness held the bus like a cage.

There was no way he was going to step one foot off this bus until he had a better idea of what was outside. Ever so slowly, he moved down the aisle toward the rear, alternating hands touching the tops of the seats as he passed. Tension built, and if this had been in a scene in a horror movie, he would have jumped out of his seat and ran out the theater.

His face neared the back window. A single streetlight a half block away cast its brightness enough to make him feel a little better about what he could see but had him still concerned with what he couldn't see.

There were two other vehicles not far from the bus, presumably involved in the same accident. It didn't look like anyone was still inside them. Where had the passengers gone?

The wet slapping sound returned, and Eric saw a dark form emerge from behind one of the vehicles. It was a man, and from the way his body shifted from side to side as he walked, he certainly was injured. The light shining behind him darkened most of his frontal features. There was something not right with the situation. Eric felt his insides shudder a bit.

The man plodded closer, and then another figure emerged from behind the vehicle. It was a woman with long hair. Her left arm had been cut off at the elbow. Her slow gait matched that of the man, and the wet sloshing sounds increased.

Something hit the side of the bus just to Eric's right. He turned and saw a face fit only for Halloween night right outside the window. Half of the scalp was missing from the head, and Eric saw brain. A large scar ran down the entire length of the left side of the face. The eyes set deep within the sockets and threatened to draw Eric into its wide-open, blood-stained mouth.

He had the urge to flee, but the sight had him anchored to the floor. More fists hit the side of the bus, and as if an early fog spilled onto a field and approached, more of the ghastly creatures appeared by the sides of the bus.

Moans rose through the thuds as flesh hit metal. The horrifying creatures wanted in, and there was nowhere for Eric to run. He was trapped, surrounded, and the very sight of these degenerate people twisted his stomach into a big knot.

"Eric," a voice said, weak and distant, but with a jagged edge that cut cold fear into him.

"We want you, Eric," another said, stronger, with unsettling desire.

"No!" Eric spun around, seeing an army only Hell could spawn in every direction.

"We want you, Eric. We want you… we want you…"

*

"Eric… Eric… wake up, dude!" Kent stood over him and shook his shoulder. "Dude, you all right, man? You don't look so hot."

Eric sat up in the dusty, old cot and recognized the room right away. Rubbing his eyes with his fingers in an attempt to relieve the headache, Eric sighed. "Yeah, I'm fine. Had a bad dream."

Kent backed up one step and put his hands on his hips. A wide grin grew under the bug-eyed aviators riding his nose.

"What the fuck are you grinning at?" Eric asked.

"The radio's back on, dude. It started broadcasting about the time when we turned on the generator."

4

The morning sun steadily rose into a cloudless sky. For several blocks on either end of the street, there was no sign of life. Abandoned and crashed vehicles remained as evidence of the aftermath of horror.

The survivors holed up at the radio station made little attempt to hide their whereabouts now that a horde of undead surrounded the building. Zombies endlessly beating the doors attracted even more undead by the minute.

Overnight, the station's parking lot had filled with an army of rotting flesh and bones. Now, torn limbs oozing pus baked under the morning sun. As the day heated, the rot of maggot-filled bones filled the air with the putrid smell of death.

"Good morning, Panama City Beach, and the surrounding Bay Count area. This is Seth, A.K.A. as the *Spider*. The time now is seven fifteen a.m. on Thursday morning, and we are broadcasting to you *live* from WKBM.

"As most of you know, the dead are returning to life, but they aren't the same anymore. They are one nasty group of individuals. They aren't your typical band of looters and street gangs. They are D...E...A...D... dead, and they want to more than just rob you. Yes, indeed. Their sole purpose is to harm anyone they find alive. And by harm, I mean *eat*. Yep, you heard me right. The undead are actually eating anyone they can get their gore-covered fingers on. This is not a prank. This is real. It's been three days since the attacks started, and there is still no word as to how far across the country this phenomenon has spread. So for now, my advice to you is to stay locked indoors at a safe location. With any luck, the military will make a move and put an end to this mess," the booming radio voice continued.

"Unlike yesterday where I played a little music and gave a blow-by-blow of the horrors I witnessed outside my window, I'll have a guest speaker from one of the survivors who has joined me. This survivor tells me WKBM is the only station that has been broadcasting for the last two days. A part of me is kind of proud to say I'm still here and kicking, but the other part is feeling the same thing that you guys must be feeling: Stressed the hell out, wondering where the help is and when it's going to arrive. Hey, your guess is as good as mine. I'm dealing with the situation one twelve-ounce beer at a time. People deal with stress their own way, *don't judge me*." A quick pull from the can resulted in air and liquid slurping down his throat, alerting the listeners that Seth had applied another dose of self-medication.

"We have now a gentleman who has been out in the shit for the last two days with nothing but a truck for cover who found the balls to come knocking on my door. I'm sure you're eager to hear a firsthand account of his story, here he is.

"Start off by telling us your name and where you're from."

"Is this the one I talk into? I'm a little nervous," George said

"Yes sir, move up a bit and speak clearly into the microphone."

"Hi, my name is George. George Wellington. I'm from the Lynn Haven area. Uh…What else do you want me to say?"

"Well man, we have all day. How about you start from the beginning? Let's hear everything starting with Tuesday morning right before the panic really hit."

As George sat in the radio announcer chair, he felt a little out of place. With a long pause of silence over the airwaves, his mind raced with what had happened those last few days. There hadn't been any time, or reason, to think about it all over again until now.

"From the beginning you say," George had said his thoughts aloud. His mind flashed to the moment at his empty home with no sign of his son other than the brief handwritten note on the stand beside the front door that read, *Be home soon.* The ache in George's heart returned, and he hoped to God that Tyler was safe.

"George…from the beginning. Start by telling us what you were doing when the shit hit the fan and how you managed to make your way to the station," Seth said.

Realizing that he had just stared blankly at the table in front of him for who knows how long, he came to and locked gazes with Seth. "Sorry, haven't really thought much about it, I guess. I haven't really wanted to." George took a deep breath and heaved the air out slowly. "Well, like I said, my name is George, and I'm from the Lynn Haven area. I guess I will start with my normal events leading up to the panic, like you said, Seth."

Seth lifted two thumbs up at George.

"Tuesday was like any normal day for me. I got up early, had my morning coffee as I read the paper in the living room. After I read the paper, I watched the news for a little bit before checking the mailbox. When you get old, it's routine, routine, routine. When I turned on the TV, the news wasn't on. Nothing was on. I just assumed the cable was out. So, I went out to check the mail. Something seemed odd about the neighborhood as I walked down the driveway. I couldn't quite place it. It seemed empty, quiet.

Normally, Miss Harvey would be up messing with her flowerbeds—likes to weed in the morning before it gets hot. She lives across the street from me. The dogs… there wasn't a single bark as I walked to the mailbox. Usually, the neighbor's dog sees me through the wood fence and barks up a storm. Not just that dog, though. There's at least six dogs on my street and not one of them made a peep. I lingered around the mailbox longer than normal—looking up and down the street—but saw nothing. After that, I made my way back to the house."

George coughed, and scratched the bottom of his throat before continuing. "I hadn't taken five steps when I caught a glimpse of Jamie Johnson, my next door neighbor, face down in his driveway. I didn't notice him on my way out because there were some boxes on his driveway blocking my view. Seeing him laid out like that did take me by surprise, even though Jamie was a bit of a late-night drunk. So I just assumed he must have locked himself out of the house and passed out the driveway. As I got closer to him, I noticed there was blood on his face and even more on the driveway. His blood. I called out to him a couple times and he didn't respond. I thought about checking for a pulse, but then I thought I was just wasting time. I don't have any first-aid training, so I ran back to my house and dialed nine-one-one. Just like the TV, the phone was dead. It was then I knew something was wrong. Was there some type of emergency and I slept through it the night before? When I hung up the phone, I looked out the front window and saw several strange walking people coming toward my house. I panicked and immediately locked the door and went into my bedroom. The people outside made their way up the porch and started banging on the door to get in. I'm not the bravest guy in the world, but I was afraid if I didn't do something, they might break in. So I left the bedroom and shouted from behind the door for them to leave. I told them I had a gun and would use it, even though I didn't have a gun. They didn't answer back, just moaned and groaned—sometimes even sounding like an animal. I had no idea where they came from. The neighborhood seemed empty before.

"I was afraid to sneak a peek at them through the window. I didn't want them to see me. When nothing I said seemed to matter,

I gathered some essentials and fled back into my bedroom. I barricaded the door and hid in the bathroom—trying the phone every five minutes to see if it would work."

"How long did you stay in the bathroom?" Seth asked.

"I guess it had been around ten hours, and not once did those lunatics let up outside. I heard glass breaking, which let me know they had finally broken in." George cleared his throat and took a sip of water. "My truck was parked in the back. I have a rear carport, so all I had to do was get to the truck. Funny, the whole time I was in the bathroom, none of the invaders came around to the back. They just stayed in front of the house and pounded away. Anyway, I put my phone and two bottles of water in my pocket and held on to a box of Cheese-Nips I took earlier and left through the bathroom window."

"And the undead, how did you get past them? How many were there?"

George laughed. "Ha, the undead! I didn't know they were undead at the time, Seth. At this point, I really hadn't gotten a good look at any of them." George dropped his gaze to the table and rubbed his temples with his hands. He moved his mouth to speak but the words just wouldn't come out at first. "The undead... those people were dead... and the whole time I was mistaken, maybe even forcibly telling myself lies that they were only mad. Looters and bandits—whatever. All I just knew was my home was being overrun and was no longer safe. That I needed to get to my son. I had to leave. I had to. There was no other way. I HAD TO..."

George realized he had unconsciously reached in his pocket. He opened his hand and saw the note his son had left him. He turned his gaze back at Seth, and said in a weary voice, "I had to leave. Don't you see? There was no other way." Tears welled in his eyes and began to fall.

"Well, I'm glad you made it out alive," Seth said, and held a hand up indicating for George to take a bit of time to compose himself. "Folks, we're going to take a little break and come back to George's story in a few minutes. Until then, stay tuned, and more importantly, stay alive."

With a few clicks of the mouse on the computer, music started to play in the background. Seth took off his headphones and leaned back in the chair. "Dude, you've got to pull it together. People out there need to hear your story. You made it out alive. You're offering them hope in a bad time. People need hope to survive. Not stress."

George just shook his head and glanced over at Billy, who was busy looking through a stack of CDs on the couch next to piles of trash that had been there when they arrived. "What are we going to do? We can't just hole up in this place forever."

"I know that, man, but right now it's not like we have much else in the way of options. It has only been like three days, dude. The National Guard or the military will be here sooner or later. We just got to stick it out and keep hope alive to those that might still be out there in a situation like ours or worse. Unless you've got a better idea, that is. I am all ears, man."

"No, I don't have any ideas."

"Then, for now, this is what we're going to do. I know that it's hard for you to rehash all that crap, man, but it could really help some others out there to know what's going on around them. Can I count on you to keep telling the story?"

Without saying a word, George slowly rose from his chair and walked to the window. Seth was right. People needed to hear his story; one reason, so they wouldn't feel alone. Just knowing there are others out there going through the same thing helps sometimes. Besides, what else were they supposed to do in this hellhole? The parking lot and the alleyway were overrun with the undead.

Even with the upstairs windows closed, George caught a whiff of the stench of rotting flesh from below. With numbers like that, there was no way the barricade at the front of the building would last much longer. And with the only other exit totally blocked off by an alley infested with rotting corpses, what else could they do other than sit tight and tell stories?

5

"Hold him down, soldier. Get him locked down already."

As Jared Clay and Rich Michaels struggled to contain the reanimated corpse in its restraints attached to the gurney, Professor Taft stood over them barking out commands. He sounded like a drill sergeant popping off order after order like it was their first week in boot camp. The cadaver they had brought in that morning was no different than the rest. Dead, rotting flesh dried out from the loss of fluids.

Though technically dead, the body thrived with some type of life. A life full of rage stemming from unquenchable hunger. While the creature thrashed about in the arms of the two soldiers struggling to lock it down, Professor Taft prepared a syringe to extract what fluids might remain beneath the skin, and more importantly, in the brain of the living corpse.

Its wide mouth snarled, and thick slobber coated its teeth in anticipation of soft flesh. The zombie's eyes glazed over in a light milky-white substance and stared eagerly at the two soldiers. Its head was tilted up slightly contorted in an attempt to reach its prey.

The room was about the size of an average living room. The walls were solid white with bright florescent lighting that cast onto every nook and cranny from the ceiling. Other than the countertops and cabinets lining every wall in the room, there was a single table in the center. A variety of lab utensils and beakers filled with various liquids were available, as were surgical tools. The floor was a filth-stained white tile, and the room was never warmer than a whopping 68 degrees.

Taft had worked with this particular Biochemical Research Lab team for six months. This was the first time he had worked in conjunction with the military, however. He didn't mind, the pay was better.

They always find a way to leave me with the clumsy ones, he thought as he situated a few things he needed on the table while studying the new recruits in his peripheral from across the room. Clay mumbled something to Michaels. Taft guessed it wasn't something nice, seeing as to how it almost never was. With syringe in hand, and two rubber gloves practically down to his elbows, Taft stepped behind the two soldiers and beside the gurney.

"When I signed up, I wasn't signing up for this shit," Clay said.

Michaels nodded. "I know man. I'm thinking we should—"

"Are the two of you done yet? Gibbs wanted these sample tests ready hours ago, and I'm not going to be the one taking hell for any of the delays this time," Taft said.

Michaels looked back and raised his upper lip as he stepped aside to make room at the operating table.

Taft didn't appreciate that Dr. Gibbs commanded more respect than he. She never seemed to get crap from anyone and that annoyed him at times.

With the zombie's gaze now shifted to Professor Taft while he stood over it, the creature began to moan and snap its teeth, and then began jerking violently.

Taft hesitated before inserting the needle into the corpse's neck, his gaze met with Clay's, who simply nodded and pressed down on the zombie's forehead to secure it from moving.

Inserting the three-inch needle and pulling back on the thumb, a very dark, thick gray substance and congealed blood filled the tube.

The door burst open, and two men rushed in startling Taft, Clay, and Michaels.

"What the hell?" Taft yelled as two soldiers entered the room.

In their grasp, they had a handcuffed female zombie in tow. She looked to be in her mid-twenties, and her awkward gait had her crashing into the table set in the center of the room, knocking its contents all across the floor.

Steel and glass implements collided with the tile floor. Taft's distraction twisted the syringe, and the needle snapped off in zombie's neck. Black, putrid blood and gray fluids shot out into the air, some found its way onto Michaels' chest and face.

"Orders were to bring her to you for test samples," one of the soldiers said.

"Can't you see we are in the process of doing that here? Who ordered you to bring that thing down here now?"

"Baker did, sir."

"We don't need her. So dispose of it, and leave at once. Look at this mess you've caused. Soon as you get rid of her, you can come back and clean—"

"Professor... Professor... PROFESSOR!"

"WHAT!" He turned his attention to Clay, who knelt by Michaels.

"It's Michaels, sir."

Michaels, on his knees, bent over with one hand supported by the floor, and the other spastically wiping at his face, sounded panicked, "It got in my eye! It got in my *fucking* eye! If I turn into one of those things, I swear I'm going to eat you both!"

All gazes froze on Michaels, who continued to spit and wipe his face.

The two zombies in the room struggled to free themselves.

Taft said, "Would you help him to his feet and take him to the MED station. And the two of you, get that thing the hell out of here." He pointed to the female.

With both men still staring at Michaels, the female zombie jerked free and lunged toward Professor Taft. She landed on top of him, eyes wide, and mouth even wider.

Taft fell backward and tripped over Michaels, who was being assisted by Clay to his feet. With nowhere to go but backward, Taft fell toward the zombie strapped on the gurney, reaching out in a last ditch effort to catch his balance. The gurney and the zombie strapped to it toppled over.

The weight of the woman was too much. The gurney came crashing down along with them. Using one arm against the woman's chest, he did his best to keep her teeth from sinking into flesh, but she extended her neck closer. The putrid stench of her breath hit his face as the bowels of her rotting insides spewed into the air. One of her eyes was missing, along with a large chunk of her lower jaw skin. The black gaping hole that once held an eye was nothing more than an empty socket with fragments of bone and scratch marks where it had previously been attacked. Slobber and bloody slime poured out of her gnashing mouth down her lipless chin, bottom teeth exposed. The clatter of her teeth crashing together echoed off the cold tile floor. Bits of mucus leaked down onto Taft's chin and shoulder as her teeth viciously chomped.

"Fucking do something, you morons!" Taft said struggling.

With guns drawn, the two men aimed at the zombie. With the zombie being pushed around by Taft, who rustled with it on the floor, neither man had a clear shot.

"For crying out loud," Clay said as he jumped forward to pull the woman off the Professor. He grabbed her by the back of the hair, pulling her up and away from Taft. In one smooth motion, he reached for his 9mm, un-holstered it, and released the safety. A single shot from the pistol hit her one good eye. The eye exploded, spraying Taft in the face with goo. The bullet split the back of her skull and bounced around inside her cranium. The zombie immediately fell limp to the floor.

Michaels staggered to his feet a little off balance and collided with the toppled gurney behind him. Losing his footing, the restrained zombie's germ-infested mouth filled with gnashing teeth met bone as they ripped right into the back of his ankle. Blood gushed from the beast's mouth, violently shaking left and right.

Michaels' scream startled both soldiers at the door. The soldier closest to him sporadically fired shots into Michaels' stomach and chest. Collapsing to the ground on his knees with blood pouring from his mouth, Michaels weakly pulled his sidearm from its holster and fired wildly back.

With a mouth full of blood, he attempted to speak as each shot was fired, life slowly fading from his body. Blood covered the tile beneath him. His blood. "You... fu...king pri...ck."

One shot was a direct hit to the head, sending one of the uninfected soldiers instantly to the ground. A barrage of gunfire exploded in the room again as shots were traded. Michaels finally lost all of his strength and fell to the cold floor, filled bullets.

The gunfire ended.

Taft, still on the ground next to the unmoving female corpse that had attacked him, sat wide-eyed and blood covered.

The one remaining soldier who had entered the room reached for his chest, taking away blood on his hand. With his bottom jaw hanging low, the man glanced at his blood-soaked extremity, fell to his knees, and then collapsed to the blood-soaked laboratory tile.

"I did *not* sign up for the crap," Clay said.

Three men and one female zombie lay motionless on the floor. Taft and Clay stared at one another while the zombie still strapped to the toppled gurney moaned with excitement.

The zombie tied to the table now stared right at Clay as it cried out, the broken syringe still in its neck. In a fiery rage to get at him, blood and pus poured from its mouth. Clay reached up and fired two precise shots into the zombie's head. A splatter of blood, black matted meat, and grey matter sprayed across the back of the silver gurney, making a loud pinging sound like two metal pipes colliding together. Its head jolted against it.

Taking a moment to look around the room at the carnage that had just taken place, Professor Taft stood to his feet, and attempted to regain his composure. "Why did this happened? This is a secure area and I have to approve new specimens to be brought here." Taft removed the rubber gloves and his lab coat. "Are you hit or bitten, Clay?"

"No, sir."

"Good. Go find Gibbs, and get her ass down here right away. I am going to start cleaning up all of this shit."

Clay holstered his weapon and disappeared out into the hallway.

Sorting through what still seemed salvageable amidst the broken glass and surgical tools that found their way to the floor, Taft couldn't believe General Baker broke protocol. *That bag of wind for a general couldn't keep his head on straight if it was screwed on*, he thought, knowing good and well he wouldn't ever be caught dead saying something like that out loud.

With his back turned away from the five bodies that now littered his lab, Taft was too furious and irritated at the irrational mistakes of others to realize or hear the movement taking place behind him on the floor.

Michaels' eyes opened, and his limbs began to rustle about with life. Dead, rotting, rancid life. The thing that was once Michaels slowly rose to its feet.

Taft cluelessly ranted to himself, while tinkering with the remains of his tattered workspace, and cleaning blood from his face and clothes at the sink in a corner of the room.

The decaying zombie, that was only moments ago human, lurched with outstretched arms toward the professor. Blood gushed from his torn ankle, spewed from its mouth, and several bullet holes in its chest and stomach. The quick loss of blood from the bite and shots left it looking pale and drained. Once it was only a few paces behind Taft, it let out a light, guttural moan.

Taft instantly knew that sound. The sound of dead life. A prickly ice sensation raced down his spine. He was afraid to turn around and face what waited behind him. The zombie lunged forward as Taft turned around to meet its milky-white gaze.

6

General Baker looked and played the part of being your typical military man of age, stature, and experience. He even had the scars to prove it. Seated in his elegant brown leather chair behind his exquisitely expensive desk, Baker slouched back, legs propped, and a half-smoked cigar steaming in his ashtray. A small glass of scotch complemented his smoke. The aromatic spirits lingered amidst his partially soaked mustache.

Photos of important men and events decorated the wall behind him. His Tallahassee office, actually rather small, still carried with it an overpowering sense of authority that commanded respect.

Rob Foster waited to report to the General for what seemed like an eternity of silence.

Despite the fact that Baker came across as a rather harsh and distasteful figure to his subordinates, he was in fact a diplomatic man by nature, and chose the right words to say and was eager to listen. Foster, still unsure as to which side of Baker he found more intimidating, waited for the General to respond to the report concerning Professor Taft and the dead soldiers. He knew Baker found Taft to be a prude little man who thought too highly of himself. Something Baker highly disliked and did not hesitate to share when in group settings.

"And where is Clay now, son?"

"In his quarters, sir. He was given a sedative to calm him."

"And the others?"

"The dead are currently being properly disposed of, sir."

"And Taft?"

"Well sir, he… he… was taken down to the holding cells for future testing, what's left of him at least. Gibbs' idea, sir."

"We need to have all of the other—"

The phone suddenly rang, cutting the General off. He set down his glass and picked up the phone in front of him. "Yes... and their E.T.A?... I see...go ahead and patch me through."

After a brief moment of awkward silence, Baker continued to speak into the phone. He kicked his feet off the table and retrieved his cigar. With a few puffs, the tip glowed like hot embers, smoke quickly clouded the space between them. The General hopped to his feet and barked out his demands, "Once you arrive, I want a full report on civilian status and threat level of the surrounding area... NO! ... The number one objective is shutting that radio station down, civilians second. Do you understand, soldier? ... Good."

Baker slammed down the phone onto the receiver. After several deep puffs on his cigar and a massive swig finishing off the remainder of scotch, he sat back down. "The chopper is about twenty clicks away from the radio station. Once we hear back from them, we'll decide the final course of action."

Foster wished he understood more of the situation. The last thing he wanted to see was the military overreaction and innocent lives lost. He brought a hand to the side of his head and rubbed his temple.

The General leaned forward in his chair. "Look, Rob, our job is to keep this thing from spreading any farther than it already has, and to keep the rest of the country in the dark. I don't like it any more than you, but those *are* our orders. I'm responsible for seeing that they are carried out."

"But people have the right now know the truth, sir."

"Oh, is that your opinion, Lieutenant? Well, you don't get paid to have an opinion. None of us do. That's the way it is. Now, back to business, and the reason I called you into my office to begin with."

Baker took one last long drag from his cigar before smashing the end into the ashtray. With one exaggerated exhale, a large cloud of smoke thickened the growing haze.

Foster's eyes began to water, but he held back from wiping them. He pulled out a folded piece of paper from his back pocket, and spread it out over the General's desk. The paper showed a complex map of the northern coastline of Florida, as well as the southern parts of Alabama, and Georgia. Red X's marked fortified locations and blockades already in place. It was Foster's job as second-in-command of operations to secure the infected zone and restrict incoming and outgoing transport within its borders. A job that he was eager to take on, despite his experience, or the lack thereof.

Rob Foster made few friends in his fast ascension to First Class Lieutenant. Though young in age, he was more than qualified on paper to handle his position. He saw no reason to be disliked by his peers.

He had known General Baker for two years. He could tell Baker had grown quite attached to him since his transfer from Wisconsin. One time, the man said he saw a lot of himself in him. Rob was honored by that compliment. The General never neglected to keep up professional appearances despite favoritism.

Foster pointed to the map. "Over the last forty-eight hours, the unknown contagion seems to have spread as far west as Mobile, into Jacksonville, and into southern parts of Georgia. We have already disabled all forms communications for these areas, excluding the radio station en route. The entire eastern border of Mississippi has been on lockdown for the last thirty-two hours, along with all of southern Georgia, and Alabama. Orlando has yet to be infected, and military personnel from that district are currently posted from coastline to coastline on twenty-four-hour surveillance. In short, nothing can get in, and nothing can get out. The media are swarming us with questions. So far, they are accepting our answers and are refraining from exploiting the situation."

"Casualties?" Baker asked.

"Estimated ninety-eight percent of the infected zone population, sir."

"Impressive, Lieutenant. Impressive."

Eyeing the outlines of Foster's map, General Baker pulled another cigar from his shirt pocket, bit off one end, and spit it across the room. He then motioned for Rob to pour himself another glass of scotch as he lit the cigar. As he sat back in his chair and propped up his feet, partially on Foster's map, Baker took repeated puffs on the cigar to help get it started.

While Rob made himself a drink, along with another for the General, Baker picked up the phone and dialed out. "Tell Dr. Gibbs that I will be meeting her in her office in fifteen minutes... I don't care if she is or not, I will expect her to be there."

Not quite in the gentlest of ways, the phone came crashing down yet again. "Now all we have to do is clear this mess out and things will be good as new," Baker said and leaned back with a grin from ear to ear.

Bringing the drinks to the desk, and taking his place seated with arm reached out passing over a scotch-filled glass, Foster had a nasty gut feeling that something terrible was about to happen. Things weren't quite over yet.

The calm before the storm, he thought.

*

Meanwhile, only two doors down from the recent accident in Taft's lab, Dr. Teresa Gibbs squinted into a microscope, examining the partial decomposition of gray decaying flesh—that of Professor Taft himself. Directly in front of her, only a few feet across the room, stood her esteemed colleague tied securely to the wall by the neck with a one-inch-thick chain. The metal pressed tightly into his skin to ensure no further mishaps might occur. His face was practically unrecognizable at first glance.

It had been a few minutes before Gibbs or anyone else had made it to the lab to see what the commotion was about. The creature that had once been Private Michaels had easily overpowered the thin, unfit professor.

Dr. Gibbs was not the easiest of people to pull away from her work, especially when potentially uncovering important discoveries. Clay had to practically drag her out of her office.

The majority of Taft's scalp had been ripped clean off, leaving only the lower part of his face left holding any skin. Both eyes had been eaten out, along with parts of his tongue. His shirt and stomach had been ripped down the middle, revealing all of his internal organs had been pulled out by hand. Needless to say, he was a mess, and if it hadn't been for the ID badge clipped to his shirt pocket, it would be impossible to guess his identity. After cleaning up the mess from the attack, most of the professor's entrails had been disposed of with the remaining bodies. General

Baker wouldn't have allowed Dr. Gibbs to use one of his men as a test subject, therefore reluctantly, she shot Michaels on-sight before having the other men restrain Taft. The room stunk of iron and festering bowels. Taft's blood-soaked body slowly stained the tile beneath him as he stood tied to the wall.

Dr. Gibbs steadily jotted down several notes while talking to herself and peering into the microscope. "I can't believe I didn't see this before. The molecular patterns are practically identical. If I'm right, this could mean only one thi—"

Two rapid, deep pounds shook her attention from the tissue sample and toward the door. Baker walked into the room, Foster no less than a step behind.

"I was told you were making your way down to see me. What do you want now?" Gibbs said as she returned her attention back to the microscope.

"Yes, we have orders to transfer you and your team to a new location outside of the containment zone. With us being smack dab in the middle of things, the higher ups find it best we move things north."

"Everything we've learned so far is in this lab. We can't just move to another location and continue where we left off. It might take weeks to set up a lab like we have. Besides, we're right in the middle of the best source of specimens. Baker, have you thought of that?" Gibbs asked.

"Orders are orders, lady. I want you and what's left of your team ready for evac in no less than forty-eight," Baker said.

*

Foster stood off to the side while Baker and Gibbs had their debate. Standing next to the late Professor Taft was a bit unnerving. Foster couldn't help but feel a wave of nausea at the stench of rot. And yet the other two arguing back and forth seemed unfazed by it.

Dr. Gibbs was an attractive woman, even in the stained white lab coat. Foster had thought about her on more than one occasion. What would she look like with the lab coat, and every other piece of clothing, tossed to the floor?

Her long, jet-black hair constantly draped over her left eye when she leaned over the table. Her light-blue eyes almost luminescent against the darkness of her hair. She was shorter than Foster but taller than the average woman. He had never seen her in anything other than her lab coat and work clothes. The huge white jacket consumed her petite frame and golden complexion, making her hands appear quite small. She was in her early 30s but looked an easy 25. Foster couldn't keep his eyes off of her, even with the smell lingering in the room.

He had tried on a few occasions outside of eating lunch together to get her to join him for a drink off the clock. She seemed interested but then always blamed her research being too important right now to spend her time that way. Dr. Theresa Gibbs was passionate about her work and was basically never *off the clock*. Foster hoped she was just as passionate in the sack. She had what he liked to call *bedroom eyes*.

"And where are we planning to relocate?" she asked.

"That information is currently classified. We are only looking out for your best interest. But enough talk for now. We'll be having a meeting after dinner to go over your current findings. And I expect something good. It's your job to figure out what's causing the outbreak." Baker slammed his fist on the table, knocking a few loose papers onto the floor.

Gibbs turned her eyes away from the microscope.

"Are you hearing me, woman! I expect a full report by day's end. Is that clear?" Baker said.

"You're not going to get a damn report anytime soon if you don't let me get back to my work, so if you please!" Gibbs said.

Feeling the tension rising in the room, Foster retrieved the shuffled papers from the floor, with a smile intended to cool the situation with Gibbs. She wasn't looking his way, though. Her eyes had returned to the microscope.

General Baker and Rob Foster left the room.

7

The three soldiers had been on missions for years but never in these conditions. The general guideline of any operation for these boys was simple and always relatively the same, an in and out operation, quick and easy.

Bo Brad Barrie the pilot, Gus *the bus* Stanford, and Willy Smith. They had been through hell and back together a time or two but nothing ever quite this literal.

"Only a few more minutes and we should have the target zone in sight," Bo said through the receiver in his helmet from the cockpit.

Attracting some attention as the helicopter loudly buzzed through the air over the city streets of the Bay County area, most zombies took notice. Attracted at first toward the aggressive noise created by the blades, then the gust of wind that suddenly rustled the trees, wreckage, and debris about in the street, and then lastly by the sight of a large black object drifting by in the sky. Zombie after countless zombie staggered out from houses and buildings, gathering in the streets, reaching to the sky as they shambled their way toward the ever-shrinking black object, the helicopter steadily moving along.

"What do you think they're doing, hidden away in those houses and yards?" Willy said, sitting at his rightful place as the gunman. He leaned halfway out of the chopper and looked back shaking his head.

"Who knows, man," Gus said. "They probably aimlessly walk around looking for something to eat, something to kill. I wouldn't doubt it if they get lost once they make their way into the buildings. Those things are dumb as rocks."

They suddenly passed a mass of zombies the likes of which they had never seen. "Holy crap, Gus. Look at this." Willy leaned ever farther out of his seat, pointing toward the crowd below.

"There must be hundreds of those things down there," Gus said as he looked over Willy's shoulder. "Why do you think they are all crowded up in that backyard like that? I haven't seen anything like it."

The mass of the undead noticed the chopper, and in an almost flawless unison, reached toward the sky.

Bo, not actually able to see what the other two had been talking about, spoke up, "Chances are there is someone alive in that house or in a shed in the back yard, or something. And they all want to get in. That's what."

"Well, maybe some of them will follow us for a few miles and thin out that yard," Bo said. "Help out whoever might be stuck down there."

The chopper continued on course for several minutes passing street after street, house after house, and countless zombie after zombie. Each one looked the same. A ghost house on a ghost street, with the living dead reaching to the sky. Each one's attention being drawn to the men in the helicopter. Many of the undead turned and followed. This went on the entire trip to the radio station, all the way from the base in Tallahassee.

"Holy shit, you guys. Look up ahead!" Bo said.

"What is it?" Willy asked.

"We're here, guys, and it doesn't look too promising," Bo said.

Gus unstrapped his belts and made his way to the front of the chopper to see what the big deal was. With such broad shoulders and height, he had to squeeze past Bo to poke his head into the cockpit to take a look.

Before joining the military, Gus had tried to make it in the pros as a front lineman. After only his fourth game in the semi-pros, he tore a muscle in his thigh. With no other real options, Gus still felt like he was called to something bigger than himself. Now here he was in the most unlikely of situations, strapped to a freaking helicopter of all things, about to face his Maker. Who would have thought?

"Well don't that just beat all," Gus said with a quirky inflection in his voice.

"I take it things aren't looking too good," Willy's voice came from the back in both their headsets as if sitting right on top of them.

"I'm afraid not," Bo said.

A mountainous horde of undead ghouls piled together in the parking lot right in front of the radio station. Something they could see over a mile out.

"That's not the place we're going, is it? There must be hundreds of them."

"I'm afraid so, Gus. You aren't going to chicken out on me now, are you? I didn't remember to pack your security blanket this time," Bo said.

Bo loved to tease the hell out of Gus simply because it was so easy to do, and the man was three times his size. Bo was the one who coined the name *Gus the bus* and was glad it stuck. Even though Gus was a big man, he was the kindest person Bo had ever met.

"Shut up and just drop the thing already. In and out, remember?" Gus said.

The helicopter closing in on the building slowed and hovered in place directly over it. Its loud powerful blades blew up dust in its slow descent to the rooftop. The overwhelmingly large crowd of zombies in the parking lot began to stir, falling on top of one another as they reached to the sky toward the large black object. A powerful gust of wind threw rocks and random trash from the station's roof to the ground two stories below.

*

Inside, still telling his story on the air, George continued, "And that was when I found Billy at McKenzie Park, in town. Shortly after that, we made our way to the beach and came up with the idea of heading to the station. It wasn't until—"

"Look outside, you guys. I just saw a helicopter." Billy excitedly danced up and down barefoot on the couch, facing away from the radio equipment, eyes fixed on whatever it was that he happened upon outside.

"I hear it," Seth said pulling his headphones off one ear. The sound of the chopper rattled the windows.

"Attention people, something's happening outside. We'll be back shortly." Seth quickly clicked a few buttons sending the next song in queue across the airwaves.

Shaking his head up and down to the song's rhythm, standing on the sofa with a grin ear to ear, Billy said, "We're gonna be rescued!"

Both Seth and George instantly found their faces glued to the glass. Dust and trash furiously danced in the air all around the parking lot. The sea of undead beneath them danced even more so.

George could barely make out his truck from the window looking out onto the mass of bodies littering the parking lot.

*

"It's too small," Bo said.

"What do you mean *it's too small*? You've done this a thousand times. Just drop this bird so we can hustle," Gus said.

"The roof of the building is too small, and that freaking oversized air conditioner is in the way. I can't land it," Bo said.

"Then what are you saying? I sure as hell ain't going to just mosey on up to the front door and knock to see if anyone's home," Gus said.

"That's exactly what we're going to have to do actually," Bo said.

"Let's light 'em up, boys!" Willy brought his gaze over to his right.

"Well crap, here we go!" Bo pulled back taking them away from the rooftop and directly over the swarming sea of death that engulfed the parking lot below.

An onslaught of automatic fire littered the parking lot of undead as the helicopter hovered overhead in a circular motion. Zombie after zombie fell to the ground, chopped in bits and pieces as blood, chunks, and bone exploded tearing limb from limb. Torsos separated from legs, and heads exploded like watermelons. The deafening sound of the gunfire Willy's battle cry. His entire body shook with force matching in rhythm, each bullet shell dispensing in the air with a spark, smoke pushed out with each release of three empty shells a second.

"Aaahhh…What… the… fuck… now? BITCHES!" Willy shouted as he shot round after round of automatic fire into the crowd of ghouls.

With most of the threat relinquished, zombies littered the ground. The parking lot was no longer visible beneath the fallen creatures. Blood and scattered remains covered everything beneath the chopper.

"That's enough, Willy. That's enough!" Gus leaned over and grabbed him on the shoulder.

Willy slouched back in his chair, muscles completely worn out from the ride.

"You got to admit, Gus. That was pretty freaking sweet." Willy grinned.

Gus just smiled and shoved Willy out of the chair. "Let's move."

The helicopter descended slowly to the parking lot, setting down on the ocean of bodies it had just utterly mangled to no end. Crushing several bones beneath its weight, the helicopter touched down in the center of the lot directly between George's truck and the front door of the WKBM station.

"I feel like an idiot for leaving the bird. But with all these zombies out here, you two loafers aren't going to make it without me. Let's go!" Bo shouted from the front of the chopper, both men scooping up ammunition and holstering weapons. All three men looked at one another, Bo unhooked from the cockpit making his way to the rear.

In unison, they all looked out at the carnage before them.

Bo took off his helmet and shouted, "Stay tight."

The others nodded in agreement before jumping from the chopper to the ground.

With a floor of bodies, the men's footing and balance was off just a little. Walking on mutilated faces and broken bones was no easy task. The scent was unbearable.

With only a few feet between them and the front door, Willy did his best to hold it back, knowing he would catch hell for it later, but it was too late. Bent over the heaping pile of rotting flesh and blood, he vomited partially on his boot but mostly on the chest of what looked like a gas station attendant. Its nametag was too hard to make out from the gore that covered it.

"Come on, we ain't got all day, boys," Gus said and grunted, who was already standing in front of the door.

Bo beside him, pistol drawn, aimed out into the parking lot past the chopper. Some of the previously fallen dead slowly began to shuffle about.

"Move Willy, we got to go."

A zombie underneath Willy's feet instantly grabbed his leg. It was an elderly woman with gray, matted hair, who somehow still managed to keep her glasses on. One lens was missing and the other was cracked. The knitted scarf she wore, blood-stained and torn to bits, revealed her naked, pale chest. The skin on her bones sagged from age and was covered with liver spots. A large chunk of her ribs protruded from her side, broken in places. The woman wrapped her mouth around his calf and bit down.

Willy shrieked, releasing a single shot into her skull, blood spraying up and away from him simultaneously. "Stupid bitch!"

He quickly shook it off and moved toward the door.

Gus repeatedly slammed all of his weight into the door, only stopping momentarily to bang on the door with his fist, shouting, "OPEN THE FUCK UP!"

Both Bo and Willy stood guard picking off stragglers. As each moment passed, more and more of the undead hoard that had been gunned down began to rise, even crawl in their direction. Each shot both men fired was precise, taking down the lead zombies each time with single shots to the head from their 9mm pistols.

One went down in front of the chopper, shot right between the eyes. Another's right eye caved in as the back of its head erupted in a fire spray of blood, bone, and brain. One by one, zombie after zombie was quickly dispatched by their stunning marksmanship.

"How's it coming, Gus? We don't have unlimited ammo in case you were wondering," Bo said.

Willy took a few steps back, joining Gus at the door, and put his weight into it.

"Nine o'clock, boys! We've got trouble," Bo said.

Gus and Willy stopped for a moment and looked. A swarm of the undead poured out from the corner of the building. More and more of them each second spilled out from the alley. All three men aimed their weapons toward the growing numbers. Shot after shot, zombies went down. With every zombie that fell, another took its place, gaining yardage to the front door in the process.

"Come up with a plan, Gus. We need to do something," Bo said, still in mid-aim, releasing single bursts from his 9mm.

"Just keep firing." Gus holstered his pistol and went back to slamming on the door with everything he had. "Time for a little front line action!" Gus took three steps back and crouched, putting all of his weight into his legs. He jolted forward hoping to smash all 280 pounds of his weight into the door, but suddenly slipped when he lost his footing. The piles of bodies underneath him prevented him from getting any solid tracking on the ground. He fell forward and landed face first into a heaping stew of rotten flesh and guts strewn out on the pavement. He came away chest covered in chunks of muck and bile. Still on his knees in front of the door, Gus began to shout as loud as he could, slamming both fists against the door over and over again with all that he could muster.

In the distance, more zombies began to appear. They made their way from down the street corners and along the sidewalks previously attracted by the flying black object. Their moans grew louder and louder as they drew closer to already alarming numbers of undead that fell upon the men in the station's parking lot.

"Cover me, I need to reload." Willy dropped to one knee, pulling a magazine from a pouch attached to his ankle. Reloading, he pressed the release on the pistol and chambered a new round. They were no longer making their way from the alley, which was a good thing, but the bad news was that Willy, Bo, and Gus were almost totally surrounded. Several zombies managed to get past the firing line and in front of the chopper.

"Shit, how many of those things are out here, and where the hell is the welcoming committee?" Willy said.

The zombies were getting closer now. Almost too close for firing range. A zombie grabbed Willy's arm. He pulled the creature in and shoved it away into a cluster of other zombies, firing three shots into its neck and face. Blood spewed out from its throat and cheek. The final shot sent it to the ground.

The double doors to the radio station suddenly swung wide open, sending Bo and Gus back a few steps.

Bo lost his footing when his leg tangled in the mess of bodies at his feet, sending him to the ground on his back. A male teenage zombie wearing an anarchy T-shirt covered in mud and dried blood knelt over him instantly, taking hold of his face and hair with both hands. Bo let out a blood-curdling scream as the creature's fingers ripped into his cheeks and right eye. Blood poured out, covering his face and mouth. Kicking and screaming as he laid there on his back, the zombie landed on top of him, tearing into his throat with its rotten teeth. As it pulled away massive chunks of flesh, Bo's screams turned to muffled, watery gurgles. Blood bubbled from his mouth and throat as another zombie took a chunk of Bo's hand, removing several fingers.

"Fucking hell!" Willy opened fire on the creatures that now covered Bo's body. Shot after sporadic shot landed in every spot but the one that mattered. Shoulders, spleens, kneecaps, and chests erupted as the fire from his pistol tore through flesh and bone.

As the door slammed closed in front of him, entirely unaware that he had been dragged into the building by Gus, the last thing Willy saw of Bo was his boots, the rest of his body consumed by a plague of the undead.

8

Eric, Kent, and Cynthia circled the radio, discussing their options. The radio had suddenly stopped broadcasting again less than a moment ago. The ravenous horde of undead desperately attempted to make its way into their fortified, underground stronghold.

"You heard what they said. Those things out there are slow and easy to get past when there isn't that many. I really do think we have a chance outrunning them," Eric said.

"Ha, *not too many*, he says. You've got to be out of your freaking mind, Eric. There has to be a hundred of those things above us trying to get in," Cynthia said, her bright red hair tussled in every direction.

"Eric does have a point, woman. Our window of opportunity is limited," Kent said.

"Oh ya, then why did they just shut off the transmission, Kent?" Cynthia said, stressing the situation even more.

"Who cares why they shut off. All I care about is what was said before they did. You heard it clear as I did. Armed men and a helicopter means *people*. People with guns. And lots of them. I don't know about you, but that sounds like the place to be. If we're going to make the party, we need to get, and ASAP."

Eric rose. "Yeah, and ever since that helicopter flew above us, there haven't been as many zombies as before. You can tell because there isn't as much moaning. Instead of sitting here while you two argue like a married couple, I'm going to get some things together. I'm heading out. That station is our best bet. If we leave now, I know that we could be there by nightfall. It's a risk I'm willing to take, because it sure as hell beats sitting here waiting to die." Eric made his way over to the bed and gathered up the few belongings he had with him. His cell phone that did nothing but produce an annoying beep when he tried to dial out, a pocket knife, jacket, and his wallet. There wasn't any money in it. Eric smiled a little as he pushed it into his back pocket, thinking to himself, *Not like any money is going to do a bit of good anyhow*.

Kent followed suit snatching up his shades, checked his pocket for his lighter, and picked up his crowbar. The weapon was covered in dry blood and had a few unidentifiable chunks on one end.

"Will you two hold on just one minute? If we are really about to do this, what's the plan? Do we even know where this stupid radio station is? Last I checked, Kent is the only one with any kind of a weapon. How do we know they'll still be there *if* we make it?"

Eric threw the sheets and pillows from his bed, then flipped the metal frame over. "We improvise." He kicked one of the metal leg posts, and after a few solid kicks, bent it enough to pry it free by force. He tossed the makeshift weapon across the room toward Cynthia and proceeded with breaking free another one of the legs.

"We'll use Cynthia's bag to bring some water bottles and anything else we might need that'll fit," Kent said. He and Cynthia hurried to fill the bag. Once filled, he said, "I'll take it."

The three gathered under the door and looked up. Moments passed without anyone saying a word.

Eric finally broke the tension, "That lady bag matches your eyes."

Kent glared up at him, crowbar in hand, shoulder bag tossed to one side. "I'll get you to tell me how it feels slammed against your balls if you don't shut up."

"Are we seriously doing this?" Cynthia asked.

The three of them peered up into the small glass opening in the door overhead. Small bits of lights periodically shown through, suggesting the sun was still out, which was a good sign. Last thing they felt was needed was to be taking this situation on in the dark. Hands, teeth, various fluids—mostly blood, and the occasional faces could be seen on the other side of the glass, blocking most of the sunlight.

"You guys ready for this?" Eric asked, attempting to come across with a laugh and smile but only sounding scared to death in the process.

"As ready as I am ever going to be," Kent said. "And besides, I'm out of smokes. Going to have to go out and get some sooner or later, right?"

Both men looked over at Cynthia, who held her weapon tightly gripped with both hands close to her chest, obviously nervous as hell. She just shrugged her shoulders; Eric and Kent looked back at one another having no words to say.

Eric reached for the latch and pulled the lever, releasing the locking mechanism on the door. All three of them found themselves looking back toward the room they were about to abandon, their sanctuary for the past two and a half days. It lasted only a moment. The thought of Tyler flashed into Eric's head. If his dad was at the radio station, then where was Tyler?

"Here goes nothing." Eric twisted the handle to the shelter door. The latched door swung open.

MOVE

1

The double doors came crashing closed, both Gus and Willy had landed on their backs in the center of the lobby. Boards, tables, and chairs, along with a single desk, lay scattered about in the room along the front. A little boy hid behind a fake tree in the corner, crouched behind its woven container, mostly exposed. The child smiled right at Gus. He couldn't have been more than ten years old.

The two soldiers surveyed their surroundings for a brief moment while standing to their feet, brushing themselves off. Chunks of gray, matted meat covered with blood fell from their black on black attire.

A large hunk of rotting skin was stuck on Willy's ammo belt, and he had to remove it with his bare hand. It was part of someone's face—the ear still attached.

While Willy spastically continued checking his gear and assessing the remaining ammunition in his guns, obviously shaken up a bit, Gus stepped toward the two men slinging boards to the front doors using makeshift hammers and bent-up rusty nails to re-barricade the room.

"They got Bo, man. What the fuck are we supposed to do now?" Willy said.

Gus immediately turned back to Willy, who had lost all the color in his face and his eyes looked glazed over.

"Stay tight, soldier. Stay tight! We've got to keep our heads in the game." Gus turned his attention back to the two men fast at work on the barricade. The door shook like crazy. Incessant moaning and banging of fists and limbs violently shook the doors on their hinges.

Gus grabbed hold of the large desk, and in one solid motion, yanked its heavy wooden frame in front of the doors—shoving it flush. "Got anything I can use as a hammer?" Gus said as calm as he could, given the situation.

"Look around and grab anything that'll work," Seth said while he feverishly worked.

"There's a box of nails on the floor next to that tree over there," George said.

Billy popped out from behind the tree, grabbed up the box of rusted, worn-out nails, and stepped out into the center of the lobby holding the box up high, excited to see the men in uniform. He always wanted to be a cop one day, because that's what his dad was and he loved his dad. He was so brave, at least, until he went missing.

Grabbing a heavy brass lamp, Gus ripped off the shade and headed for the door. "Let's see if this will do the trick," Gus said as he stepped past the little boy, taking several nails in hand as he did.

Billy's eyes never veered from Gus, not once.

The three men continued throwing up board after board, nailing in each piece quick and sloppy. Luckily, there were no windows in the room, leaving the doors to be the only thing worth worrying about when it came to barricading the place.

"Let's get these in, and then go back and reinforce it after," Seth said, pulling his long dark hair out of his eyes, sweat making it cling to his face a little.

Willy perched himself against the wall opposite of the doors, sat on the floor, and watched the three men hastily work. Looking confused and unable to focus, he had elbows propped up on knees with both hands covering his face. Several reloaded weapons tucked at his side. Two 9mm pistols, a mini machete, and an M-4 rifle all set ready to fire, safeties off.

"Your friend over there going to be all right, Mister? He doesn't look so hot," George asked, hammer in hand, swinging it as he spoke.

"Ya, he'll be fine. He just needs a minute," Gus replied. "We just lost one of our own out there. They were close friends, and besides, what the hell took you guys so long to let us in anyway? You do realize that we were getting run down out there, right?"

"You're looking at it, man. We had this whole thing boarded up. We saw you guys landing and immediately ran down here and started taking all of this crap down," Seth said.

*

Once upstairs, the five of them rewarded their hard labor with rest. The front entrance was once again boarded up and as secure as it would ever be, given what they had to work with.

Zombies pounded at the newly reconstructed blockade, ever persistent in quenching their hunger.

Willy sat next to Billy on one couch, Billy's age really showing. He sat wide-eyed and giddier than ever as he asked question after question about what it was like to fly in a helicopter.

Seth sat at his broadcaster's chair, discussing the situation with George and Gus.

Gus kept turning his gaze toward the window, his jaw tight with an ever-growing scowl on his face.

Even after the brutal display of fire from the sky and countless bodies falling to the ground, meeting their Maker never to return, never to rise again, the parking lot still managed to be just as full as ever. A hundred zombies, if not more, gathered below, with more gathering each minute from the adjacent streets.

The hoard of undead shuffled atop the countless remains of their fallen brothers and sisters. Moans grew as their numbers swelled. The chopper was completely surrounded by the undead, only the top half showed.

Gus abruptly rose and stood by the window, gazing out as if he were looking for something, someone. "Bo..." he whispered.

Nothing.

"Hey, are you listening to me, Mister?" Seth asked. "What's the plan? How are we going to get back on that helicopter and get out of here?"

Gus squinted his eyes and scratched his chin stubble, pulling himself away from the window. Barely fitting himself on the empty loveseat across from Willy and the boy, Gus' arms found both armrests as if it was a seat built for one.

"We aren't getting back on the chopper," Gus said very matter-of-factly.

"And why? You were sent here to rescue us, right?" Seth said.

"Bo was our pilot. He's gone, so we are just going to sit tight for now. Pilots usually stay with the bird and don't go on missions. We're so shorthanded we didn't have that luxury. And now we'll have to face the consequences. Don't worry, though. I've already radioed reinforcements. There's no telling how long it will take them to gear up and be on the move. A lot of roads looked congested with zombies and wreckage. I imagine that might slow up the cavalry a little. Until they get here, we're sitting ducks, and there's nothing else we can do. And besides, even if we did have the pilot, we wouldn't have enough ammo to get back out to the chopper anyhow. Sit and wait for the extraction is our only option."

"Why would you come here without enough ammo? Didn't you know how bad things are out here?" George asked.

"Bad intel. We were told we could land on the roof. Our primary objective was to shut down this signal, not fight an army of walking dead."

"What... you mean like shut down the station? Why in the hell would you need to—?"

"*Ccchhhsss...* Blue Bravo, this is Red Tango come in...over...*Ccchhhsss...*" Willy's radio chimed in, cutting off Seth. Willy unclipped the handset from his hip and tossed it across the room to Gus.

The radio looked half its actual size clenched in Gus' grip. He brought it up to his face with all eyes in the room on him. "This is Blue Bravo, what's your E.T.A.? Over."

There was a moment of tense silence as the group eagerly awaited reply.

More static.

"O'four hundred. Civilian status?"

Gus looked around the room for a second, then held down the button on the handset before continuing. "Three. Uninfected..."

More static.

The same voice came back over the radio from the other end but with a different tone to it; a less robotic more human one. "Sorry about Bo. I know you guys were close."

"Yeah," Gus said locking gazes with Willy.

The same man's robot inflection came back almost instantly. "Red Tango out."

Gus clicked the receiver again, still holding it close to his face. "Blue Bravo out. Stay tight."

Gus slung the device back to Willy, whose obvious fatigue had intensified. As he snapped the radio handset back to his belt, a bead of sweat trickled down his right cheek. His eyes looked dark with eyelids that looked like half-open shades. His skin had turned slightly pale. Hiding a cough under his sleeve, Willy sat up and looked about, as if realizing he was the center of attention. "I'm fine, I'm fine. I just need to rest for a second. I've been up for the last forty-eight. Give me a break."

"You don't look so good, Mister," Billy said.

"Why don't you sit over here and let Willy lay down for a bit." George motioned for the boy to sit on his lap, in front of all the colored lights and buttons.

"Willy over there lost his lunch when we jumped. In all our time out, I've never seen him do that. You wouldn't have anything to drink, would you?" Gus asked, standing to his feet, looking around in the room. "You're not going soft on me, are you, Willy?"

"Ya, I have a few bottled waters and a shit-ton of beer in the mini fridge over there," Seth said.

Gus opened it up and glanced over at Willy now laying sprawled out on the sofa. One foot rested on the floor, the other knee up, boot on the couch cushion, blood dripping down his ankle hidden out of sight, blood slowly starting to soak into the fabric.

"Ha, do you really have to ask?" Willy said as if to read Gus' mind.

Gus smirked and reached in the fridge, pulled out a cold beer, and handed it to Willy.

"Now that's what I'm talking about." Willy grinned as the beer reached his hand.

"It's going to be dark soon." Gus was back at the window again, the horde of undead still growing below. "The boards and chairs downstairs aren't going to hold those things out forever. There's just too many of them."

"You still haven't told us why you need to shut down the station. What do you think that's going to accomplish?" Seth said, sounding none too happy.

"Look, pal, we don't make the orders, we just follow them. Our orders were to come in, shut you down, and call it a day."

"So, is that what happened to the other stations and phone lines then? I take it that I'm right, because we still have power, which tells me the phones would be working as well," Seth said pulling a beer from the mini fridge, eyeing George to see if he would like one as well.

George shook his head and went back to preoccupying Billy.

Willy lay eyes closed, drink emptied, cold can pressed against his forehead with one hand.

"Number one," Gus stepped away from the window and stood in the middle of the room. His massive arm stretched out, and he shook his finger forcibly in Seth's face. "I don't appreciate the attitude, and second... well... there is no second."

Pulling his hand away from Seth's face, Gus calmed down. He pulled out his sidearm, released the magazine, examined it and slid it back in, then glanced down at Willy, who was looking worse by the minute. "Willy, are you feeling any better?"

The soldier's eyes had closed. Willy appeared to be asleep.

Gus turned to the others. "This thing, whatever it is... all of those people coming back to life like that. It's not everywhere. It's just here in the south. That much I can tell you. The rest... well, the rest is classified, some of which even from me. All I know is we've been flying that bird back and forth from town to town for the last two days, and every place is the same. You are the first group of survivors we've come across. Most signals we have shut down were on auto pilot with distress signals."

"Well isn't that just some peachy news," Seth said. "Once the cavalry does show up, how the hell are they supposed to even get to us, let alone us to them? We are fucking trapped in here."

2

The door to the shelter latch swung open, Cynthia, Eric, and Kent instantly jumped back into the room looking at one another not really sure what the actual plan might be, weapons held tightly.

A rot festering body plummeted down into the room, and then another and another. As each fell, the crushing sound of bone and flesh slammed against the cement. The third one landed on its neck the entire twelve feet face first. Its neck made a teeth-grinding crunch as the zombie's flimsy body met the solid floor below.

The three blood-soaked creatures slowly began rising to their feet, blood and other mess stuck to the ground from their bodies as they rose. The room filled with the stench of decay and mildew. Not a single one of the creatures was fully intact. Each one had been obliterated in some disturbing way. The one that had cracked its neck upon entry walked with its head cocked to one side.

The closest zombie now fully stood, lurched forward, both forearms missing. Biceps outstretched, bloodstains from its wounds, and bone peeking out from both limbs. The zombie's eyes instantly grew wide with excitement. Several more of the undead fell into the hole.

"Shit!" Kent leaped forward, crowbar in hand. With a thrust, the metal punctured the zombie's soft skin. Its chest caved in, giving way to the crowbar rupturing its heart. Kent furiously pulled the weapon from the creature's sternum and took a step back. Thick blood splattered over the floor. The monster wasn't even fazed. It kept coming toward them.

With not much room between them, the wall and the zombies, Cynthia started screaming. She dropped her makeshift club, the metal clanged against the cement floor, and then backed into the corner.

Eric remembered when Kent had rescued him. He came up from behind him and smashed that little zombie girl's head in. Her brains and chunks of something else all over the street where she fell.

"The heads, take out their heads!" Eric yelled as he confidently darted toward the armless zombie in the lead. Several more continued to fall from above through the open latch, each one moaning as they slapped the pavement floor. The room was now crammed with bodies. There had to be ten or more of those things in the room with them.

Eric's bedpost effectively met with the creature's face as he leaned in with all his weight, thrusting the object deep into its skull. Blood and tissue shot out onto Eric's arms, hands, and the floor. He aggressively yanked the metal post from the zombie, the dead thing now surely dead as it lay motionless with a gaping hole and blood dripping from what used to be its right eye.

Kent and Eric hesitated for a moment, both staring down at the dead creature on the floor. Eric had never killed anything before in his life, except for the one time that he accidentally ran over a cat. That, however, wasn't really his fault and he knew it, because had that stupid animal not randomly darted back in his direction as he passed it by, it would have been fine. But instead, it practically committed *kitty suicide* and jumped right back in front of the oncoming motor vehicle, both wheels giving it a good once over. Eric still felt bad about that, at least a little.

"Look out!" Cynthia shouted from behind them as a tattered zombie, who clearly had previously worked for UPS, came down on Kent.

With arms stretched out, the creature grabbed hold of Kent by the shirt. Its germ-infested mouth swung open, teeth flared, Kent unable to shake free. The zombie's brown shorts and shirt were covered in blood, grass stains, and something chunky. Its face was ghostly white, and its mouth was covered in blood. It almost made the thing look like a show clown covered in dried paint, who for some reason decided to eat all the paint.

Right as the creature's teeth started to descend upon Kent's tender, juicy flesh and muscle-filled arm, Eric's weapon came down on its back with full force, knocking it away from them both.

As it staggered for a moment, Kent's adrenaline caught up to him, and he instantly snapped. Gripping the blood-drenched crowbar, Kent fell upon the staggering creature, shouting relentlessly as he did so.

"You stupid UPS asshole! Fucking die already! Aaaahhhh…"

Kent's weapon repeatedly met the zombie's head as he shouted. The other zombies that had fallen into the shelter, with outstretched arms, made their way toward them, moaning.

Cynthia jumped up, grabbing her metal bedpost from the floor, following suit with the others.

With all three of them shouting and swinging, dull *thuds* and *thunks*, wet splatters, and bones cracking sounded in the underground room. Undead after undead fell to the floor covered in more blood than before.

With just about each reanimated corpse that fell to never again rise, another fell into the hole taking its place. The small room was beginning to get claustrophobic.

"There's too many!" Cynthia shouted.

Almost completely cornered to one side of the room, the three would-be warriors clung tight to one another's side, weapons drawn. A very large, overweight male zombie closed in on them, fifteen or more right behind it, others still were falling into the shelter from the open latch, one by one.

The dead man's shirtless belly shook with each step toward them. The dead man was only wearing a dirty old pair of whitey-tighties and one half-loose sock. He seemed to have nothing really wrong with him. No bite marks or blood. He was just pale and bruised on one side of the chest. Then he stumbled and slightly turned showing bite marks on his back, torn muscle and tissue exposing the backside of his ribs.

Behind him, the pantry shelf crashed to the floor. Several zombies fumbled over the shelf and its contents, pushing forward among the small crowd, trying like the rest to get at Eric, Kent, and Cynthia. Canned food and toilet paper now littered the floor.

With the overweight zombie almost on top of them, Cynthia screamed and took two steps forward, slamming her weapon into the beast. The zombie's head shot back as its neck exploded. Blood rained out like a struck piñata full of children's candy. Her metal rod lodged in its throat, extending out of the back of its neck right under the skull. The weight of the zombie overpowered her as it fell forward, teeth and eyes still fixed on her during its descent.

Trying to hold the putrid thing back, she stretched out her arms, thrusting hard in a forward motion still holding the lodged weapon, with a firm grip. As she screamed, eyes closed, landing back against the wall from the mass of dead flesh falling upon her, the creature dropped at her feet.

She opened her eyes, arms still outstretched before her. The weight of the zombie's body was too much for its own skin. The zombie's head was attached to the blunt object, body motionless on the floor before her. She screamed even louder.

The weapon was lodged between bits of the zombie's spine. Its milky-white eyes and coffee-stained, blood-filled teeth still busy at work chomping in midair. She dropped the weapon, still attached to the amputated face.

To the ground it fell, and she vigorously kicked the bodiless head. It bounced toward the other end of the room, getting lost between the legs and feet of the other ghouls still walking toward them.

Eric and Seth continued fighting for their survival, delivering blow after blow to heads, puncturing eyes, mouths, and skulls.

The overweight body on its stomach now, revealing its wounds, was partially leaning against Cynthia's leg. She bounced to one side giving a little room, quivering at the sight of the lifeless, headless body.

"This isn't going to work. We aren't going to make it," Cynthia screamed hysterically, flailing her arms about aimlessly in a panic, standing next to the oversized corpse.

"She's right, there're too many of them. We have to do something." Kent heaved out of breath in mid-swing, crowbar cracking a zombie's skull wide open. A litter of bodies lay before them, but every second seemed like more were in the room than before.

"I got it! The generator!" Eric lunged forward with all of his might—knocking down several zombies and taking one down for good with a solid blow to the face from his broken bedpost. A zombie's eye popped out as he retrieved the weapon.

"Get to the bathroom," Eric shouted, completely surrounded by the undead making its way across the room toward the fallen supply of food.

"What are you doing?" Cynthia huffed as Kent pulled her by the shirt toward the bathroom.

Swinging wildly and pushing to keep the zombies off of him, Eric furiously kicked the PVC pipe from the ventilation system to the generator and pulled out his pocketknife. He stabbed both drums of gasoline next to the generator and jammed the knife into the generator's fuel tank.

He turned and hastily made his way for the bathroom door, Kent and Cynthia already behind it. Totally surrounded by the undead, Eric forced his way through the crowd, pushing with everything he had to get to the door unscathed.

One zombie got a solid grip on Eric's wrist and used the leverage to lunge forward. The monstrous jaws wide open fell upon Eric's shoulder—biting down hard. Eric flinched but didn't let it slow him down. With the creature still holding onto him, it came down for another bite. Eric turned and punched it square in the jaw, separating its jaw all together with his right hand. A few loose teeth glided through the air.

The zombie stumbled back releasing its grip, as Eric reached the door, shouting, "Open the fucking door!"

The door swung open, and without breaking stride, Eric fell into the cramped bathroom, slammed the door behind him. Instant pounding erupted from the other side.

"Are you out of you ever-loving mind?" Kent said, shoving him on his shoulder.

Eric instantly winced as a jolt of pain shot up his shoulder to his head.

"What are we supposed to do now?" Cynthia asked with a flustered tone. She stood in the bathtub to make room in the already cramped area.

The room was pitch black, the light off. It took Eric a moment to collect his thoughts. "We wait."

"Wait, and for what exactly?" Cynthia again asked with the same flustered tone.

"Please tell me you have your lighter on you," Eric said, standing next to Kent at the door.

A moment later, Eric felt something small and hard push on his arm. He took the lighter. Eric flipped back the lid and pulled down on the flint wheel with his thumb. The flint sparked and lit the wick. Shadows danced wildly around the three of them in the room, each one's face looked menacingly evil in its golden glow, twice over reflecting in the bathroom mirror. They all stared at the flame as it danced about, sounds of the undead moaning and pounding before them, nowhere else to go, trapped.

With a very unsure look on his face, Eric smiled at Kent, and said, "It works in the movies… here goes nothing!"

He reached for the doorknob, one hand holding the lit Zippo.

"What worked in the movies?" Cynthia asked.

Eric quickly opened the door just a crack, it was slightly heavy to push open with the restricting mob pressed against it. Eric tossed the lighter out into the other room and slammed the door shut holding the handle tight, pulling back on the door with all his weight.

Nothing happened.

"What worked in the movies?" Cynthia shouted over the sounds of their oppressors trying to get it.

Kent said, "Would you just chill out for at least one—?"

BOOM… the fuel fumes from the generator caught, catching the two drums in a blaze. Instantly, the bathroom door blew from its hinges, sending Kent and Eric flying back into Cynthia. All three of them came crashing down into the tub, bathroom door on top of them. Eric still held the doorknob in his grip, the door no longer attached.

Zombies lay scattered about in the other room. Some of them had caught fire, and others fell to the floor with fewer limbs than they had previously. Arms and legs were tossed about among the strewn bodies. The room was filled with black smoke that bellowed out into the back yard from the open shelter latch.

After a moment, Eric and the others finally came to.

"Everyone okay?" Kent shouted.

"I'm okay," Cynthia mouthed.

"Me too." Eric nodded, realizing that if their ears were ringing half as bad as his, they too could hardly hear a thing.

The three of them shook it off, and after a moment, gathered themselves together, and made it out into the main living space of the shelter. It was a disaster. A thick black fog covered everything.

Stepping over bodies, the three hurriedly made their way across the room toward the door. A large ray of light beamed into the room from overhead.

Around them, zombies started to shuffle about. At the foot of the ladder, Cynthia made eye contact with a bodiless head, eyes still fixed on the group as they began to climb the ladder. Its chubby cheeks and punctured jugular bled out on the floor, her makeshift weapon still lodged in its neck. The beds, or what was left of them, were blazing behind them.

After climbing the ladder, the three stood in Tyler Wellington's back yard filled with bodies covered in black ash and red gore. Behind them, smoke poured out from the underground shelter that had held them safe from the outside world up until now. It was a miracle they made it out alive. They could have easily been blown up, eaten, or choked to death from all the oxygen being removed from the shelter during the explosion.

Eric thought of the door that lay on top of them in the tub. It had been their saving grace.

As they dusted themselves off and took in the surroundings, Kent slapped Eric on the shoulder again, looking happier than ever. "You have got to be—"

Eric winced and grabbed his shoulder, startling both Cynthia and Kent. He slowly removed his shirt and jacket.

"I got bit," Eric said, a defeated intonation in his voice.

After examining the shoulder, Cynthia smiled. "Didn't break the tissue."

Eric was too shaken up to really want to take a good look at it. The skin wasn't broken, sure. But it still hurt. It was bruised to hell and back, but the flesh hadn't been torn. No blood. Feeling slightly overwhelmed in a good way, Eric put his shirt and jacket back on, and looked around at the yard.

They all did.

Zombies littered the ground around them as they stood next to the door, some now slowly starting to move. They must have been standing around the shelter opening when the generator blew, because their top halves were blackened. One zombie was on fire.

Several zombies lingered in the street closer to the front of the house, but didn't pose any immediate threat. The rest of the yard was empty. Despite the lack of numbers before them, the grass was almost nonexistent. Footprints tracked the entire yard, turning most of the landscape into a mud path.

As they soaked in the events of the afternoon, they stood dusting themselves off, black dust puffing out around them as they patted themselves down. Eric pointed to the house connected to the back yard, gesturing they make in that direction.

As they made their way across the yard, spirits lifted and the sun shining, no one even took notice of the bloody cut on Eric's right hand, discoloration already setting in on his knuckle. It was going to be dark soon.

3

The front yard had a few stragglers shuffling about in the grass and driveway. Quite a few more were in the streets. Scattered mud tracks led from the Wellington driveway out into the street heading in practically the same direction Kent and the others had intended on going. Kent wondered if the tracks were from the mass of zombies that had been in the back yard trying to get into the shelter. Whatever had gotten their attention, causing them to leave the yard, Kent was thankful.

The sky had changed from a baby blue to a multitude of colors. Purple, pinks, and yellows blossomed in the sky as the sun prepared its descent.

"We need to get a set of wheels if we're going to try for the station," Kent said as he glanced out the front window through the blinds. He walked into the other room to join the others, realizing he had been mostly speaking to himself.

They spent the first few minutes rummaging through the house. No one was home, and surprisingly, the back door was unlocked. The three of them found themselves in the kitchen discussing what to do.

Kent sat on the countertop, and Cynthia was snooping in the pantry for something to eat.

"I know we probably don't have a ton of time to waste, but my house is only a few blocks away. I have to go there, see if my parents are alive. I just have to know," Eric said with a lukewarm Dr. Pepper in one hand, the other rubbing his sore shoulder.

"We need a car and some real weapons," Kent said and eyed the gory crowbar on the countertop beside him.

"For now, I think we can grab a baseball bat or two. When we make it to my house, I'm sure I can find my dad's revolver—assuming it's still at the house. Nothing else comes to mind."

Cynthia stood munching on a bag of barbeque chips, looking out the window in the kitchen above the sink. There wasn't much to look at other than the adjacent house and the fence line. "Whatever the plan is, I think we need to do it now. We're burning daylight."

"Hell, I'm ready when you are," Kent said, hopping down from the counter, purposefully bumping into Cynthia, but trying his best to make it look like an accident.

He reached up to catch her as his bodyweight sent her a little off balance. Kent wasn't born yesterday, he knew good and well how to read the ladies—regardless if the world was going to hell. As he grabbed hold of her, he slowly let her go, bringing her into himself slightly while making sure to maintain eye contact for as long as possible. It was obvious she liked it.

Eric exited the kitchen and started pulling everything out from the hall closet. He found what he was looking for and even knew where to look. He retrieved two baseball bats. One was made of wood and the other was aluminum. The countless sleepovers in middle school came in handy. Before they stepped a foot into the house, he was aware that there would be zero guns in there, so he didn't bother checking things out upstairs. He only yelled out to anyone that might be home, and after a moment without any response, he went about his business, looking through all the rooms.

Cynthia and Kent made it into the living room at the front door of the house. Eric held both bats up, smirking at Cynthia, wondering which one she would choose.

"The aluminum one is lighter," Eric said.

She nodded and took it from him. They stood by the front door, weapons at the ready, eyeing one another. "Déjà vu anyone?"

Cynthia laughed as they all stood there crouched in close, weapons up high.

They all smiled.

Something about Cynthia was starting to change. She seemed more relaxed than when they first met, but more in an unhinged way than from building confidence. She smiled a lot more, and given the current set of situations, that just didn't seem right.

"We're following you, dude man," Kent said from behind Eric.

A few steps out the door and Eric immediately met a zombie's face with the business end of his wooden bat. Blood exploded into the sky as the wood collided with the zombie's nose, breaking its face. The zombie fell back, knees bent.

The race was on. Several zombies in the yard and along the street took notice, but they didn't bother pursuing. All three noticed the massive mud trail leading off down the road to their right as they passed up the adjacent street and continued down the block headed left. The mud led out into the street from the back yard onto the driveway and into the street.

Eric pointed and they all nodded in agreement, faces thankful for whatever had aided them in thinning the horde.

Mmm... I don't normally date older women, but damn that's nice. Not really taking into perspective that she was only a few years older than him, Kent trailed behind Cynthia as they swiftly made their way down the street, along the sidewalk, at a quiet, yet steady pace. Her ass shook vigorously with each step. Her clothes ragged and stained, the pant leg on the left side split up the seam slightly past the knee, revealing the back of her silky white leg.

Must have happened when that obese zombie fell on her, Kent thought.

Her shirt was partly covered in dried blood and most of her was covered in soot. Handprints covered each cheek of her pants from where she had patted herself down before. Kent was slightly turned on just watching her tote that baseball bat. It made her seem all business, red hair bounced down her shoulders onto her thinly built frame. Sure she might have been a little out of shape, but who wasn't at her age.

"Would you quit looking at my ass and pay attention?" Cynthia said.

They had stopped on the sidewalk. Eric was crouched behind a thick tree, pointing his blood-stained bat at a red, one-story house only a few mailboxes down. This part of the neighborhood was closer to the main road, only a block and a half from the Publix grocery store off Highway 77. There wasn't a single zombie in sight. However, they heard the sound of their cries from where they stood. Fire crackled in the distance, and the smell of something burning was apparent.

Motioning them in close while keeping his voice low, Eric said, "We probably have less than thirty minutes of daylight left, and there's no telling how long we have to get to the radio station. When we get to my house, there are some backpacks in the closet in the living room. I want you to both get one each and make for the kitchen. Get some dry goods. If we get stuck out there, I want to be able to eat tonight."

"But I was beginning to like my man-bag," Kent said, yanking at Cynthia's bag filled with bottled waters strapped over his shoulder. It made them all smile a little.

"While you two get the food, I'm going to see what other weapons we can get and check on my parents. But, *yes*, lose the bag. *I'm sure one of the backpacks will match your outfit*." Eric had ended the sentence with a nod and led them toward his house.

*

Eric sat on his parents' nicely made bed, looking over the small revolver and four boxes of ammunition. Ninety-six bullets in all. Defeated, Eric sat there, muscles and mind finally giving way to the emotional and physical stress of the last several days. His parents were nowhere to be found in the house. For all he knew, the whole town, possibly the whole world, was overtaken by cannibalistic madness.

The last time that he had talked with his parents was at the dining room table while playing dominos and telling stories. Despite his age and the statistical B.S. that went with it, Eric was very close to his parents, even in the middle of his teenage angst. He missed them greatly.

Looking over at the gun on the bed, he thought about the day that his dad decided he was old enough to learn gun safety. He was still only a little kid then but remembered it clear as day. The fancy case with foam insulation on the inside, and the just-like-new smell that had filled his nose with its aroma. His dad wasn't ever really big on guns, but with Eric's mom being highly allergic to dogs, they decided some type of protection would be a good idea.

Eric recalled the several times that his father took him to the gun range, to teach him how to properly use a weapon. This, of course, wasn't until later when he had gotten a little older. Eric loved doing things like that with his father. This one-on-one time reminded Eric of the movies and television shows he saw on TV and how they depicted life should be. His dad was generally quite busy, so what time was given to Eric was cherished.

Eric let out a big sigh, picked up the gun and ammo, then headed out of the room, but not before glancing in the mirror. His face was filthy; his entire body was too. Covered from head to toe in dried blood and soot, Eric finally caught a glimpse of his jacket. The shoulder that had been bitten looked beyond repair. That sucked, because that was his favorite jacket.

Shrugging off his appearance, Eric stepped out into the hall and into his room across the way. Posters of sports players and girls in bikinis covered his wall, along with several gaming posters. A few finished and unfinished model cars sat atop his dresser. A small television hooked to a gaming system was stacked in the closet above his clothes. Eric was a typical American kid and he knew it. He never got into drugs like some of his other friends and was better off for it. That's probably why Tyler and he were close friends. The older Eric got, the harder it was to keep good friends around that didn't want to try getting you into something not worth messing with.

Eric grabbed a change of clothes from his dresser and tossed the torn jacket into the closet. He threw on a clean pair of jeans and a plain white undershirt, with the same sneakers he had on before. After sifting through the closet for his backpack, Eric realized that he had left it on the school bus. Luckily, he had an extra one in the closet. He filled it with a change of socks and underwear, along with the ammunition for the gun. He checked the gun to make sure it was loaded and clipped the holster to his belt. He thought it a good idea to have extra bullets on hand and reached into the bag to pull out a few to stick in his front pocket.

"Well, shit, man. You clean up well," Kent said as he stood in the doorway, Cynthia right behind him on her tippy toes peering over Kent into the room. They both had on backpacks and had their weapons in hand.

"We ready to do this or what, dude?" Kent said looking down at Eric, who was on his knees in the room, stuffing his backpack, shoving bullets into his pocket.

Regardless of him changing into a new pair of clothes, Eric was aware that he looked just as outlandish as the two that stood at his door. The water was off at the Wellington house, so they didn't even bother trying it here. He stood, tossing the bag around the unsore appendage, face and arms covered in muck, and not a single spot of dirt on his attire.

"Almost." Eric grinned, pulling the mattress up and away from the wood frame exposing several magazines and a single key on a key ring. "Anybody want to go for a ride?" Eric stepped forward, tossing the key into the air, then snatched it back in midair with the same hand.

"We found a few extra waters, some chips, mixed nuts, and an apple for each of us," Cynthia said as the three of them made their way down the hall. A dozen frames hung on the wall with photos of friends and family, along with the occasional photo of a happy moment in life. One of which was a picture of Eric and his dad halfway leaning over the hood of a junked out car, each covered from fingertip to elbow in grease, smiling. That picture was a few years old.

"Hey, this must be you and your folks. You look just like that man," Cynthia said.

Both Eric and Kent had made it into the kitchen and looked back to find Cynthia still standing in the hallway eyeing a photo. Having lived in that house his whole life, Eric didn't need to see what picture she was looking at. He could just tell by where she stood in the hall as to which picture she was referring.

Slightly agitated, and with a hint of distress, Eric snapped off, "Ya, that's my dad and mom, we had just ridden the Tower of Terror. Are we going or what?" Eric stood by a door in the kitchen that led into the garage.

"Gosh, sorry I even brought it up." She made her way into the kitchen; the garage door was already open.

Eric stepped into an old El Camino. Kent stood at the passenger door with the door open.

"Ladies first," Kent said raising one hand palm up.

The car didn't look like much aside from the new paint job, but it cranked up, not quite just like new, but good enough. Eric clicked the headlights *on* and pressed the garage door opener. Nothing happened. He pressed it again.

"Shit, the power's out. I totally forgot." Eric opened the driver side door and stepped out.

With the rev of the engine, and the headlights at his back, Eric's shadow shot up one side of the garage door as he leaned in pulling it over his head. The darkness startled him, unaware that night had fully arrived. The headlights instantly illuminated the outside world. Eric stood for a moment trying to let his eyes adjust as he looked out into the street. He didn't see a single zombie. *Where could they be? Where did they all go?* Eric thought of the muddy street by Tyler's house for a moment.

"What's he doing?" Kent asked, sitting in the passenger seat with Cynthia beside him, his left arm across the headrest behind her.

She just looked back at him as confused as he was.

A zombie lunged out from the shadows beside the house and landed on top of Eric. The creature wrestled Eric to the ground, snarling and biting. His back to the floor, he had his arms out trying to keep the thing's teeth at bay. Both Eric's and the attacker's shadows stretched across the driveway from the headlights. With the headlights beaming down right in front of them, Eric could see everything perfectly clear.

The zombie's skin was white as a ghost and tight to the bone. Its cheeks caved into its face, along with its eyes. Both of the creature's lips looked as if they had been torn off, or even eaten off, revealing most of its teeth, and a good amount of its gums. The corpse's gum line was discolored. No longer its natural red, they looked puffed up, a grayish purple. Blood was caked around its mouth and chin. Its thin frail arms reached out at him, Eric held onto them both without much trouble.

The zombie must have been small to begin with, because it didn't seem to weigh much at all. It was more being startled that brought Eric to the driveway than the actual attack. With its arms stretched out, Eric saw that it was missing an index finger and thumb on one hand. It didn't seem to be bleeding. The area around the flesh was a puffy gray and red. The blood was clotted, preventing it from bleeding out. Then again, this thing could have been dead long enough that it already bled out everything it had.

Eric heard the sound of the passenger door open and footsteps headed in his direction from behind the car. The steps passed him and kept on going. While still wrestling with the small zombie, Eric caught a glance of Kent in the yard swinging his crowbar.

The frail zombie flew from atop Eric and onto the driveway beside him. As Cynthia's aluminum bat came crashing down, her legs in a wide stance practically straddling Eric, he flinched covering his face with his left arm. A cold, wet fluid splattered across Eric's arm and chest as the bat slammed into the ground beside him. After only a few swings, the bat made a pinging sound as cement met aluminum. It had only taken two solid hits for the zombie's rotting skull to collapse, shattering in two. The remaining hit from her bat cleared the zombie's skin, bone, and brain colliding with the driveway beneath it.

"Fuck, me," Eric spat as Cynthia helped him to his feet in front of the El Camino.

Kent still stood in the yard, swinging his metal club furiously, attacking the lingering zombies that had finally started to make their way up the road. Several other zombies began to gather from the other end of the street as well, making their way toward the Micson household.

"Let's go," Eric shouted dashing around the open driver side door.

Kent quickly turned and made for the car. The three of them jumped into the vehicle, slamming both doors simultaneously. Eric gripped the steering wheel, and hit the gas, taking them out past the driveway into the street.

More than a dozen zombies littered the street in front of the house, something Eric was unable to see before from the garage, the street pitch black, no streetlights to brighten them.

As the car barreled down the neighboring streets toward town, Eric frantically took turns left and right, speeding past stop sign after stop sign, the gas gauge well past *E*. The car slammed into a wandering zombie as it reached out for the oncoming car—sending the zombie barreling over the hood of the car into the back bed. As the zombie stood up in the back of the car, it instantly lost its balance and fell out of the car, smashing into the road.

The gas light suddenly lit up, getting their attention as they flew down the street at nearly 50 mph, passing house after house with not a single sign of life.

4

The Rhino Runner tore down Highway 231 southbound at a steady 65 miles per hour, which was saying a lot for the oversized armored bus. The two-man extraction team consisted of Megan Linkouscie and Luke Beal.

Megan was a spitfire of a woman with more skeletons in her closet than Saddam Hussein. She had served two terms in Iraq, dealing in civilian and VIP transport in and out of the Green Zone, without a single fatality to count against her during each term. That is if you are only counting the lives she was commissioned to protect. The truth was, she had more kills than skeletons. Her favorite weapon of choice had been the M-4 carbine compact rifle, with its variable selective fire rate and lightweight casing, never left her side. *It's my visa*, she would always say, knowing she could hold her own in any situation.

Luke wasn't quite as cocky as Megan; it wasn't part of his personality. He had an inborn air of confidence. He had worked one term in Iraq alongside the infamous Linkouscie, transporting civilian contractors, military personnel, and the press, generally from one base to another. Although Luke was a natural marksman, he usually took the wheel when handling missions involving the Rhino Runner, leaving Megan to handle the odds and ends of each extraction. Of course, that had been years ago. The Rhino Runner they piloted was military surplus. These vehicles weren't meant to be driven on American highways. But with the rise of the undead and the situation becoming critically chaotic both politically and globally, they had been sent in to help the Tallahassee base contain the spread. But they both knew better. Something this viral would eventually be uncontainable, and quite possibly already was well beyond the borders they were sent in to help protect.

"Slow it down some! You're going to need to veer right onto Fifteenth Street in a second." Megan sat in the passenger seat bouncing up and down, pointing at the road ahead of them, as the massive civilian cargo bus barreled down the highway.

Even though they were both equal in rank, Luke didn't mind that she barked orders at him. He actually liked it, even when in front of other officers. Sure, he caught some flak for it, but it didn't bother him because he knew where Megan's heart was. And at the end of the day, he was the one who reaped the rewards. Luke was the one who held the cards both on the job and in the dark.

They had been a serious item for the last eight years. The trash-talk attitude Megan had toward Luke in public was their attempt at keeping up politically correct work-related appearances. They both found that the closer they became, the smoother the operations went on the job. Funny thing was everyone knew about their relationship. No one cared. Not even their commanding officer. The Commander knew a good team when he saw one.

With the Rhino Runner now racing down 15th street after veering right, Megan scanned the GPS tracker to determine the next turn they might need to take.

"I think we're going to be on this road a while," said Megan, eyes examining the gloomy city streets as the scenery rapidly changed from an emptiness of the murky highway to a ghost town of congestion. Wrecked cars and abandoned storefronts all without power sat in wait, ghouls lingering in its wake. As the armored bus drove deeper into the city toward the Panama City Beach Hathaway Bridge, a presence of the living dead became more and more manifest.

Zombies staggered in the streets and in abandoned parking lots, all turning their gazes toward the oncoming vehicle, high beams lighting up the night as it rolled down the winding road. 15th Street was dead; Panama City was dead. It was exactly what they had expected to see and had seen for the last few days.

In the still of night under the half-lit moon, the bus slowly came to a halt, parking in the middle of the street. The bridge was in sight. The bus headlights revealed what they didn't hope to find. So far, the zombies they had passed along the way had been relatively spread out and low in numbers, but this was no longer the case.

"It never can just be an *in and out OP*, can it?" Megan said looking over at Luke behind the steering wheel.

"Well, shit. What do you suppose we do now? I haven't seen so many in one place like this before," Luke replied.

"Ha… You remember when we escorted the U.S. Secretary of Defense across the Baghdad International Airport and the confinements?"

Luke smirked, nodding, gripping the wheel a little tighter. "Yes, but don't forget we had two Humvees with us. Let's also not forget that one of those vehicles blew the hell up."

"Oh come on, Luke. You act like there's going to be landmines on that fucking bridge."

Megan and Luke sat there, bus idling, the engine's hum lightly roared at a steady rate. Beyond the headlights, what they could see was unmistakable. An ocean of the dead slowly made their way across the bridge, most likely headed to the same destination as the Rhino Runner. Easily a couple hundred rotting corpses meandered across the manmade construct. There were so many of them it was hard to tell if the bridge was congested with vehicles too. With the way things had looked on their way in, it was more than likely going to be the case.

With more undead still pushing against the passing hoard that hadn't made it onto the bridge yet, some attention toward the idling bus started to form. Several stragglers in the streets making their way to the bridge took notice of the Rhino Runner, quickly making a U-turn. Their moans and hissing helped attract the attention of several others as the inevitable trend began to take effect. A steadily growing mob of zombies trekked in their direction, features becoming clearer with each step forward as the bus lights beamed down on the growing crowd of putrid flesh and bones.

The milky-white gaze of a handful of zombies lit up from the headlights of the bus as they crept closer and closer to the idling vehicle. Megan and Luke glared into the eyes of death as the creatures slithered toward them and surrounded the front of the bus. The zombies' torn flesh and bones visible. All hands stretched out ready to attack the people inside.

One zombie walked toward them, with only one hand outstretched, unlike the rest. The lights divulged its reason. It diligently kept hold of a severed limb. As it paced toward them, it instinctively refused to release the partially devoured arm.

Megan glanced at Luke again as they both witnessed in horrifying detail the atrocious mob falling upon them. Luke reached for the bus radio and clicked the receiver while holding it to his face. "Blue Bravo, this is Red Tango come in…"

Static, and silence.

"Blue Bravo, this is Red Tango come in… Over."

The undead mob reached the vehicle pressing their bodies into it, beating and pushing against its sturdy hull. The bus shook violently from side to side.

"Blue Bravo, this is Red Tango, come in…"

More static, and silence.

"Red Tango to Blue Bravo, what's your E.T.A?" the voice said.

*

Nothing had changed at the radio station. Gus, Willy, Seth, George, and Billy sat upstairs twiddling their thumbs, waiting for the extraction to happen. Seth had run out of cold beers by this time. Between him and Willy, they had both drunk a good eight or nine beers apiece.

Gus refused to have any alcohol, knowing that things were going to get a little hairy once the secondary team arrived. Gus originally didn't feel it to be a good idea that anyone drink before getting back to the base, but Seth was persistent, with saying *Might as well drink up, don't want to let them go to waste.*

Gus had also opted out on telling Willy not to drink, against his better judgment, but knew that he had taken Bo's death a lot harder, so Gus let it slide.

Billy had fallen asleep on the floor surrounded by tons of open discs. He had decided to sift through almost every last record in the room, feeling the need to pick out the best song to listen to before they were rescued. This, of course, was only if Mr. Seth was willing to let him do all of the button pressing. He had fallen asleep before even picking out the song.

George stood by the window watching the steadily growing mob outside. "Hell," he said.

"What?" Seth asked.

"They had to come from Hell," George said with one hand in his pocket holding tightly to something.

"Ha… yeah, that and then some, old man," Seth said slurring his words a little as he leaned over the empty mini fridge.

Willy had passed out on the couch in the same spot he had been laying when they first arrived upstairs.

"We've got another delay," came the robotic monotone voice on the other end of Gus' handset. Familiar grunts and hissing came from the background noise of the radio. Moans of the dead echoed beneath the static.

"Details," Gus replied.

"We are approximately thirty clicks out but have a delay. There's a mob of zombies who would like nothing better than peeling this vehicle open and eating us like sardines," Luke said.

"Take your time. Don't compromise the mission. Just be safe. I'll inform the base of the delay," Gus said.

"Roger that, Red Tango out."

Gus immediately radioed in headquarters speaking directly with First Class Lieutenant Rob Foster. While he relayed details of the extraction delays, he couldn't help but wonder what was in George's pocket. The man had pulled it out eyeing it several times but had turned away from Gus preventing him from seeing it. Not only that, but the old goat kept fidgeting with it.

*

"You ready to light these mothers up?" Luke asked.

Megan unbuckled her seatbelt and made her way to the back of the bus. The Army had confiscated a number of flamethrowers offered by a survivalist company. She had minimal training on the torch's use, but she was a disciplined soldier and had full confidence in her abilities. The safety goggles went on first but as the most basic form of protection. The two tanks were on a backpack and she struggled to get the straps secured around her shoulders.

With the device in place, she ascended the ladder to the hatch on the roof. Releasing the latch and pushing open the hatch, she stuck the upper half of her body out.

"Fuck you, bitches!"

With a pull of the trigger, the bright flame erupted from the nozzle. Its bright golden glow lit the world around her, exposing what lingered out in the near distance previously hidden by shadows. An ambush of zombies steadily approached the idling bus. An easy twenty had already made their way up alongside the vehicle, frantically attempting to get inside.

"Let's do this!" Luke steadily gave the Rhino some gas, sending the armored monstrosity across the field of walking corpses.

Megan narrowed her aim in on the cluster of ghouls surrounding the front of the bus. The flame shot out as she pulled the trigger and swung the nozzle from side to side. Instantly, over a dozen bodies were drenched with the near thousand-degree inferno. Skin crackled and popped like puffed rice as it blistered and burned.

Luke watched from the driver's seat as the mob of angry flesh-crazed zombies ignited. The zombies scattered about, flailing their limbs in the air. Flesh scorching on their bones sent a few to the ground. Others bumped into one another, catching who they touched on fire. Dead flesh popped and sizzled like bacon cooked in a frying pan.

As the bus inched forward and zombie after zombie burst into a fiery glow, the stench of burning rotten skin and hair filled the air. Megan swung the flame back and forth, dousing the zombies along each side of the bus. The decomposed smell of rancid tissue as it melted on rotting bones reached Megan's nose. The stench had her gagging. She forced back the vomit as it raced up her throat and let out a gasp from holding her breath. Thankfully, everything stayed down.

The numbers of the mob directly in front quickly dispersed, allowing the bus to move forward toward the bridge. Zombie bones crushed and heads popped shooting brains along the road as tires rolled over. Meagan's body swayed as the Rhino trekked over the fallen dead.

The vehicle passed down the street leaving behind a wake of zombies still chasing the bus. The goal wasn't to get rid of the problem but to simply get past it.

The bus made its way up to the bridge and forced its way through the crowd as far as it could, running over countless zombies. As the bus slowly moved forward, blood and gore drenched the windshield and splattered across the grill as faces met its force.

Once at near center of the bridge, the mass of zombies around the Rhino Runner brought it to a halt. The bus shook more violent than before, zombies ten and twenty deep on all sides pressed against it. The moans and screeches from the undead plague grew so loud that when Megan squeezed the trigger of her flamethrower, the roaring hiss of its blaze was drowned out.

Zombies lit up the night, and their screams grew louder.

5

People filled the cafeteria. Most wore green and gray uniforms. A select few dressed in black and sat together apart from everyone else. An even smaller number of men and women wore slacks and white coats. Those, too, separated themselves like a small flock of birds. Almost everyone had a weapon of some kind, but generally just the standard issue 9mm sidearm holstered at the hip.

The room was quite loud, filled with the chatter of small talk, and a movie playing in the background on three separate television sets all positioned in different corners of the room. The movie was of no real importance and no one showed it the slightest bit of attention.

Dinner time was taken in two shifts, one at 7 p.m. and the other at 7:45 p.m. Theresa Gibbs generally took hers along with the first batch and took thirty minutes to eat, spending the remainder of her time back in her lab, which she deemed of the utmost importance.

Not one to follow trends, Gibbs found herself seated with General Baker, Lieutenant Rob Foster, as well as a few others, one of which was missing. For a moment, she had forgotten that Clay had been sedated earlier that day due to stress and lack of rest. The man needed it, and she was glad to see that he was getting to sleep it off.

Gibbs didn't really get along with Baker, but he generally held his manners at the dinner table and liked to keep to small talk. To her, that said a lot about the man's character.

Even though Foster could be a bit annoying at times, she had to admit, at least to herself, that he was quite adorable with his boyish charm and witty sense of humor. She was on to him and appreciated his attempts to win her favor, but just didn't want to take the time away from her work to build a relationship. She did, however, enjoy the attention.

She and Baker talked about their favorite jazz singers, while Rob strutted down the aisle carrying two trays of food, one of which belonged to the lovely Dr. Gibbs.

"Here you are, little lady," Rob Foster said as he handed her the plate of food.

Gibbs did her best to push work into the back of her mind, deciding to take the entire forty-five-minute break today, knowing that after dinner they would be having a meeting. "Thank you, kind sir."

"Why don't you two just hook up already?" Clay said at his abrupt, unexpected entrance. He pulled out a chair and flopped down on the seat.

"Jared Clay, what are you doing up already? I didn't expect to see you until tomorrow," Gibbs said coolly.

"A man's got to eat sometime," Clay said, ending his sentence with a mouthful of whipped potatoes. He swallowed, and said, "Thanks, by the way, for the shot. I feel tons better. I really needed the sleep."

"I'm glad to hear it, son. We're going to need you tonight too. Going to be a late night for some. That's if you're going to be up to it, of course," General Baker said.

Gibbs frowned and narrowed her gaze. "He should take things slowly."

"I'm fine," Clay said with food in his mouth. He was a southern boy through and through. Born and bred in the South, the rest of the world remained a mystery for the most part. After getting into trouble a time or two with the law and the inevitable knock down drag out he and his folks had, his future didn't offer many options. Working for his old man the rest of his life as an electrician, despite the decently sized pay, didn't seem like the life he had always hoped to have. Clay *wanted* to see the world, wanted to meet different ladies of all nationalities.

One day, sitting in the rundown trailer park in the rundown trailer he rented from his uncle, Clay decided his life had to change. It had to change *now*. As he sat back in the rickety old recliner watching the black and white television set, an Army commercial came on promising that he would see the world. Two days later he joined, and see the world, not so much. More like *see that next few states over*. Originally from Mississippi, Clay was stationed just down the block in Florida. Now, only two years remained on his enlistment contract.

"Ha-ha... check that out. If I found a cookie that big, I would be set for life!" Clay pointed to the television set playing *Honey, I Shrunk the Kids* and laughed out loud. A mashed potato mustache outlined his upper lip.

The four discussed small topics, keeping the conversation light between bites. Gibbs felt out of place at times when the men treated her like she wasn't there.

Her eyes eventually wandered over to Rob. She watched him as his muscles flexed and his facial expressions changed back and forth between a series of emotions while the guys shared stories. He might have come on too strong at times, but she did find the man rather handsome. After a few moments, she caught herself staring at him, mostly because he had caught her staring too.

Awkwardly and spastically, she gathered her things up from the dining table. "Um... I... I um, I need to go back to my lab and gather my notes and go over a few samples before the meeting tonight." She stomped off heading out of the cafeteria.

"Man, what the hell was that all about?" Baker asked.

"Mr. Romance over here has got the lady all flustered," Clay said and lifted his spoon from his plate, mashed potatoes covering it as it pointed toward Rob.

Rob's face was beet red. He excused himself from the table following after the perturbed Dr. Gibbs leaving his half-eaten plate of food on the table.

"You think he's going to be back to eat that?" Clay asked.

Baker shrugged his shoulders.

Clay smiled, shoving his spoon into the Lieutenant's remaining mashed potatoes.

*

"Hey." Foster dashed up behind Gibbs in the hallway, catching her on her way back to her lab. She seemed anxious. "Everything okay?"

She turned around and met his gaze. She reached up and lightly grabbed his wrist. As she looked up at him, her breathing slowed, and she began to calm. "I'm fine, Rob. I'm just overwhelmed with my work right now. You're a really nice guy, and I mean that… but…"

"I think you're beautiful, and I don't even have to tell you that I think you're smart."

Blushing from the compliments, Gibbs smiled, realizing she still held his arm. "Thanks, Rob. That is really sweet. You're really sweet." She leaned in having to step up on her toes to reach his face. She gave him a light peck on the cheek, then turned and walked away, leaving him to stand alone in the hallway perplexed. As she rounded the corner disappearing from his sight, she stopped and ducked into the women's restroom. Overwhelmed with emotions and clashing rationalities, it all came down to one thing. She felt giddy. A feeling she hadn't felt since junior year of high school.

But my work is too important. I just don't have the time for this, she thought to herself as another lady exited one of the stalls. Realizing she seemed out of place just standing around, she left the restroom and continued making her way to the lab, blushing still.

6

The El Camino set under the gas station pump covering, the big seashell gas station sign no longer fully illuminated as it laid shattered half in the street. The pole that supported the sign was now bent all to hell as a crashed car had met its base. A single body slouched over in the driver's seat covered in blood was still strapped in by the seatbelt. What was left of the giant shell flickered and sparked, electricity dancing free into the street along with the once tall sign. At least that meant there was still hope that this part of town still had some form of power, though the gas station itself remained in the dark.

Eric drove past several other gas stations that had way too much undead activity for the three of them to handle, deciding to stop at this one because it seemed to have fewer zombies wandering about than the rest, and because the car started sputtering only a block up the road from where the car now sat entirely out of gas, engine off.

Cynthia stood outside the car, eyeing the creatures in the distance making their way toward them. There was only a handful of them out in the open. Without any lighting to illuminate the gas station's small parking lot, she was unsure as to how many zombies might be lingering in the distance past her point of view.

Eric had already released the gas cap on the car and inserted the pump nozzle. "I hope this station has a backup generator for the pumps." He stood on the opposite end of the car as Cynthia also watched the zombies as they crept ever closer as each moment passed.

Revolver in hand, Eric's head constantly looked over his shoulder toward the gas station doors and kept a good eye on the action out beyond the parking lot.

Eric had never shot anyone or anything that actually had a pulse. The idea of causing pain or inflicting an injury made him uneasy. Sure, it was very possible zombies no longer felt pain. Eric thought this as he watched a tall, thin man, obviously undead, walking toward them.

The man's right arm was gnawed up to the elbow, flesh and torn tendons still held his hand. His left hand reached out toward Eric while the other hand lay lifeless at his side holding the entrails.

Even if those things didn't feel pain, Eric was having a hard time getting used to the idea of pointing the gun and pulling the trigger. He had no problems with the bat and bedposts, but something about this still seemed to bother him.

With the gun raised, Eric looked back over his shoulder again, first eyeing the storefront, and then meeting Cynthia's gaze. "What the hell's taking him so long?"

*

Kent had only been in the store for a moment and couldn't see a thing. The room was dark, the moonlight not helping him to see inside. Shelves and food were scattered all over the place. Bottled soda and beer, along with chips and candy, lay everywhere. Kent crept quietly through the room watching his step, attempting to not crunch a bag of Doritos under his feet. He didn't think there were any zombies in here, but the place smelled something awful, and that was a sure sign that there had been at one point.

As he made his way across the entrance, passing the first few aisles taking a peek down each one to make sure it was clear, he noticed a body lying on the floor to his left. Only the lower part of each leg poked out, the checkout counter blocking his view from seeing the rest. Undoubtedly the source of the smell, he inched closer to it, the smell became stronger.

He reached the edge of the counter leaning forward to get a peek at the body behind the counter, crowbar at the ready. It was the store clerk. *Andrew Minner* was written on the nametag attached to the right shirt pocket under a small shell emblem. The male was at least in his early twenties and had definitely seen better days. His lower torso was torn wide-open, revealing several broken ribs and an empty hole where guts had once been stored.

The ribs looked as if they had been pulled back by hand. Guts and chunks of meat hung to one side of his body, spread out along the floor, most of which looked like it had been partially devoured. Blood-stained the walls and floor around him, along with scattered papers, and cigarette packs, cases still unopened. A shotgun lay on the floor next to Andrew's corpse, loose in his hand. The barrel cocked open, two shells tossed along the floor beside it.

Kent imagined a story of what might have played out in the store. Andrew came into work early, unlocking the place, and getting things in order. After a few unexpected cannibals let themselves into the store and totally trashed the place, he went for the gun, but fell to his doom before ever getting the first shot off. Poor guy.

Kent heard a loud bang from right outside. It startled him. He jumped up from behind the counter and looked out into the parking lot from the gas station's open door. He could see Eric holding his gun out toward the street. Cynthia instantly appeared at the door very disheveled and out of breath.

"What's taking you so long?" Cynthia asked, halfway leaning into the door, both hands up holding onto its frame.

"Fuck, I'm on it. Just give me a second." Kent glanced around sporadically until his eyes fixed on a set of buttons that controlled the fuel pumps.

"Well, hurry your ass up. It's starting to get crowded out here."

Another shot went off, causing Cynthia to look over her shoulder. She disappeared back into the parking lot. The only glimpse he got of her before going back to the register was her long flowing hair, still redder than ever in the pale moonlight.

*

Eric heard an engine fire up from behind the store. He instantly reached over and checked the nozzle on the pump. It worked. Kent had found the switch to the emergency generator. Eric motioned for Cynthia to take over. She quickly made her way around the front of the car.

Eric stepped out, back into open view of the zombies heading their way. Two had made it halfway across the parking lot.

"Shit," Eric murmured to himself, bringing the gun up in both hands, and sighting in the lead zombie. He hesitated for only a moment, still uncomfortable with the idea of blowing out a human brain with the weapon. Target shooting had always been a pastime event with his father at the gun range, the thought of seeing blood spatter out the back of someone's skull somewhat diminished the relished memory. With four shots remaining, Eric dispatched the third zombie making its way into their forbidden zone.

The gun bellowed a loud blast, sending a single bullet rocketing through the air. Eric's eyes, still sighted down the barrel, watched the zombie's head kick back violently. Blood shot out the back of its skull, ripping bits of flesh and brain out along with it. A single hole dead center of its eyes lightly bled down the zombie's nose. It fell to its knees and then to its face. It lay still.

"How we doing?" Eric said to Cynthia.

"Good enough, I'm sure." She ripped out the nozzle and spun on the gas cap.

There was no way the tank was full, but there was enough in there to get them where they planned to go. The Hathaway Bridge was only a few miles out.

Cynthia darted around to the passenger side of the car and craned her head looking back at the store.

Eric raced back into the driver's side, and Cynthia got in too.

"What in the world could that boy be doing in there?" the worried red head said.

Eric honked the horn twice looking past Cynthia toward to open door of the store.

Nothing.

He honked again looking over his other shoulder, unconsciously picking at his slowly swelling knuckle. Half a dozen zombies had breached Eric's unspoken forbidden zone making him a little uneasy. He honked the horn again. The passenger door slammed shut startling Eric so much that he jumped up bumping his head on the roof, eyes still fixed on the zombies outside.

"Sorry I'm late. Got us some goodies." Kent sat in the passenger seat straddling a shotgun and lighting a cigarette. A brown bag landed in Cynthia's lap with a few candy bars, numerous packs of smokes, and a handful of shells to go with the shotgun.

Slacking back in his seat, smoke from the very first inhale of the day breaking into the air before him. "What's the holdup? Let's make like a show and gig the hell out of here."

Cynthia popped him one good slap on the back of the head as the car took off, passing the handful of zombies in the parking lot.

Eric's outstretched hand gesturing a middle finger salute as they passed making their way into the street.

"Ouch. What the hell was that for?" Kent said.

"You had me worried. I didn't know what happened to you in there. Why don't you try being a little more considerate next time?" Cynthia shoved her back into the seat, both arms tightly crossed, and hands under her armpits.

"Cheer up, honey. I got you a Milky Way, right?" He reached into the brown bag on her lap and pulled out three candy bars. Not one of them a Milky Way, one was sugar-free. "It was dark in there, what can I say?" Kent pulled up the shotgun and aimed it out the window. The wind blew his hair about above his aviator shades.

"I'll take one of those," Eric said after glancing away from the road for a moment to look down at the bag of treats.

Cynthia had unwrapped a chocolate bar and was about to devour it.

Zombies in small clusters littered the road ahead. Two or three here, and one or two there, scattered about along the side of the road, in the street, and sidewalks. Stiff walking bodies temporarily lit up in their headlights as the car passed. Wrecked and abandoned vehicles were obstacles that had to be avoided as well.

With his sight down the long neck of the shotgun barrel, Kent eyed the dark street corners as each adjacent street passed by. They had just passed Jinks Avenue, which meant that the bridge would be coming up within a few more blocks. Kent watched as the zombies relentlessly attempted to reach out for the passing vehicle, pretending to shoot each one in the head with his newly acquired gun as they passed.

"Thanks, Andrew Minner," Kent mumbled to himself, right after making a *POW* sound with his mouth mimicking the backlash of an actual shotgun. The gun jerked up a bit in his hand a few more times, synchronized sound effects with each jolt of the gun in his hand.

"So assuming this rescue crap does go down, what do you think we're going to do next, just go on living our lives like none of this stuff ever happened?" Kent asked, gun still out the window.

"I'm going to look for my family," Eric said.

"Oh yeah, and your friend Tyler, too? Dude, I hate to break it to you, but chances are they ate *the shit*. Fucking zombies, dude," Kent said.

Eric instantly slammed on the brakes. The car slid a little to one side, jarring the three of them in their seats. No one had buckled in. Eric opened the driver's side door and stepped out.

"Dude, I'm sorry," Kent said. "Get back in the car, man. They could still be out there somewhere. It's just that—"

"No... Look!" Eric said and pointed.

Before them, hundreds of lifeless zombies laid in the street. The car's headlights showed countless bodies burned black. Smoke rose into the air; the stench gut wrenching.

"What's that awful smell?" Cynthia asked as she pulled her shirt up over her nose.

The bridge was on fire. A dozen cars scattered across the bridge had been totally engulfed in flames. Now only a remnant of those flames existed, black smoke billowed out from each of them.

A few zombies lingered in the street alongside the lower part of the bridge, partially on fire, and moaning. The stench of burnt skin and rotting flesh mixed with something else was just too much.

Cynthia was still gagging. The shirt offered little filtration.

"Who or what could have done this kind of damage?" Eric said still standing between the open car door.

"Your guess is as good as mine. Something tells me that whatever it was, it's on our side, and we need to catch up with it," Kent said.

"You think it could be the people the radio had talked about? The ones coming to help?" Cynthia asked.

"Could be... and if it is, I sure as hell don't want to miss the first train outta here. So let's get," Kent said.

Eric agreed with Kent on that one and didn't take any time to think it over. He hopped back into the car and slammed the door, putting the car back in drive. Numerous zombies staggered about in the roadway in flames lighting up the night as the car cautiously made its way across the bridge.

7

General Baker, Lieutenant Foster, and two other highly decorated men sat together at one end of an oval desk. The room was small and very plain. The walls were bare. The conference room sat approximately 30 people but never occupied more than a handful. At one end, opposite the men, the brown leather desk chair placed at the head of the table was missing. In its place a video prompter faced the whitewashed wall. A projector screen hung across from it. The four men had already been together chatting alone in the room for several minutes, discussing various important topics of the day.

"—and as long as there are no further delays, I think we should be expecting them back with the new arrivals in roughly zero-three hundred hours. All other reconnaissance teams and helicopters have reported back. The bombers will be going in Monday to start with the clearing," Foster said.

And exactly how many civilians are there, Lieutenant, with the delayed team?"

"Three, sir."

One of the older men seemed a bit on edge about the upcoming arrivals. "What are we going to do with them? I didn't expect there to actually be any—"

"I already have a few men clearing out some space for them in the barracks. They will be shipping out first thing Saturday, along with Gibbs, and the other scientists," Baker said.

"To what location?"

"We have a more secure area outside of the infected zone at one of the smaller bases. They will be working alongside Professor Simon and his team," Baker said.

"Oh, in Tennessee?"

"Yes, orders from the White House are to evac the scientific team immediately, but Gibbs is stubborn. I reluctantly provided her with a little more time to continue her work. She seems to be on to something important," Baker said.

"Hell, all those science types are always on to something. That's just their way of letting us know they are kissing their own asses."

Baker lit a cigar, triggering the other men to follow suit. The three older men all sat around puffing and huffing the room into a smog of secondhand smoke. Rob Foster sat there with eyes tearing.

One of the other men reached into his coat pocket and nodded at Rob. The Lt. lifted his hand, and with the shake of his head, said, "Thanks, I'm all right."

Rob never was a smoker. Didn't really care for it. His mom was a heavy smoker, and in middle school got picked on a time or two because his clothes smelled so bad as a result.

"Any updates for me, son?" General Baker asked with one eye wincing from the smoke in his face from the cigar in his mouth, both hands locked together, elbows on the table.

"No major updates to be too concerned with as of yet, sir. The media coverage has escalated a substantial amount, though." Rob took his gaze from the General toward the other men in the room. "Higher ups have been working on a detachment story for the press. Word is the President's speech should go live sometime tomorrow."

"Really?" Baker said.

"Yes, sir, and I haven't the slightest clue as to what he plans on saying."

"What has the press reported?" one of the other men asked, still enjoying his cigar while swiveling in the chair.

"Just a bunch of nonsense, honestly. I think America is just getting tired of being in the dark on things. They want answers, and they still haven't been given anything substantial," Foster said.

"Oh, and you think that what Washington is going to cook up and feed them from the President is going to be enough?"

The man farthest from Rob suddenly stood from his chair, shoving an index finger into the air in Rob's general direction. The cigar between two fingers, palm flush against the table as he leaned in, smoke steadily rising. "Wake up, kid. This is a war. If America really wanted to know, they would have already figured it out. This country feeds on being left in the dark. Leave it up to us to clean up the mess. Hell, don't even bother them with what the mess is, just as long as it doesn't get in the way of their happy little McMansions."

"Ha!" Rob shot both legs up, crossing them as they landed on the tabletop. His chair kicked back as he did this, throwing both hands behind his head. An aspect of Foster that Baker liked about the boy, making him see a bit of himself in the young man. Rob's tone remained calm and unfazed by the older man's sudden outburst.

Rob said, "And shutting down borders into three states isn't getting in their way? A lot of people are being affected right now and the least we can do is—"

The door swung open. The smoke that had collected above the men quickly shifted across the room as a light breeze blew in.

"Just set it over there... Hi gentlemen," Gibbs said as she stepped in. Her assistant trailed behind her, holding a small projector under one arm.

"Where have you been?" General Baker said, and rose from his chair.

"I know I'm a little late, and I am sorry for that. I just couldn't break away. I really think I'm onto something substantial," Gibbs said.

The older man that had been standing as Gibbs entered the room sat back down, but not before giving General Baker a spotty glance regarding her *substantial* remark. The lab assistant readied the projector, plugged it in, and turned it on.

Gibbs sat at the far end of the table away from the men, mostly because of the obnoxious smoke cloud that lingered over them, but also because she needed to operate the slides.

"Well, if what you have is so vital, then let's skip the small talk and get down to business. We don't have all day. Do you have the written report?" Baker asked.

Without a word, a manila envelope slid across the elongated table, not quite making it to the General. Rob kicked his feet back down taking hold of the folder while briefly glancing at Gibbs. She smiled and nodded. All business.

The General opened the folder and quickly flipped the pages before closing it back; it was obvious he hadn't bothered to read a single word in it.

"Well?" One of the other men shrugged and lifted his palms.

"Where to start..." Gibbs opened her notes and an identical folder as the one she gave the General. After glancing at them for only a few seconds, she reached for the remote to the projector without her gaze leaving the papers before her. The projector shot an image onto the screen. She eyed Foster, giving him a nod to dim the lights. Once the lights went out, the image of Professor Taft in all his rotting glory became clearer, much clearer.

"Thanks for setting it up. That will be all for now," Gibbs said.

Gibbs' lab assistant left the room, his young face looked unusually haggard.

"*Cordyceps Unilateralis,*" Gibbs said. A red dot popped up on the screen from the pen Gibbs currently waved in her hand. The red dot circled an open sore inside the exposed eye socket. Clotted blood and gray mucus covered the man's face on the screen.

"After examining the non-vital soft tissues secreting the originally unknown gray mucus, I have been able to identify several common traits between the cause and effect, along with that of a parasitoid fungus known as *Cordyceps Unilateralis.*" The slide changed to another photo. A close-up microscopic split-screen view of two nucleuses showed. The one on the left normal; the one of the right infected and deformed.

"The fungus' spores enter the body of the host through its respiratory spiracles. In this case, the host is our recently esteemed, but no longer viable, Professor Taft. The bacterium then begins to consume the non-vital soft tissues. When the—"

"Wait a fucking minute here. Back it up. Respiratory what? You mean to tell me, that shit is fucking airborne?" one of the men said.

Baker and Foster looked at one another but didn't say a word.

"We'll get to that," she said, dismissing his question. "When the fungus is ready to produce spores, its mycelia enter the host's brain and changes how it perceives pheromones, causing the host to violently attack its victims. The decomposition of the body is a direct result of large amounts of bacterium in the body. Steady consumption of what the parasitoid considers non-vital tissue quickly decomposes, allowing the vital organs to shut down entirely. Rigor mortis quickly sets in, leaving us with what we know as stiff legged walking corpses, General."

The room was quiet for a few moments. General Baker said, "A fungus is responsible for all of this? A fungus is making people eat each other? You have got to give me more than that. But let me guess, destroying the brain destroys the fungus. Is this correct, Dr. Gibbs?"

She pursed her lips and took a deep breath. Then, removed her glasses and wiped them on her coat.

"You expect us to believe a fungus is causing the outbreak, Gibbs?" one of the older men said. "Like I said, these lab rats are good for nothing but hot air. Give me a break."

Gibbs went to another slide and acted coolly. The slide was that of an ant hanging from what looked like a large leaf, the ant took up most of the screen.

"The fungus I'm talking about… gentlemen," she straightened herself in the chair, adding a bit more authority into her words, "has been previously documented in nature. Global habitation of *Cordyceps Unilateralis* in tropical forests, including Africa, Brazil, and Thailand are very common. The ant you see in this image had been overtaken by a close member of this same parasitoid. Our parasitoid. Our fungus. The CU entered the ants, just as is has in Taft, and caused the ants to go crazy. Mounds of dead, walking ants have been reported."

The slide changed to a closer view of the same ant. Similar abrasions to that on Taft covered its entire body. Gray specks covered it from top to bottom. Gibbs now had the attention of everyone in the room.

Baker said, "So you're telling me that you have found the source of our problem… is that it?"

"That is correct, and a search through our plant fossil databases revealed similar ant marks on a fossil leaf believed to be forty-eight million years old. With that said, I don't think that this fungus is currently airborne. If that were true, then we would all be infected and would have been a very long time ago. But the truth is, we are still here. Which leads me to believe that what we're dealing with here is a manmade strand of the fungus."

"If it's not airborne, then how could it have even spread to begin with?" Foster asked, finally speaking up for the first time since Gibbs entered the room.

"I'm glad you asked. I was just about to get to that." Gibbs switched to the next image. It was of an average man in his mid to late 60's. Nothing unusual stood out. "This is Grech Vonhinkly, founder of GCUR-TECH. He can be easily traced over the internet, along with anything and everything about his organization."

"Get to the point, Gibbs." Baker smashed the butt of his cigar out on the table.

"GCUR stands for Global Cordyceps Unilateralis Research, and you wouldn't believe where one of his top three bases of operation is located."

"Where?" Baker asked.

All four men leaned in closer.

"Jacksonville, Florida."

"Son-of-a-bitch! Foster, I want my best men ready and airborne headed to that facility first thing tomorrow morning."

The men in the room stood and looked at one another.

Rob instantly left the room and radioed someone on dispatch as the door closed behind him.

*

"Is there anything else for us, Gibbs?"

"No, sir, that is all I have for now."

"Excellent work, Doctor!" The three men exited the room, leaving Gibbs to gather her things alone. She took a deep breath, feeling the weight of a day's stress instantly lift from her body knowing that the harder part of the day was finally over. She just hoped that they would find something of substantial value at GCUR-TECH.

She had heard of the place once before, back when she was a grad student, and left the conference room a little disappointed for letting it take so long to put things together. With the materials she needed gathered up, she made her way back to the lab where a restless Taft awaited her arrival.

*

After taking a long, hot shower and feeling refreshed, Rob Foster ran the five-blade razor down the side of his left cheek, finishing a clean shave. He wiped his face with a towel and checked for any errant hairs or nicks. None. His face was smooth and tight.

The mirror showed a man in his prime. Young, vital, with unquenchable dreams and aspirations. The outbreak, though, had darkened the future. The enemy didn't lay across the waters, but resided on U.S. soil. Their weapons deadlier than guns and bombs.

At least now there was a lead to the outbreak's origin. It would take time for the story to unfold. Time best spent getting some rest. Work hours were flexible on the base. Essentially, everyone was on duty twenty-four hours a day. It was up to the individual to grab some shuteye when an opportunity presented itself.

A soft knock came from the barrack's door, which in itself was unusual. Normally, a cohort's arrival was announced by a harsh pounding of a fists and a loud demand. Grabbing a robe from the counter, he dressed as he stepped to the door, his bare feet on cold tiles.

Foster opened the door about halfway. His jaw dropped in surprise. "Dr. Gibbs?"

"Theresa. You don't have to call me Dr. Gibbs all the time," she said. She turned her gaze from his and bit her lower lip. "I'm sorry, I didn't mean to catch you at a bad time."

Foster saw a longing in her eyes slowly fade. Indecision obviously chasing away the reason she came. "It's not a bad time. I just got out of the shower. You're about the last person I expected to find outside of my door—not that I'm complaining." He chuckled, leaving a shy smile on his face. "Is... is something wrong?"

"Uh, no. Nothing like that. I've pushed myself so much lately that even I realized I needed a break. I wanted to take you up on one of those offers to go have a drink." Theresa Gibbs looked back up with her big eyes glowing and her dark cherry lips moist.

"I'm not dressed for going out. Although, I did notice you put on a clean lab coat to come here."

Gibbs shrugged. "I didn't pack anything fashionable for my time on the base. A white lab coat hides my dreary wardrobe."

"You know, I've always wondered what you were hiding under that coat. In fact, I've wondered what you looked like wearing nothing at all." Foster stepped closer, feeling the warmth of her personal space.

"I..."

Before she could speak, he pressed his lips against hers and kissed her deeply. Theresa melted in his arms, sighing wantingly.

"Let's step out of the hall. We wouldn't want to distract others from their work," Rob Foster said. He pulled her by the hand into his room and closed the door.

8

The Rhino Runner slowly crept up the street less than a block from the radio station. The blades of the chopper remained visible by the moon's natural light; the bus's headlights were off to not attract attention. Putting the bus in park, Luke and Megan sat across from one another staring at the mammoth crowd gathered in the parking lot pouring in from the streets. The chopper engulfed in a swarm of bodies, each zombie in an agitated totter, pressed against one another. They moaned and screamed out as if in writhing pain. An ocean of arms outstretched to the sky. Countless arms and hands clawed at the building and its entrance.

Luke slowly pulled his handset to his face and clicked the button. So on edge after dealing with the bridge, he forewent the team call names, "Gus, come in Gus. We're in the Green Zone. I repeat, we're in the Green Zone," he whispered.

The cab was silent for a moment and then startled both of them when the radio called back, Gus' voice on the other end. "Status?"

"Front and center. Way too much activity. Need an alternate route of entry," Luke said.

*

Seth stood at the window opposite of the one Gus was currently looking out of. "Back here, man, I don't see any of them in the back. Plus, we got the gate blocking them off on one side by the alley."

"I can see you from upstairs," Gus said into his radio holding down the button. "Think you can make your way around the back of the building without getting noticed? Very little interference detected from that end. The dead seem to be concentrating on the front of the building."

Luke's voice came back over the handset again, "Roger that."

From the window of the second floor, Gus and George watched as the large bus slowly crept out of sight and into the shadows in reverse. None of the zombies appeared to even notice as the vehicle slipped away and out of sight.

George walked over to Billy, waking him from his nap on the floor. "It's time to get up, Billy. We're going to leave now and go someplace much safer."

"But I like Mr. Seth and his music," a groggy Billy replied as he leaned up, both fists rubbing in his eyes.

"Mr. Seth is coming with us," George said.

"YAY!" Billy jumped with joy.

"Now we are going to play a little game," George said. "We need to keep real quiet so that those bad people out there don't hear us leaving." George ran a finger across his lips, sealing them shut.

"You mean the zombies?" Billy asked.

Willy was sitting up now. He looked like hell. Pale and bursting into a cold sweat just from the exertion of sitting up, he let out a ferocious hack, shooting a small bit of blood on the floor. Willy looked around the room and no one had taken notice. He quickly tossed a magazine over the blood-soaked couch cushion, his leg no longer bleeding. The area around the wound was clotted and puffy. His slightly torn pant leg covered the injury as he slowly stood. He ambled over to the back window next to Seth, who was working the window open.

Both men eagerly looked out into the dark. Gus sat on the loveseat, gathering up the gear that he had taken off, allowing himself to be a bit more relaxed during the wait. George and the boy seemed as ready as they would ever be. Billy grabbed a few CDs from the shelf and motioned to George, taking a few along as he eyed the old man's bag.

"You all right, dude? You look like you have seen better days," Seth said, taking his eyes away from the window.

The sounds of pounding and moaning were still just as strong as it had been after the two armed men joined the group upstairs. The relentless mob of zombies outside lingered on with the infernal beating and banging at the lobby door.

Taking a deep breath, Willy said, "Yes. I'll be fine. It took a lot out of me to see Bo go like that. He was my best friend. I just need a shower and some rest. I'll be fine, seriously."

"So exactly how are we going to get down there from way up here?" George leaned in looking over their shoulders out the window at the back lot of the building. "Seems kind of high, don't you think?" A light draft blew in his face as the three men peeked out the open window.

"The Runner is made to handle situations like this, boss. They will have us covered. Don't worry," Willy replied, stepping away from the window and heading toward Gus.

"Hey, look! There they are. I can see them!" Seth looked back into the room and motioning with his hands.

Gus' radio kicked on. "This is Luke. We made it around back undetected. I take it you're at the window with the lights on in the upstairs room. We can see you. Moving into position... Over."

"Copy that." Gus handed back the radio to Willy, who latched it to his hip alongside the holstered 9mm, rifle, and machete strapped to his back.

With the five of them at the window, they watched as the very large bus slowly moved into position, backing in directly under the window. Billy held George's hand.

All of a sudden, the double doors at the front of the building gave way. The sheer weight of zombies had overwhelmed the barricade, causing it to weaken. Innumerable zombies stumbled into the lobby, falling over one another as they gained entrance into the building. The crack of wooden doors was followed by countless footsteps traveling up to the second floor.

"Uh oh, I think I know what that is." Gus broke away from the window toward the door. He swung it open and ran to the steps leading down to the lobby. He listened for a moment and instantly knew what he heard. The grunts and moans of the undead had made it inside. He could see their shadows along the wall as they made their way to the stairwell. Crashing sounds and thuds thundered as the mob of endless zombies staggered through the building, colliding with numerous things. The fake tree, a few lamps, the phone that had been mounted to the wall... all trampled in their wake.

"Shit!" Gus darted back into the room with the others as the first of the undead reached the stairs. "We've got company." Gus dashed to the loveseat, and with a single thrust, flipped it over on its side. "Give me a hand!"

Seth and George quickly stepped over, grabbing anything they could to put in front of the door. Willy stood at the window watching the Rhino Runner as it backed up. The bus was big and the window was only two stories up, but it still looked like a long way down. The Runner's sunroof popped open revealing the top half of Megan, waving him to come down.

Willy looked back for only a second before deciding to step out the window. Two couches, the desk, and a shelf stacked with scattered CDs quickly covered the door. The three men frantically looked around in the room for something, anything to help wedge the door from opening. The sounds of the undead drew even closer with each moment as they crept up the stairs. Their footsteps getting louder as they drew near.

Willy was gone.

THUD!

Billy on his tiptoes looked out the window. Willy was climbing into the bus from a hatch in the roof. The horde of zombies in the alley trapped by the enormous fence became antsy as they watched. The sudden thump startled the other men upstairs still hunting for anything possible to block the door. The door started to move. The creatures had made it to the second floor. Their moans were louder than ever as the door shook. The couches and desk bounced about in place.

"It's not going to hold! It's not going to hold," Seth said.

"Go! Go!" Gus, with all his might, leaned against the sofas and with one hand up, pointed to the window.

George and Seth rushed over to Billy and leaned halfway out the window, looking at the ground below. A woman motioned for them to jump. George looked out past the bus. There were no zombies.

None.

"Okay, Billy, you ready to do this?"

"I'm scared."

"You can do this, son. We're going to make it." George picked up the child and leaned him out the window, lowering him as much as he could before letting him go.

"I'm scared," Billy shouted as he dangled in the wind over the bus.

"You can do this. You're going to be fine," George said. George let him go.

Billy landed atop the bus. His footing wasn't firm and he began to slide off the side. Before tumbling to the ground, a woman reached over and grabbed his leg, and pulled him in.

George tossed out his duffle bag and then stepped out onto the window ledge. "Hell… I'm getting way too old for this kind of crap." George safely landed on top of the bus, also being escorted down the ladder by the same lady.

*

Inside the big bus, George met gazes with Willy, who had a seat in the back. Billy sat next to him looking around and taking it all in. The bus was dark but not dark enough to keep from telling who was who or where was where. There wasn't a single window on the sides or the back. The front was slightly sectioned off with just enough room for one person to squeeze in and out at a time. A ladder descended from one side of the bus opposite a large side door. The seating reminded George of an ambulance. He hated riding in those contraptions and hoped to never do it again after losing his wife a few years back. The grueling 30-minute drive in the back of that ambulance was the hardest thing he had ever had to do. Several shelves lay strewn along one wall with a few guns and a large pack of some kind that looked like a flamethrower.

Suddenly, bright lights flashed in from around the street corner. An El Camino peeled out as it slid to one side, breaking itself center of the lot. Dust and dirt poured through the air around it as the car came to a stop. Seth was hanging from the second-floor window lit up in the night from the car's bright headlights. Three people instantly jumped out of the car. Two men and a woman all wielding weapons darted for the bus.

"They're right behind us and headed this way," the young male with dirty blonde hair shouted, both hands gripping a revolver.

The older man following looked twice the boy's age. He carried a shotgun.

The woman held a crowbar and trailed behind.

"Did you not hear me? They're coming this way," Eric said. As he got closer to the bus, countless zombies pushed the massive gate holding them back. "Hoooollly shit."

Luke stuck his arm out of the driver's side window and motioned them to come.

Eric came to a stop by the vehicle. Cynthia and Kent came to his side.

The side door to the bus slid open. Megan stepped out with weapon drawn, eye sighted down her rifle. She took three or four long strides forward not even paying attention to the new arrivals. "We need to move," she said.

Three-burst rounds blasted from her rifle as she squeezed the trigger, aiming in the direction the old car had just come from. An unending swarm of the dead poured out from the side street in their direction. Megan kept taking step after step forward while firing round after round. With each burst of steady shots, a ghoul dropped to the ground, only for another to take its place. Five zombies had fallen within a few seconds, but it made no difference. Their numbers were too great.

*

Seth stood at the window, paralyzed while he watched the horde of zombies descend upon the bus. The bulky, metal gate adjacent to the building shook violently from the relentless mass of zombies pushing against it. "Well, crap! I think I changed my mind about joining you guys after all." He looked back at Gus, who had left the wall of furniture, no longer bracing the door with his girth.

One of the couches fell over, and then the other, the door sliding open just a hair revealing several outstretched arms rotting and festered with worms and bloody bites. One hand was missing most of its fingers. The door inched open from the pressure of the growing numbers behind it. Gus couldn't help but imagine the numbers that now filled the lobby, crammed like sardines leading up the stairs. Shoulders and legs were in view, the door opening even wider, the desk sliding slow and steady along the carpet.

*

Eric and Kent joined the military woman in a barrage of fire outside. Eric steadied his hand, missing the first two shots as they went wild into the crowd. The third and fourth shots sent one to the ground. His fifth shot was a dud. The gun was empty. He reached into his pocket and pulled out several more rounds but fumbled them, dropping them on the cement.

Megan momentarily glanced down stepping aside to give him room, doing what damage she could.

Kent stood to Eric's right a few feet over, holding out his shotgun. A loud blast erupted from the weapon kicking back in his hand. He almost dropped it. Holding the shotgun tighter, he pulled the trigger again, holding the gun more at waist level. The gun kicked, but this time, he was ready for it. The shot was more controlled, nailing an old frail zombie that had to have been in her late 80's right in the neck. Her neck and the lower part of her chest exploded. Bloody, gray pus blasted out, spraying on the other zombies around her.

An echoing thud from behind them surprised Cynthia, making her drop the crowbar on the ground. The metal clanged against the concrete a few times before coming to a rest. A man from behind her had just jumped on top of the bus from the window. He lost his balance and slid to one side. She looked back watching the man fall from the roof of the vehicle. His long hair bounced in the air as he crashed to the cement below, landing on his shoulder, and what looked like his head. It was hard to tell. He hit really hard and wasn't moving. Cynthia instantly jogged over to him. As she reached him, she caught a glimpse of a large man standing at the window yelling something down.

The gunfire, the zombies falling on them in the lot from the side street, the man at the window, the man on the ground. He was bleeding. Blood poured out onto the lot right where he had fallen. He reeked of beer.

She looked up and saw the zombies at the gate. She was only a few feet away from them. The gate shook and rattled, tons of hands gripping it violently trying to get to her. Countless fingers enthralled its woven mesh.

*

The upstairs door slid open wide enough and more than a few zombies entered the room. Gus struggled to fit through the window. His shoulders were too broad. He leaned out the window, pushing with everything he had to get his upper half to squeeze out. The zombies moved in. The room quickly filled. One zombie after another entered the room. Gus gave up on the window and turned firing on the zombies. With his 9mm out, Gus did his best to make each shot count, the close range making this easier to do. After seven pops of the gun and five zombies down, more kept coming. They just kept coming.

Gus knew that this wasn't going to get him anywhere. He shot three more, taking them all down each getting hit where it counts. Blood and brain splattered everywhere in the broadcasting room as he took out each zombie. After emptying the magazine on the undead and littering the floor with more than a handful of ghouls, he frantically looked around in the room for something, anything that could help him. He grabbed a tall floor lamp from the corner to his right. Holding it sideways, he lunged into the mob and pushed them all back. Several of them fell over landing on others causing a domino effect. Seeing his opportunity, Gus dropped the magazine and popped in a fresh one, then turned, making for the window.

Giving it everything he had, Gus pushed and pulled trying to get both shoulders through the window, the panel too narrow for his body. Something grabbed his leg and pulled him. He heard the moans and felt them crowding around at his back. He pushed harder, kicking and flailing. Another hand on his other leg. Gus' foot collided with what had to have been a face, because one of the arms gripping his leg instantly let go. The adrenaline pumping through his body gave him the extra boost needed. His shoulders scraped against the sides of the window panel as he exited.

Gus came down hard and fast. He reached his hands out to catch his fall. Something in his right hand snapped upon impact.

*

George held tight to Billy. Both of them sat at the back of the Rhino Runner. George could see the woman standing outside shooting at something, an unknown headlight beaming on her in the distance. She had left the side door open when she stepped out. The guy behind the wheel was occupied. He was talking with someone over a radio almost identical to the one that Willy had on his hip. Willy sat next to George, and Billy leaned back, head propped against the seat, eyes closed.

"Shouldn't you be out there helping them?" George said.

Willy didn't move and acted like George hadn't even spoken to him. The sound of gunfire coming from more than one person stressed George out. "Why aren't we leaving?" he shouted at the man in the driver's seat.

Luke didn't respond, focused on the radio.

*

Seth was out cold.

"Kent, help! I can't get him up!" Cynthia yelled at Kent, who fired at the mob steadily drawing closer from the side street.

As Kent looked over to see Cynthia leaned over the fallen man, the gate behind her suddenly gave way. To Kent, it wasn't as sudden as it should have seemed. It was almost in slow motion. As he turned his head to see what she was yelling at him for, he watched as the lining of the gate to the alley tore open from the bottom. It bent up and out, the horde moving forward. Kent heard nothing. All sound had vanished as he watched, as if nothing else existed except this single moment. Kent looked back at Eric, the others still firing in slow motion, unable to hear their guns. He could see the flashes of light on each gun as they were fired, but no sound.

The crowd of creatures clambered out from the broken fence as it gave way. Cynthia jumped to her feet, darting away toward the front of the bus. Kent watched in slow motion as bullets tore into their flesh, the busted fence behind them. Blood splattered and sprayed. Heads jerked and zombies fell. Kent's view widened to see a very large man standing on top of the bus firing a rifle into the oncoming crowd. Things suddenly snapped into real time, and Kent abruptly comprehended that he had been held in the cold hands of shock.

"It's time to get the hell out of here," Gus said, getting Megan's attention. The bus steadily became surrounded by zombies. The spark of their gunfire shined in the night, each person doing their best to drive the mass of undead creatures down.

Megan retreated back toward the confines of the big vehicle, motioning for the other two shooting alongside her to follow suit. Eric, Megan, and Kent jumped into the Runner from the side door.

Luke, half out the driver's window, fired single shots from his 9mm pistol. Each pull of the trigger was a direct hit, sending its victim to the ground.

Cynthia screamed and shouted, banging on the opposite side of the bus that didn't have a door. Zombies poured in behind her from the alley. A large cluster of them immediately fell on Seth and feasted on his body. Seth never let out a single scream as they tore into his flesh, ripping him into bits, devouring him bit by bit. The creatures' hands came away bloody as they ripped and tugged. Chunks of the unconscious man's flesh came away from his body, shirt now totally ripped apart.

The bus started to move forward, Gus still on the roof. He reached down and grabbed Cynthia by the hand, pulling her up with little effort, the mob of zombies behind her only inches away from dragging her down. A sharp jolt of pain shot through Gus' hand.

She looked back as the large man held her close, the bus bouncing forward toward the street. "He's... gone."

Seth's body was covered with bloody, rotting, putrid zombies all leaning over him, undoubtedly feasting on his remains. Dozens of others shuffled past those feeding, arms stretched out toward the bus.

Countless zombies still continued to spill out into the back lot from the alley and the side street. The second-story window was filled with the undead. As Luke looked in the side mirror, he saw the building and the horde. One zombie fell from the window as they drove off. Before taking his eyes away, he thought he saw Bo Brad Barrie, the pilot, standing at the window, bloody and mangled. It couldn't have been. It just couldn't.

Gus lowered the red-haired woman down into the bus from the roof latch as it slowly edged on trying to make its way passed the ghouls that approached on either side. He followed her down into the crowded space, grabbing the torch gear, and then made his way back halfway up the ladder.

"Do you know how to use that?" Megan called from below.

"It's two valves and a nozzle handle. How hard can it be?" Gus said.

"The igniter is automatic. Don't squeeze the nozzle unless you want to burn something," Megan said and headed back to the cab.

Luke drove the Rhino Runner up the infested streets as fire rained down off to the side. "Things will clear up once we get back to the interstate. Who all do we have back there anyway? I told headquarters three civilians but looks more like six or seven."

Megan said, "Just an in and out OP, eh?" She smirked and stepped away.

The bus now moved at a steadier pace. She went to the refugees, and asked, "Anybody injured?"

No one said a word. They all seemed spent and lost in their own thoughts, their own nightmares. As Megan stood over them, one hand holding the railing over her head to keep a steady balance, she noticed that Willy was out cold and didn't look in the best of health. She let go of the rail and moved closer to get a better look at him.

After shaking his leg and saying his name a time or two with no response, she pulled out a small flashlight and shined it in his eye, while peeling the eyelid back with her finger.

"Willy... right? *Willy...* You there? Willy?" She put away the light and continued to examine him, taking out a first-aid kit. After opening the box and putting on some thin rubber gloves, she continued checking his vitals. She wrapped the cuff of the blood pressure monitor around his arm and proceeded to pump it tighter.

"Mr. Wellington? Is that you?" Eric leaned up in his seat, talking over the woman in the middle of the cab checking the other soldier. "Hey, Wellington!" Eric spoke louder leaning out from his seat a little more. The old man looked like he was in a trance staring at the floor, his arm around a kid that Eric had never seen before.

"Hey, George!"

George looked up and across the seats, right at Eric. "Eric! How in the world did you end up here?" The old man's face lit up showing a sense of hope, his eyes lightly watering as he recognized the teenager across from him.

"Yeah! So that *was* you on the radio this morning. I had my doubts, but thought it might be you. I recognized the voice. Where's Tyler?"

Any glint of hope instantly evaporated from the old man's face upon hearing those words. After a moment, George met the young man's gaze again, this time, his voice frail revealing his true age. "Tyler? Well... I... I was kind of hoping you would—"

Megan got shoved to her back against the wall of shelves and guns, Willy on top of her gnashing his teeth. His mouth sank into her throat, squirting blood onto Kent's shoes as Megan fell to the floor.

Cynthia screamed. Everyone panicked, shoving on each other and trying to move toward the front of the bus, Willy's undead corpse now feasting. Megan's body twitched violently on the floor, a pool of blood formed around her.

"Stop the bus! Stop the bus!" Eric shouted.

Luke looked back, craning his head. Everyone crowded toward the front. Everyone but Megan and Willy.

Gus shot down the ladder, hearing the screams and frantic yelling. The bus stopped. Gus tossed off the flamethrower pack dropping it at his feet. He reached out, pulling Willy up by the back of the shirt. With his other hand, Gus slammed Willy's head into the side of the bus. His hand was the size of Willy's entire face, covering it all. Two more slams against the wall. He shoved the former soldier away, pulling out a large hand blade from his hip. In one flawless motion, he drove the knife under Willy's chin and up. The metal blade penetrated the flesh sliding through the mouth and into his skull. Willy's limbs instantly went limp.

Gus dropped the zombie to the floor, blade still lodged in its skull, blood pouring down the handle. He retrieved the 9mm from his hip and aimed it at Megan. Blood spilled heavily from the open wound. As he lifted the pistol, Luke's arm reached up from behind him grabbing the large man on the wrist. Everyone else stood to one side of the bus as far as they could, huddled together in fear and shock, silent.

"No, wait!" Luke said.

"It has to be done and you know it!" Gus said.

The gun went off twice without hesitation. Her head shot back, two holes instantly appeared leaking blood from them. One hit the chest above her breast, and the other dead between the eyes. She lay still no longer convulsing. The puddle of blood beneath her steadily grew.

No one moved. No one spoke a word.

Cynthia held tightly to Kent. Billy had George's arms wrapped around him. Eric had frozen in place, stunned as everyone else.

Gus lowered the gun. "I'm sorry, but it had to be done. It's best to end it quickly."

Luke looked up at the bulk of a man and glared with pure rage in his eyes, arms shaking. Gus grabbed him by each arm and pulled him into his chest. Luke lost it. Crying uncontrollably, he broke out into tears, mourning the sudden loss.

Very shaken up and hardly uttering any real words, Luke looked up at Gus. "Not... like... this..."

"You need to be strong, soldier." Gus pulled Luke away and shook him. "We need you to be strong. We need to get to base. Can you do that?"

Luke rubbed one hand through his hair and glanced at the civilians, all of whom looked scared out of their minds. "Ya, I can do this."

Luke turned and got behind the wheel, putting the bus back in drive without even looking back.

George opened his bag and pulled out a plain shirt and covered the dead woman's face. The ride back to base was long and quiet. Very long and very, very quiet.

REGROUP

1

The sun rose early Friday morning just like it had every morning in the past. The Tallahassee sky was a bright baby blue without a cloud in sight just like the day before. It was officially day four of the outbreak and things weren't looking any better for General Baker and his men. He had already lost more lives than expected and began to feel like the higher ups might be leaving him in the dark about a thing or two. Maybe this outbreak was more than they could contain.

Between the twenty choppers sent out daily to survey the infected zones and conditions, only fourteen had made it back. His best flight team was MIA, and the General was starting to think he needed a new strategy, a new approach to this chaos.

Baker sat in his office not seated behind the desk, but standing at the window, watching a single chopper be loaded with supplies. He decided to cancel all outbound missions for the next two days. They weren't going to find any significant lives to matter. The risk wasn't worth the reward. The five civilians that now found themselves on his base were the only survivors they had come across.

The chopper getting prepped before him was scheduled to depart in less than an hour, headed for Jacksonville. A biochemical organization could very well be behind this catastrophic plague, and if so, he felt the higher ups in the military might have something to do with it as well.

As always, Lieutenant Foster was close by, sitting behind him and awaiting orders for the day. Baker's ashtray sat on top of the desk with a freshly lit cigar, unattended.

"Have the civilians examined by Dr. Gibbs as soon as they are up and about. No need to wake them, I'm sure the last couple of days have been long. Let them rest. I'm going to want a full report of their physical exams and history. I want to know who we have staying with us. Full background checks. I also want an update on Luke Beal. I heard word he had a mental breakdown last night with the loss of Megan."

"And Gus, sir?"

"I want him saddled up and ready to lead the Jacksonville team."

"But, sir, he fractured some bones in his right hand, not to mention he came in rather late last night and lost both of his teammates. I don't know that it's a wise idea sending—"

"He is the best man for the job, hand or no hand, Lieutenant. I want him on that chopper leading that team! Is that clear?"

"Yes, sir."

"Hell, while you're at it I want an assessment of Luke Beal, pronto. If he feels fit for duty, then I want him on that team too."

"But General—"

"No butts! That's an order!"

Baker turned from the window and glared at the Lieutenant.

Rob stood, tossing up a half-hearted salute, one that the General did not return.

Taking his seat at the desk, Baker shooed Rob out of his office with a flick of the wrist while picking up the phone.

Foster exited.

*

After leaving the General's office, Rob made his way down the hall passing door after door to several other offices. He finally made it to the laboratory building after crossing the courtyard centralized within the military base. The small building set across from the barracks. He made his way into the building after crossing the small courtyard leading into the double doors to the small construct.

The courtyard was also not quite that big, or that much to look at. It was the only actual designated smoking space on base, a section of the fortified compound the General never seemed to visit. A large oak tree with several benches surrounding it grew in the center. Several soda machines and one empty snack machine set against a barracks' wall. Rob had been working at this facility for a while now and only once saw that machine filled. It lasted all of three days before being emptied again. The courtyard reminded Rob of high school for some strange reason.

The small laboratory building was only a one-story box, housing five office spaces all of which were labs except for one. One of the rooms was actually designated as an office space used for group meeting between the different directors. Its door read *Dr. Theresa Gibbs*, she being the lead scientist and medic on the team. His mind raced back to finding her at his door and sharing a few hours in the dark. Her smell, her taste, the intimate moments had him longing for the next encounter.

Rob passed the labeled door, taking a left down the hall toward the group of lab rooms knowing good and well that the doctor would not be in her office. She never was. He was actually even surprised it had her name on it. He couldn't recall a single time that the office space had ever been used by anyone. Most of the scientists kept to the labs or the cafeteria.

To Rob's right was a single person restroom with both a male and female logo next to the door. To his left, he passed Professor Taft's lab space. As he passed by, peering into the room from the door's small horizontal window, he saw the room was empty. The image of Taft that was shown at the meeting, the enlarged image of the dead man's mutilated face, skin torn to the bone and eyes missing, instantly popped into his head. He tried to shake the thought as he passed Gibbs' door by only a few paces. He stood at the door for a few moments, still lingering on the thought of Taft's rancid decay of a form. He prepared himself, knowing good and well the man he had just thought of was dead and yet still somehow continued to function as if still alive.

*

Dr. Gibbs had just finished taping the fractured hand of Gus *the bus* Stanford. It was obvious how the man earned his nickname. He sat on top of the metal desk in the center of her workspace, taking up more than half of the table.

"Your bones will heal with time. You shouldn't be using it." She turned from him, making her way to the sink. "I'll take a look at it again Sunday before I get sent to Tennessee."

"Oh yeah, I thought you had to leave tomorrow," Gus said.

"No, the team and I were supposed to, but I talked the big wigs into giving us another day. We leave sometime Sunday. I'm not exactly sure when."

After knocking on the door with two quick taps, Rob stepped into the lab.

Gus sat up high on the table, his shirt off, holding his busted hand out in the air.

Gibbs had her back turned to both men with her hands in the sink that was set across the room from the door.

"What can I do for you, General?" Gibbs said, sarcasm dripped in her voice.

Rob loudly cleared his throat as he stepped into the room, making eye contact with the man who sat on the metal table, smiling. He slammed the door a little harder than intended as he stepped in. She turned to see who it was, half-expecting Baker to be traipsing into her workspace pitching a fit at her for not being packed and ready for the lab team evacuation even though she had been granted extra time.

Taft stood against the wall, still tied like before. His wounds looked worse than the previous time. It had only been a short while and his skin seemed to be tightening up, drying out and turning a flaky gray. The restraints dug so deep into his neck and ankles that they looked almost nonexistent, sunken beneath the skin to the bone. The skin on one arm had been peeled off revealing blackish blood and gray muscles, along with bits of bone. The dead man stood chewing on something, and it looked like it might be a bit of his own flesh that had once hung in front of his mouth. The man was beyond a mess, beyond dead. He was hell.

"Oh, hey Rob," said Gibbs with a little pep in her step, not at all fazed by the corpse of a man standing tied to the wall across from her. She smiled, drying her hands, stepping toward the two men, happy to see him. "What can I do for you this fine morning?" She gave him a furtive wink.

Gus watched as the two would-be romantics got lost in each other's gaze for a moment or two. "Is it just me or can you cut the sexual tension in this room with a knife?" Gus said.

Rob instantly broke from the glance and stared down at the floor, cheeks a light red.

"So, Lieutenant, what brings you here?" Gus asked.

"I came to speak with Dr. Gibbs about you, but since you're here, that will make my job a little easier. I came to check the status of that hand of yours." He looked away from the shirtless man, still holding out his hand and focused on the lady. "What's the damage looking like long term? I'm going to need him back in rotation ASAP."

"I've sent the report in. His hand is fractured," she said.

"Yeah, I'm aware of that. I've gone over that with the General. That is why I'm here. Gus, you have been selected for another OP. It leaves in less than an hour. Can you handle it under your condition?" Rob pointed at the man's damaged extremity.

Gibbs said, "I don't think he should be going back out like this. His hand needs to be immobile, and that could take several weeks."

Rob kept his gaze on Gus. "The truth is, things are falling apart around here, and we are running low on qualified men. Well, soldier? You're the best man for the job, and we need you. This is the last OP before we send in the bombers."

Gibbs threw down the paper towel she was using to dry her hands, irritated at Foster, irritated at this whole system. "You can't be serious! They're just going to blow everything up. Just wipe their hands of it and call it a day. You can't do that, it's unethical."

Foster continued, "Gus?"

"Yes, I can do it. What's the job?"

"Jacksonville. You will get a short debriefing as soon as you are done here, so put that shirt back on," Rob said before turning to Gibbs.

With distress in his eyes, she could tell that he didn't like the situation or the way it was being handled anymore that she did. "Where's Beal? He's possibly getting sent out too."

"Yeah, right! That guy is a mess. After what I did to his woman, after what I had to do, there is no way in hell that guy is working with me. He might snap and try to take me out when I'm not looking or something... No way," Gus said as he put on his shirt. "That guy has lost it!"

"Speaking of being *one to snap*, how are you doing by the way?" Rob asked.

"What do you mean?"

"Well, you lost Bo and Willy last night. I just wanted to make sure that you're able to handle it," Rob said.

"I'm fine. What's past is past. It's old news, water under the bridge and all that shit. Let's just go," Gus said with a slight hint of hostility.

Gibbs gave Rob a concerned look as the two men stepped out of the room.

2

Kent stood in the hall right outside the barracks. He and the others had gotten in late last night. After they arrived, several armed men escorted them to a secure set of rooms with bunks and blankets. To Kent, the rooms looked like they had once been storage closets or even an old office, but he couldn't have cared less. He was happy to finally be some place safe, surrounded by tons of armed people, with plenty to eat. They hadn't had anything in the way of food as of yet, but lunch was definitely on the agenda for him today. He was starving.

He still wore the same thing he had on the day he met up with Eric and Cynthia. His shirt was torn in places. Blood and soot covered his wardrobe from head to toe. A guard had mentioned throwing clothes in the wash sometime this afternoon. At this point, it didn't seem like a wash would do his clothing any good. It would be better if they could find him something new to wear.

Two men dressed in fatigues rounded the corner, both armed with guns at the hip. Kent leaned over a water fountain as they slowly headed in his direction. The stream of water sprung up at the push of the button, meeting his lips.

"—and that's just ridiculous. I can't believe the President, of all people, would bald-faced lie like that on national television," one of the men said as they walked up.

"What do you expect? Why else would he have given a speech at seven a.m. in the morning? They make announcements early in the day so that most people are unable to see it. Give them time to make some edits. Show the five o'clock news what they want them to see, leaving out the details," the other officer replied.

"What exactly was said, if you don't mind my asking?" Kent turned away from the fountain and faced the two men.

"What, you didn't see it?" replied the taller of the men.

"No, I was asleep. I came in with a few others just last night," Kent said.

"Oh, shit. You came in with Luke and Megan?" The man talking suddenly got jabbed in the side by the other soldier's elbow.

Kent said, "Yeah."

"Well, the President just had a press conference talking about this little epidemic and totally lied. He said that what we have going on in the Southeast is the result of an oil spill off the Gulf coast or something stupid like that. Said they quarantined things to keep us from exporting poisoned fish and other seafood. Made it out to be another BP-type incident. Sent in teams to clean things up, people already really sick and what not. What a crock!"

"Quarantine? So you're telling me that the rest of the world is okay?" Kent stood wide-eyed, his shocked expression partially hidden by the massive shades he still wore.

"Where the hell you been, man? Under a rock?" one of the men asked.

Kent shrugged his shoulders and looked to the ground. He chuckled, "Yeah, something like that."

The two men looked at each other and shook their heads. One of them said, "Look, we don't have time to go into it. Find whoever is in charge of you and ask them. Now, excuse us." With that, the two walked off.

Kent pondered the situation for a moment. He grabbed the backpack from the floor and then made his way to the storage space that had been converted into sleeping quarters.

Stepping quietly into the room not expecting the others to be awake yet, Kent closed the door, slightly surprised. Eric, Billy, and George were all up getting dressed and ready for a day filled with who-knows-what. They hadn't been told much more than *this is your room, see you tomorrow.*

First thing on the agenda for today was something about getting a checkup with the medic. Kent wasn't too sure when, because he was half-asleep when the bus got in last night. He was never one for long drives even if it was under three hours. Something about the motion of the road just put him to sleep every time. Even with the two bodies on the floor, the lady's throat ripped open and a knife in the other man's head, he still managed to fall asleep.

Kent nodded to George and Eric. He took a few more paces past the two men, opening another door that led into another room. The rooms were small but provided what the survivors needed. They connected to one another by adjacent doors, reminding Kent of a hotel room. He imagined that one of the rooms might have once been an office that led into a large storage janitorial space or something. Both rooms looked exactly the same. Each room had three cots that sat low to the ground, one coffee table with nothing on it, and your basic dim overhead lighting. It was obviously thrown together in hurry-up fashion. Pipes ran outside of the walls into each room leading out into the hallway. The pipes weren't visible in the hall, so that must have meant that the ceiling was higher in these two rooms. They smelled of mold—like an old gym locker.

With the door closed behind him, he dropped his bag to the ground. Cynthia lay partly covered by her blanket still on her cot asleep. Suddenly startled by the abrupt noise as the heavy bag collided with the floor below, she quickly sat up in the bed holding the covers partially over her chest, revealing her naked shoulders and bare back.

"Honey, I'm Home," Kent said as he dashed forward pulling her blanket away, exposing her breasts as he landed on top of her, wrapping the covers around them both as he fell.

"Yuck, get off of me. You're filthy!"

She pushed him away, tossing him over and off of the cot. He landed on the floor, taking the covers with him. Covering her well-rounded chest with one arm, most of her voluptuous bust popped out around it. Sitting up in the cot, she glared down at Kent, giving him an ugly look.

"What? I just got out of the shower!"

"You might be clean, but those clothes are disgusting. You're covered in blood, for Christ's sake." Cynthia climbed to her feet, stomping across the room, gathering her clothes from the otherwise empty table.

Kent remained on the floor as he watched her dress with her back turned to him. Kent was still getting a solid view of her round bottom, cheeks peeking from under her underwear as she pulled each leg into one pant leg at a time.

"I ran into some men outside, and they said this place was quarantined and the rest of the world is uninfected," Kent said while enjoying the view.

"Really, what else did they say?"

"Something about the President giving some speech or something. Said he lied out his big fat ass about what's really going on."

"Like that's a surprise."

With not much else to see now that she was dressed, Kent made it to his feet, slung the backpack over a shoulder, and pulled a fresh cigarette from his pocket and then lit it.

Cynthia followed his lead grabbing up her things. "You know, I don't think you're allowed to be smoking in here." She opened the door leading into the other room where Eric and the others had slept.

"Oh yeah, and what are they going to do, shoot me?" A puff of smoke poured from his mouth as he spoke.

*

George raised an eyebrow as the two entered. "Well if it isn't the two love birds. You two were up late last night," he said and smiled.

Kent's chest puffed up along with a wide smirk crossing his face as he took a seat on Eric's cot next to him.

Cynthia just stood there obviously a little embarrassed, her face turning almost as red as her hair. Last night things definitely moved a bit quicker than she would have liked, but it had been quite some time since she had been intimate with anyone besides herself. Other than that, the last thing she wanted to do was send a mixed signal pushing Kent away. She liked him, even though he was already starting to change in little ways. Ever since they had gotten a little snuggly with one another in the car, things with him were different. He seemed cockier and arrogant. Not at all romantic.

She wasn't exactly sure how she felt about him yet. At first, she seemed overwhelmed with a mixture of emotions and hormones. Now, something in the back of her head was telling her to slow down, and that he was going to be more trouble than he was worth. Still, last night was nice, and she knew that everyone else in the room knew as well.

George just smiled. He and Eric went back to what they had been doing.

"I heard you telling her something about a quarantine," George said, his stuff gathered up and at his side.

"Yeah, man, I ran into a couple of dudes out in the hall talking about it. They said this thing, this plague, was just in the Southeast. *The pestilence of man* and all that jazz. The President said it was just an oil spill and they are getting it cleaned up, or something like that. I'm not too sure," Kent said.

*

Eric knelt and tied his shoes with his backpack strung over one arm. His shoulder still throbbed a bit but was feeling much better. His wound on his hand from punching that zombie in the jaw was another story. It had gotten rather sore since the shelter and was a little discolored. It looked and felt infected.

"So, have you guys been formally introduced yet?" Eric reached a hand out palm up toward George while putting his cut hand in his pocket to hide it away. Out of sight, out of mind. "This is George, Mr. George Wellington. *The* Wellington." Tossing his arm across the air, he pointed it at each person as he spoke. Everyone made eye contact, waving hands at each call of the name to signal who was who when each name was called. "George, this is Cynthia and Kent. Kent and Cynthia, this is George and Billy."

"Cool, so you're that guy that was on the radio, right? Telling your story about finding the kid and driving to the station. That's some crazy stuff, man. Crazy," Kent said as he brought the cigarette up for a puff.

Seeing that the two had not actually caught on right away, Eric decided to spell it out for them. "We stayed in *Mr. Wellington's* back yard for the last 3 days. The shelter. This is George, my friend Tyler's dad. He is the one that built that shelter."

"Oh snap, that's what's up, dude. That place saved our lives. Too bad we had to blow it to shit to get out though." Kent shook his head letting out a stream of smoke.

"So your Tyler's dad, right?" Cynthia asked. "Eric here has talked about him a lot. He seems like a real nice kid."

George sank into his cot, depression and anxiety shown on his face. Everyone in the room was quiet for a moment. George sat there taking in deep breath after deep breath, staring at the floor.

Billy sat beside him. His eyes wandered around the room. George was sad. In a way, everyone was. Billy missed his mommy and daddy. Eric missed his parents. George missed his son. Billy leaned over and hugged the old man. No one said a word. The room was silent and filled with tension.

Kent looked over at Cynthia and shrugged, mouthing the words, *Nice going, dude.*

Cynthia's head shrank into her shoulder.

Knock, knock, knock...

The sudden interruption broke the silence like a train wreck startling everyone in the room. The door swung open a moment later. A short, hefty man dressed in slacks and a white lab coat stepped in. He smelled of cheese and perspiration. His glasses were thick, making his eyes look gargantuan against his already buggy little round head. His hair, or the lack thereof, thinning badly and brushed to one side. The man looked like he might be in his late thirties and seemed like he may be an avid believer in super powers in some alternate reality. The kind of guy that longed for a *lab accident turned superhero* kind of vibe just emanated as he entered the room.

"Good morning, everyone. I hope you all slept well. If you all are ready, we'll head over to the lab for a few simple tests."

"Tests? What kind of tests?" Eric asked, his hand throbbed in response, hidden in his pocket still.

"Just some standard tests, young man. We want to make sure none of you are sick or in need of immediate medical attention before relieving you to the cafeteria," the man said.

"Hell, that sounds good to me. When do we eat?" Kent shot to his feet and stepped toward the door, walking right past the man dressed in white.

"Excuse me, but you need to put that out. There is a designated smoke area outside in the courtyard." He grimaced, waving a hand in front of his own face as Kent passed, smoke trailing behind in his wake.

Eric stood, giving George a tap of encouragement on the shoulder, and then walked out of the room meeting Kent in the hall.

Cynthia followed, scrunching her nose up at the man as she passed him at the door. It wasn't the smoke that made her make that face, but the cheese smell lingering on the man in the lab coat. She kept her head straight, eyes to the door, not glancing over to George. She met Eric and Kent in the hall.

With the lab assistant in the lead, the five survivors were escorted out of the barracks and into the courtyard, where several people stood smoking and chatting under a large tree. The sun was out, the breeze felt fresh, and there wasn't a single zombie to stress over. Everyone had a gun. The place was clear and secure. A sense of refuge and ease came over all of them as they made their way across the grass toward another smaller building. On the side of the building next to its double doors, a little sign read *Laboratory Research Facility*. Over the double doors block letters spelling *LRF* hung on the brick wall.

Billy grabbed George's hand.

"So, if you could have one superpower, what would it be?" the man asked as he led them down the hall and around the corner, not directing the question at any particular person.

3

Gus had one foot propped on the helicopter's landing skids as he peered into the cockpit, holding a clipboard in his good hand. With his injured hand, he struggled with the grip of his pen, double-checking the supplies before setting off on the Jacksonville operation.

The pilot, Jesse Watts, sat in the cockpit gearing up the bird and checking all the gauges. After firing her up, the large overhead blades kicked on, steadily picking up momentum.

Gus mumbled to himself as he checked off each set of items from the list, making sure he didn't miss anything he might need.

"—check. Four M-fours, check. Plenty of additional ammo, check. Three gas masks, gloves included, check. Extra fuel cans." Gus leaned in reaching up with his white wrapped hand, shaking the canisters to ensure that they were filled. "Check."

The chopper blades now in full swing hummed loudly with a whooshing sound over the big man as he continued down the list on his clipboard. The heavy wind created by the blades blew the man's short, slightly graying hair. With his black pants tucked into his black boots and his black V-neck shirt tucked tightly into his pants, Gus' clothes clung tightly to his body.

Watts leaned back from the cockpit reaching his arm out to get the big man's attention, pointing at the airfield directly behind Gus. He was unable to hear Watts, the man's mouth steadily moving. He turned back at the hip leaving his feet in place and taking a glance over his shoulder to see what Watts was pointing at. With the bright asphalt glaring in his face from the clear, sunny sky, Gus lifted the clipboard over his head using it as a visor. The paper blew frantically in place between his thumb and the clipboard.

"Name, soldier?" Gus shouted leaning in to greet the unexpected visitor.

"I'm Jared Clay. I'm taking Luke Beal's place on the Jacksonville OP," the slightly younger and obviously inexperienced man replied.

It was a little hard to hear with the blades buzzing over them, but what Gus got from the shouting was that Luke was out and he was in. Gus was thankful for that, because Luke was in no shape to be on duty, let alone work with Gus. He kind of figured that this was going to happen because the man was running late. He, however, half hoped for someone a little less green around the ears than this guy standing before him now.

Gus couldn't think of a single time when he had ever seen this young buck on base. Sure, there was something like four hundred people on base at any given time, but still. You would have to run into one another sooner or later, right? He had met every team that ever ran on a bird at that base for the last few years, and this kid for sure wasn't one of them. Gus turned to face the unanticipated guest, and out of habit, reached out with his bad hand for a handshake.

He did a good job of not showing his first impression of the kid, keeping a stern and steady look. Feeling it too much effort to shout over the noise, Gus just smiled and nodded, stepping out of the way to allow the newcomer onto the bird after awkwardly shaking hands.

Clay's jacket fluttered abruptly for a few moments right before jumping into the chopper, neck bent slightly showing his personal concern for the blades overhead, a clear sign that this guy had no helicopter experience.

The pilot ready to go, shot his hand in the air, spinning his index finger around and around mimicking the blades. Gus got the cue and hopped in taking his helmet and tossing one to Clay. He took a seat across from Clay, facing him, and buckled in. He glanced up at Clay who was already strapped in and struggling to get the helmet on. Gus just smiled, trying not to look too tense, knowing good and well that this trip was going to be an interesting one to say the least.

Gus leaned up and popped the top of Clay's helmet shoving it down onto his head the rest of the way. His hand instantly throbbed with pain sending a jolt up his elbow, making him realize he had just used the wrong hand for the job.

Clay gave him a thumb-up for the help.

"We clear for departure?" Watts asked, his voice rang out in their headsets as if he was right on top of them.

"Roger that, take us up," Gus replied as he slapped the side of the chopper with his good hand. *Stay tight*, he thought to himself as he brought his hand back, not feeling the need to engage the others. His last mission with Bo and Willy came back to haunt him, his mind racing with the loss.

*

The chopper slowly leaned forward and up as it ascended off of the ground and into the air, leading the soldiers toward Jacksonville. As the chopper reached a higher altitude, what was originally not visible from the ground instantly became otherwise, Clay seeing it for the first time.

The base was surrounded, surrounded by the undead.

Here he was for the first time, getting a firsthand glimpse of the situation; how bad it truly was. Sure, he had his run in with the infected earlier that week, when Michaels ate the dirt and that wacko professor Taft had him strapping down a zombie to the gurney. It was just another shit detail job assignment. He had been sent in on several occasions to do grunt work for the white coats, but never anything that outrageous. After that day happened, he knew he was out in two years, no questions.

Peering over the buildings and across the base to the fences that surrounded it on all sides, zombies had gathered around ten and twenty deep in some areas, clinging to the fence line. It was out of control. There didn't seem to be a single spot of the visible fence line that didn't have at least two rows deep of those creatures trying their best to get in.

The chopper took a sharp turn to the right and then eventually straightened back out flying over the main gate. Four armed guards stood in control towers on each side of the large retracting electric gates. With each armed man wielding an M-4 in hand, the men held their weapons out and at the ready.

As the chopper flew directly overhead, Clay saw that soldiers were taking shots into the crowd from the towers. From the looks of it, he could almost swear that they had made a game out of it. With that many undead at the gates, it was a futile effort and essentially a waste of ammunition.

Breaking away from the base now pushing forward over the city, Clay also noticed that the majority of the dead were younger people. With Tallahassee being a major college town and the state's capitol, it was at one time well populated with college kids and people in their early thirties trying to make it in the bigger city. But they were dead now, and reanimated as the undead. The city streets and alleyways were cluttered with walking corpses.

*

With Clay leaned over the side of the chopper just a tad as he looked out at the ravenous plague, it took Gus a few times to get his attention. Having seen it all first hand, Gus didn't bother even the slightest glance overboard. It was day four for the big man and that was more than enough.

"Clay… Clay… Clay…" He tapped the guy across from him on the knee getting his attention from what lay out there on the streets. "I didn't see you in the debriefing room this morning. What do you know of this OP, exactly?" Gus asked, aware that Watts could also hear their conversation.

"Nothing, sir. I was told I would get my orders once we took off," Clay replied slightly distracted, his eyes still fixed on the devastation outside as they passed over it.

After making sure that he had Clay's undivided attention, which took a little work, Gus started going over what the young man had missed in the debriefing. He started by producing a wallet-sized photo of an old man from his shirt pocket and handed it over to Clay.

"This man is Grech Vonhinkly, founder of GCUR-TECH."

The two men swayed and bounced in the chopper as it cut through the sky.

Gus continued, "The man is sixty-two years old, but don't let his age fool you. He is believed to be the mastermind behind more than a handful of biochemical warfare agents, including the one that has currently wiped out almost all of Florida and its two connecting states. Despite that, I don't expect the man to be dangerous."

Clay jumped in asking, "How do you know that?"

"Because he's the scientist type, that's why. How many white coats do you know carry a gun?"

"Dr. Gibbs carries a gun," Clay said.

"Besides Dr. Gibbs? None. That's how many," Gus said. "Now, the facility we're dropping at is a secure location. What that means is that we don't actually know a whole lot about it other than where it's located. How big the place is or what to expect is unknown. What we do know is that this facility contains large amounts of biochemical agents and bacteria. Not sure on how well guarded the place is or what the staffing situation is either."

"So basically you're telling me that we are going into this thing with our eyes closed. Is that it?" Clay asked.

"Unfortunately, yes," Gus replied.

"So what's the mission? Seems like checking the place out for the sake of checking it out would be a big waste of time," Clay said, still glancing out of the cockpit occasionally, watching the city streets pass by congested with abandoned cars. It was like a huge ghost town.

"Find Vonhinkly, retrieve any useful data on the bacteria or disease or whatever it is, and make it back unscathed all before dinner," Gus said.

Gus noticed a change in Clay's body language. It suggested something that he saw couldn't have been good. He stopped his little speech to peer out the same side of the chopper at what had Clay's attention.

Watts, the pilot, chimed in for the first time since taking off, "Ashley Fox's team! Straight ahead."

The three men peered out as they passed, slightly cutting off course to take a closer look. The black bird, an exact replica of the one they currently rode in, sat atop a large building. The structure looked like it could have been a small mall, but Gus couldn't think of there being one of those out this way. On the side of the building, the word *Sears* identified it.

The parking lot, along with the streets from above, looked fairly safe, no major signs of the infected. A few stray zombies meandered about here and there, but nothing they couldn't handle.

"Fox Trot, this is Blue Bravo. Come in. Over," the pilot said holding his hand up to his helmet with the radio. "Fox Trot, this is Blue Bravo. Come in. Over."

After a few seconds of watching the lack of activity on top of and around the building, Gus spoke up, "Let's move on. We have a job to do. Call radio dispatch and make the report." Without a word, the chopper redirected to its original route, Watts calling in the unexpected find.

"I didn't realize they didn't make it in last night. I wonder what happened," Gus said, still looking out at the helicopter, watching it get smaller and smaller the farther away they got.

"Quite a few didn't report in last night, actually," Clay said. "Rob was telling me about it. Something like five or more of the teams didn't report back in. I imagine they had the same set of issues that you ran into last night as well. I heard yours was rough."

"Get ready, kid, because the shit is probably about to hit the fan again," Gus said.

"Speaking of about to hit... what time are we expected to arrive? Feels like we have been riding in this thing for a while."

Watts chimed in to answer that one before Gus could even speak up, "Not long, maybe another thirty minutes, forty-five at the most."

When we get there, if for some reason there isn't a good place to land, we're turning around and calling it a day. I'm not about to land knee deep in that mess twice in less than twenty-four hours. If Baker has a problem with that then he can eat it, because I don't care. Just not going to do it. Gus thought of his lost friends and that was the last thing he needed right before another jump.

*

The three soldiers flew the rest of the way in silence. Clay sat there wondering what it might be that was eating the older, bigger man up so much. It was written all over his face, whatever it was.

Clay glanced down one last time at the photo still held tightly in his hand. Nothing unusual stood out about the man in the photo. He looked like an average civilian. How was it that such an ordinary man was responsible for all of this? He handed the picture back to Gus.

Everything looked the same for miles and miles on end. Large fires billowed out from buildings and in small forest areas. Cars of all kinds littered the roadways. The walking dead scattered everywhere in the streets, the parks, the parking lots. It was all the same.

Clay couldn't help but wonder if there was anyone left within the quarantined zone. Could this much destruction and chaos actually spread this fast in a few days? This type of power in the hands of man gave Clay a gut-wrenching feeling, one that made him a little lightheaded and overwhelmed. Realizing that he was only a short way out from landing in this stuff and possibly meeting face to face with the creatures drove sharp pains into his stomach. He was having a panic attack.

Clay suddenly unlocked his safety straps and proceeded to vomit out of the aircraft. His hair and jacket fluttered in the wind with half of his body hanging out of the helicopter while he held to the sides with both hands. The light brown heave poured out pushing away from him horizontally. Most of the puke made its way out of the chopper, but almost all of it splashed across its side.

When the moment passed, he sat back down and harnessed himself in again, making eye contact with Gus, helmet slightly lopsided. "I'll be all right. I just need a minute."

Gus didn't say a word. He just leaned forward pushing the thumb and forefinger of his good hand on the bridge of his nose and rubbed it between them.

He let out a big sigh.

4

"So tell me, Gibbs, what did we find out about our visitors?" General Baker asked.

"You can at least wait for me to sit before barraging me with questions. I'm not one of your subordinates." Gibbs had just entered the General's office after administering a basic check up on each of the civilians. She held in her hand a manila folder with files on all five of the survivors.

As she sat down in front of Baker's desk, he turned from his mini-bar with a freshly poured glass of scotch on the rocks. The ice bumped the side of the tumbler as he took a seat before the slightly irritated doctor.

"It's a little early for that, don't you think, General?"

"When you're the general and the world around you is in chaos, you can make up the rules as it suits you. Now, down to business. What can you tell me?" Baker asked, setting down the drink without taking a sip.

She placed the folder on the desk and opened it.

The General raised an eyebrow. "That doesn't look like a whole lot of intel, Dr. Gibbs."

"That's because there wasn't much to find, sir," she said, her words frostily. "They're average civilians."

"Average civilians who managed to avoid the plague that's affected most of the population in this area. Something's different about them," Baker said.

She flipped to the first name in the file. A small profile photo of a young, rebellious-looking man slid across the table finding Baker's hand as he scooped it up before allowing it to come to a stop.

Gibbs thumbed through the notes for a moment reading over a few details. "Kent Kingsly. Thirty-four years old. Six-foot-two, blue eyes, brown hair. One hundred ninety pounds. Originally from Illinois, picked up and moved to Florida five years ago with a rock band. Spent a couple months in juvenile detention for grand theft when he was younger. Honestly, from what I can tell, this guy is harmless. He plays the card but doesn't have an ounce of gut to actually back anything up. He's all talk. Beyond that, he's as healthy as most Americans. "

General Baker leaned up from his seat passing the picture back, then sat back down, picking up his drink. Spinning the ice around and around for a moment, he eyed it with great appreciation. While taking a deep gulp, he gestured with his other hand for her to continue with the next civilian's report. Coming away with a half-empty glass from his mouth, the cup reached the tabletop of the desk, leaving a smirk across the General's face where the alcohol had recently just finished touching his lips. "Ah, that's some good stuff."

She continued, "Cynthia Smith. Thirty-eight years old. Five-foot-five, hazel eyes, red hair, one hundred and eighty-seven pounds. Originally from Texas, raised in Florida almost from birth. She's a local." She retrieved the photo of the red-headed lady and tossed it across to Baker. "This one is mentally unstable. Several reported cases of attempted suicide. If she is a threat to anyone, it is most likely only to herself. I'm not the slightest bit concerned with her. All she needs it medical treatment to keep her from having any episodes. I have one of my assistants filling out a prescription for the woman. The hardest part will be to get the lady to take them."

Without feeling the need for Baker's approval, she just continued moving on to the next person. She tossed out another photo.

"George Wellington. Sixty-eight years old. Five-foot-nine, gray hair, brown eyes. Two hundred twelve pounds. Local, born and raised. Nothing special about his medical history. The man has a son named Tyler, still missing. His wife died a few years ago in a car accident. Worked the same steady job his entire life straight into retirement. I'm surprised the man is still holding on. He's been through hell. He requested to speak with you in person. Something about needing to look for his son. I told him I would see what I could do," Gibbs said, hoping the General would be sympathetic enough to give Wellington some time.

"I'll be sure to speak with him after dinner tonight," Baker said, propping both elbows up on the table, looking a little bored.

"Thank you, sir. I know he will feel much better if you can offer him a little hope." Gibbs was surprised Baker seemed concerned for the man. Maybe it was the scotch talking.

"Moving on," Baker said.

"Oh... right." She flipped a few pages and landed at Eric's section of the folder. "Eric Micson. Age seventeen, six foot, blond hair, green eyes, one hundred and forty-five pounds. Also a local born and raised. Still in high school, an A-B student. No record that I can find. The all-American teenager every parent wanted but didn't get."

"And the boy," Baker asked.

She closed the folder and slid it to the side. She recited it by memory. "Billy Woods. Age nine. Other than his height, weight and eye color, we have no other information about him. Parents are unaccounted for. George said he found the boy locked in a public bathroom, screaming for help at a park. George saved the kid and ended up at the radio station with him where we picked them up."

"I'm surprised there wasn't something that connected them. And you say they're in good health?" Baker asked.

"Other than a little malnourishment, everyone seemed fine. Nothing to be alarmed over," Gibbs said.

*

They sat there for a second in Baker's office staring at the air between them. The General knew she was hiding something, but he wasn't sure why.

He picked up his tumbler and proceeded to refill it. "You know... Dr. Gibbs, sometimes I wonder." He stepped away from the mini-bar and turned his back on Gibbs, casting a quick gaze over a multitude of photos and medals that hung from the walls in his office, stopping at one photo in particular.

"Sometimes you wonder what, sir?" Gibbs asked as she grabbed the folder and held it tightly.

Baker reached up, taking the framed photo from the wall to get a close look. In the black and white photo, a much younger, more vibrant Baker stood with three other men near his age, all wearing matching uniforms. The men were smiling as if a funny joke had just been told. The backdrop to the seemingly playful moment was a B-52 bomber.

Baker spoke while wiping the accumulated dust from the photo and setting it back on its hanger against the wall, "It takes a team to stay alive, Gibbs. A *team*. Leaving out the slightest bit of details can be detrimental to the safety of the entire operation. You are a part of this team, are you not?" he asked without taking his gaze away from the old photo.

Before she could reply, he continued, "Have you ever heard of *Han Anderson*, Gibbs? The story of a king and his new clothes, are you familiar with that story?" Baker turned, glaring down at the woman, one hand still straightening the replaced photo frame.

"No, sir. I can't say that I have." She swallowed deep and dryly.

"An emperor, who cared for nothing but his appearance and attire, hires two tailors who promise him the finest suit of clothes from a fabric invisible to anyone who is unfit for his position or just hopelessly stupid. Do you see where I'm going with this, Doctor?" Baker sat down picking up the cigar from his ashtray, flicking ash all over the table in the process.

Gibbs took off her glasses, rubbing the lenses with her white coat.

The General again continued, but this time with a lot more grit and tenacity in his voice, "The emperor cannot see the cloth himself, but pretends that he can for fear of appearing unfit for his position, or stupid, for that matter. His ministers do the same. When the swindlers report that the suit is finished, they mime dressing him and the emperor then marches in procession before his subjects. A child in the crowd calls out that the emperor is wearing nothing at all and the cry is taken up by others. The emperor cringes, suspecting the assertion is true, but holds himself up proudly and continues the procession assuming that the people in the crowd are the ones who are stupid." Baker slammed the cigar back into the ashtray, smashing it beyond recognition.

"Do you think I'm *stupid*, Dr. Gibbs? Are you playing me for a fool?" he shouted. "Now what is it about these civilians that you are neglecting to tell me? Do you think I can't see past your magical clothes, Doctor?"

She sat there for a moment. In as soft voice, she said, "One of the civilians… one of the civilians… is… is infected."

"Is what?" the General asked.

Stronger, she said, "Infected. One of the civilians is infected. It's Eric, the teenager, sir."

Relaxing a little, he propped himself back in his chair. "A few minutes before you arrived, one of your assistants informed me that he suspected as much. I blew him off at first—failing to see what advantage you'd have in keeping a secret like that. But when you walked in, I could tell you were hiding something. I have a gift for reading people, Dr. Gibbs. So, you have some explaining to do. First, where is Eric now?"

"In the mess hall with the other civilians," she replied. "I gave him a shot that should stop the spread of the bacteria. I'm still—"

"What do you mean *should*?" Sitting forward again, leaned over his desk, Baker's face returned to that awful glare. His fists clenched tight atop the table.

"It works in the lab. Eric is the first carrier I've been able to work with who hasn't fully changed over yet and took the opportunity to test out the formula," Gibbs said. "I'm going to personally keep tabs on him. If the infection spreads, I'll report it immediately."

Baker shot to his feet pushing his chair calmly into place under the desk. He slowly walked around the desk making his way behind Gibbs.

She shifted left and right in her seat. Baker's hand suddenly landed on both of her shoulders. She leaned forward and tried to stand.

He pushed her back down, sending her right back into place. Holding tighter than ever, he spoke again calm and collectively, "So let me get this straight. You, you of all people decided to let an infected person into my base and thought it okay to have them mingling with my men. You intentionally put *my men*, the soldiers I am accountable for, in harm's way without my consent. All for what Gibbs? A little fucking science experiment that *should* work?"

"I was afraid if I told you, you would have killed him. General, we're running out of time. We don't know what caused the outbreak, yet we put ourselves right in the middle of it. What happens if *we* come down with this... this condition? Time is running short, and I thought the risk was worth the reward. I believe we're living on borrowed time. Not just us, but the whole United States—even the whole world."

General Baker shoved her back down with both hands still firmly clasped onto her shoulders. "What you have done is nothing short of treason."

Gibbs contorted her face as if she were in fear of being struck. She sat squashed between Baker and the seat. Then she said in a small voice, "I would like to leave now. Please."

"Of course, of course you would. And you should." Baker stepped back, releasing his grip. The General then made his way around her and took a seat at the desk, pulling a cigar from his shirt pocket. He lit it the same way he had done it every time before. After a few puffs, Gibbs jumped to her feet and grabbed the manila folder, then turned away to swiftly make her exit.

An electronic click sounded from the door.

Baker picked up the phone almost instantly speaking with someone on the other end.

As he muttered something, Gibbs reached for the door. It was locked. She shook the handle reputedly. "What's going on?" She dropped the folder and grabbed the door handle with both hands. The papers and pictures scattered about the floor.

"Yes... send them in," Baker said and hung up the phone.

The electronic click sounded from the door again. The doorknob began to turn, and then the door opened.

Two armed soldiers entered the room, forcing Gibbs to retreat. She stepped on the contents of the folder strewn on the floor.

"Take her down to the cells and lock her up. I'll deal with her later, personally," General Baker said from behind his big desk. He waved and gave a mock smile to Gibbs as the two men grabbed hold of her. The smoke from his cigar clouded around his face.

"You can't do this! I still have work to do. I need to watch Eric," Gibbs shouted. She flailed about in the arms of the two soldiers, trying to break free of their grip. Her efforts were futile.

The two soldiers exited the room closing the door behind them as they went. The folder of spilled files had a photo of Eric turned right side up. The General left his seat and retrieved the photo of the teenage boy and glared at it a moment, then blew a heavy gust of cigar smoke into the photo as he held it.

"Not on my watch," he murmured to himself before crushing the photo in his hand.

5

The cafeteria was practically empty. Kent, Cynthia, George, Billy, and Eric sat together eating and carrying on in conversation. The only other people in the lunchroom beside themselves were the cooks, who kept themselves busy prepping things for the next meal of the day. One other person walked around the mess hall, gathering up empty trays and cups on a roll cart, undoubtedly the designated dishwasher. They found themselves seated almost center of the very large room.

Everyone had clean clothes on, feeling fresher than they had felt in days. All but Cynthia still wore what they had shown up with. She, on the other hand, had received a new pair of camo pants and a plain gray shirt. With almost all of her original wardrobe tattered beyond repair, she was happy to be issued something new, even if it wasn't her style. Her long flowing red hair now clean was wrapped tight in a long ponytail, running down her back.

Kent looked her over, feeling like it made her look as if she belonged in the military. It turned him on. Cynthia was aware of it and disliked his lack of manners. The entire time they ate, he wouldn't keep his hands off her, and it was getting annoying. He was acting like a child, she thought and that he needed to show some dignity and respect for the others at the table, if not for her.

With almost everyone's plates nearly emptied, they just sat there talking amongst themselves and watching the television.

With Billy in the group, a cartoon station was the channel of choice. Something about the moment just seemed right, seemed real. For the first time in days, the group of survivors felt normal. There was a renewed hope buzzing about in their midst. Everyone was cheery and giddy, laughing at stories and one another. Things were going to be okay. Sure, they had all had their fair share of loses, but who didn't? Optimism was alive once more.

"—and that's when Eric here just snapped. He ran through a pile of those things, straight across the shelter, and started kicking the generator pipe like some sort of WCW maniac."

Cynthia cut Kent off, finishing the story for him, "Yeah, had he not pulled that crazy stunt, we wouldn't be here today. We ended up nearly blowing that shelter out of the ground. It was freaking crazy," she said and laughed, shoving Eric playfully.

"Ha… It was nothing, really. Do or die, right?" Eric shrugged his shoulders at her boastings and blushed at the same time.

The sound of the television echoed in the background. Billy moved his attention over to it. His legs swayed back and forth, his feet too short to reach the tile floor.

"So where do you think we will go from here?" George asked and brought a glass of soda to his lips.

"Hell, this outbreak is only in one area. Chances are, the government is going to pay us a pretty penny to keep our mouths shut. Soon as that happens, I'm hopping on a boat and hitting the islands," Kent said.

"Oh, and what islands would that be, Kent?" Cynthia asked pushing him off of her for the fifth time in the last few minutes.

"Any island," he said reaching down with one hand to get a palm full of Cynthia's bottom.

She glared at Kent and pulled his hand away. "Really now, and what if the government doesn't pony up like you think they will? What then?"

"I know what I'm going to do," Eric interrupted while he looked down at his bandaged hand. The bandages wrapped around all four knuckles. Some blood and other liquid lightly soaked the top of it around the cut. He flexed his fingers as he spoke, slowly taking his eyes from his wound and toward his comrades. "I'm going to retire."

The cafeteria suddenly filled with laughter at the thought of a teenager already set on retirement. Billy turned and smiled along with the laughter. The mirth lasted for only a few seconds.

"How's that thing holding up?" Cynthia asked pointing at Eric's bandages. "Looks like it hurts."

Before Eric had the chance to speak, Kent butted in, "Man, you sure were in there for a long time. What did they do to you in there?"

"Fixed me up, of course," Eric said. He looked down at his hand a bit longer in thought before continuing. "And yes, it freaking hurts. The doctor stabbed the hell out of my knuckles with a big needle. She sucked out some liquid from it to do some testing of some kind she said, and then gave me a shot. That was painful. Her assistant had to hold my arm down to do it," Eric replied, his eyes fixed on what little was left on his plate. The fork in his hand mixed the last bit of food around as he stared. "Since she gave me that shot, I kind of feel funny. Like sick to my stomach or something. I just want to lay down when I finish eating."

"What about you, Mr. Wellington? What are you going to do now?" Eric asked.

"I was hoping to speak to the General sometime today. I plan to continue searching for my son and want the Army's help," George said looking down at the little boy sitting beside him. "And for Billy's parents too!"

Billy immediately joined the conversation as if listening in the whole time, "My parents? I watched daddy shoot my mommy at home. She was attacking him in the living room. After that, my dad took me through the woods behind the house and across the street into a park. Daddy locked me in the bathroom there. I could hear him shooting some more and then it stopped. He left me there."

The room was suddenly quiet. Billy went right back to watching the television as if what he had said was nothing at all. He leaned forward taking a sip from his straw without taking hold of the cup of soda. Both of his hands lay tucked to his side, hands gripping the bench as his legs swayed.

George sat in silence thinking back on when he happened upon the young boy locked away in that park bathroom. He had recalled one time Billy mentioning that his father was a policeman. George instantly flashed back to the moment when he drove up to the park. Several zombies littered the area meandering about. A few intently clung to the restroom door trying their best to get it. George vividly recalled one of those corpses being a uniformed officer, gun still in hand. Blood covered the victim's throat and shirt, along with several chunks of flesh missing from its upper arms. With the gun in one hand, the zombie pounded at the locked door alongside a few others. Lost in thought, George was surprised that this detail had not clicked before.

George's train of thought suddenly was interrupted by Billy's giggling. Something on the television must have been funny to the little boy.

6

Luke Beal hovered over the sink in the joint bathroom that he shared with another military officer from across the hall. Looking at his reflection in the foggy mirror, hot water running in the shower behind him, Luke stood in the room with only a towel draped around his waist with both hands pressed against the sink holding him upright. He was a mess. Beside his thoughts, the only other sound he heard was that of the high-pressure water spraying into the tub from the showerhead behind him.

The main barracks were more like a set of college dorms than anything else. There was a main hall with rooms on each side. Every other room shared a full bathroom with the adjacent room next to it. Each set of sleeping quarters was generally shared with a roommate and had previously been furnished for them. With two beds, a couch, a mini fridge, and a television, each room was identical. Luke had the luxury of not having a roommate. He wasn't the only soldier to be so lucky. With the chaos and the content losses, a lot of people didn't have roommates these days. It was quite common to have one person per living quarter, despite the setup. Luke also didn't have to worry about the tenant from across the way barging in on him in the bathroom. They both kept up with each other's schedule, and Luke was well aware that the other man was on guard duty today until late.

He and Megan used to spend Fridays relaxing in his apartment if they were off. They would watch television, talk about anything and everything, and just enjoy each other's company. He missed her scent, her touch, but most of all, her laugh.

Lost in thought, Luke imagined the two of them in the shower, like several times before, making love. Each bead of water splashing against her bare skin as it dripped down her chest tightly pressed against his. Her heavy breathing deep into his ear while he held her close, each leg tightly wrapped around his hips, her back pressed against the tile wall.

He took a deep breath and sighed even deeper. The train of thought broke as he stared at himself in the mirror. Unable to make out his face, he wiped the heavy condensation from it. Staring straight ahead, as if into the darkness of the abyss, Luke glared at his own reflection, sick to his stomach with anger.

His lover and friend was dead.

After a few moments of heavy breathing, he found himself lost in thought once more. He found himself inside the Rhino Runner peering over Gus' shoulder. The big man had his pistol drawn same as before. As he watched from behind the big man, he witnessed Megan pleading on her knees for mercy in the eyes of her executioner. She cried out for help, and before Luke had the opportunity to—

CRACK!

Luke suddenly snapped out of the daydream of the *nightmare* as he slammed his fist into the mirror. Bits of glass fell around his bleeding hand into the sink and onto the floor. All he could think of was that big man's stupid face. *You know it has to be done*, he had said before he murdered her.

With those words playing over and over and over again in Luke's head, he felt enraged. Angry at Gus for shooting the one woman he had ever grown to love. But more so, angry at himself for not doing something, for not taking action.

What had made him just sit back so reserved in the briefing this morning? He had the opportunity to step up, to say something to that big prick of a man. Gus had it coming! Yet, Luke just sat there, mouth closed. Megan deserved some type of retribution, and he just let it slip away so easily. Why?

Luke also couldn't help but think that he was taken off of the Jacksonville operation because Gus had it out for him. Sure, Luke could admit to himself that he was a little out of it and couldn't say he actually took a single bit of information away from that debriefing. But, Gus was surely the reason he was removed from the mission. Why? Was Gus too little of a man to face his victim's lover? That must be it, that son of a bitch!

Luke stood there thinking these things, watching the blood drip from his hand down the drain. The red color popped against the white of the sink as it ran down one side in slow motion. Luke turned on the water, watching the blood and water quickly mix together. The blood began thinning out as it poured down the drain from his cut hand.

"Stupid son-of-a-bitch!" Luke mumbled under his breath.

Taking two steps back, knowing the distance by memory, Luke sat down on the leg at the edge of the tub. The water emanated heat against his back, steam steadily filling the room around him from the still-running shower. To his left was the door which led to his room, and to his right was the door leading to his neighbor.

With elbows resting on his legs and face buried in his hands, Luke cried like a baby. His loss was more overwhelming than he had even initially realized. He finally cracked, sobbing for a handful of minutes, while seated on the edge of the tub. The water behind him slowly began to cool, the heat gradually subsiding.

After a while of crying, he cried some more. The image of Megan's beautiful face haunted his thoughts; her short naturally silky hair and bright eyes. Her dimples just so, making her always seem to have a little smile tucked away. Those rosy lips, they haunted him. She haunted him. How could he ever live like this? Alone?

In the middle of thinking these things, Luke glanced over noticing his holster. Just a few feet over, on the floor next to the toilet, his discarded clothes lay strewn. His 9mm handgun lay amongst them, tucked away in its designated place, strapped around a black leather belt.

He kicked up, leaving the stooped position, leaning forward toward the clothes. Still bent at the knees and not moving his footing, he reached the belt and pulled it in close. Falling right back onto the tub, he sat there eyeing the holstered weapon; eyes, beet-red and slightly swollen from all of the emotional stress. A fresh tear leaked out with a sniffle. Luke quickly wiped it away with his forearm while un-holstering the pistol. He clicked the release, dropping the magazine out while catching it with his free hand. After confirming that it was full, he slammed it home and racked a round into the chamber. Clicking off the safety, Luke eyed the weapon with a furious stare. Blood slowly poured from the cut on his hand. He held the gun, paying no attention to the bits of glass lodged inside the cut.

He put the 9mm up under his chin, leaning his head back. His hand tightened around the grip of the black pistol, trigger finger slightly starting to add pressure. *You know it has to be done, you know it has to be done, you know it has to be done, you know it has to be done.*

Water fell from the shower like rain, offering a gentle symphony into the future.

7

BANG!

With one leg extended, Gus' boot slammed into the metal door, shattering the lock. The door swung open, spinning around as it crashed against the wall, swinging on its hinges.

The two soldiers stared down the stairwell leading into the building. Only the first few steps in the light, the rest swallowed in darkness.

The chopper had set down on a large building. The three-story building had been a lot more secluded than Gus had anticipated. This was a good surprise. There were no real streets to speak of, mostly just woods and dirt. That meant no infected ghouls to hassle with. The three-story building sat alone, hidden in the outskirts of downtown Jacksonville, a few miles to the east. Whatever was going on at this place was intended to be a secret.

After safely landing the chopper on the roof, Gus and Clay geared up, moving as quickly as they could. The objective was to get in and out with enough time to spare; just an in and out OP. Gus' motivation—the cafeteria; he wanted to make it home in time for dinner. But, lately, it hadn't seemed to be turning out in his favor.

Watts had shut down the helicopter. His job was to sit tight and send word if anything dramatic changed outside. Armed with enough ammo for a small army, he was happy to stay atop the relative safety of the roof. It was a tough job, but someone had to do it.

Aware of the limited visibility when wearing the gas masks, Clay suggested they go in wearing one. Gus agreed, immediately strapping on the mask. Clay did likewise.

Each armed with an M-4 and two 9mm handguns, they both carried as much ammo as was practical. Clay threw an ammo pouch around one shoulder and across his neck and filled his cargo pockets to the brim with magazines for his rifle.

Gus had the same setup as Clay, along with a slim back pouch loaded with even more. If, by any chance, they were going to run into as many of the undead as Gus had crossed in Panama City Beach, he was sure as hell going to be ready.

"Let's do this just like I said before!" Gus shouted, his voice muffled under his gas mask.

Clay nodded, bringing his rifle up, slamming in a fresh magazine, and racking a live shell into the chamber. He pulled the weapon up to his shoulder at the ready, clicking the safety off.

Gus nodded in response, turning on the flashlight attached to the end of his rifle. Clay shrugged, shaking his head, as he reached up to do the same.

With a flick of the wrist motioning them to move, the two-man army moved forward into the building, descending the staircase toward the top floor. Trying to enter as quietly as possible, the two men slid down each step with ease. The bottom of the stairway appeared to open up into a large room or hallway, and they wanted to avoid attracting any more attention than they already had when kicking in the rooftop door.

As Gus reached the bottom rung of the steps, he turned back toward Clay at the rear. Quietly pointing at his own eyes, then, shooting his index finger toward the right, Gus silently gave the order. Gus shot straight-as-an-arrow up against the wall at the bottom of the steps, peeking out ever so slightly.

Signaling Clay once more, with the same set of hand motions, Clay darted out from the stairs to the right. With rifle at the ready, his flashlight swiftly covered the right side of the room up and down.

From behind Clay, Gus burst out from the hiding spot against the wall, checking the left side of the room; his motions practically mirror-imaging Clay's simultaneously.

Nothing.

It was just a storage space leading to the roof; a few dusty cases and a lot of unfiled papers. With only the sounds of their muffled breathing, Clay flipped through a handful of the dusty files. With one in his hand, he looked over his shoulder noticing that Gus was still scanning the room with his light. Glancing to no particular spot on the paper, he began to read, "…received the new shipment of Brazilian…"

"Watts, radio headquarters that we have arrived and are sweeping the place now. I'll keep you updated," Gus said, and clipped the radio back to his hip. He stepped up and pulled the paper from Clay's grip. "We have a lot of rooms to cover, kid. No time for reading." Before crumpling it up and tossing it to the floor, he, too, glanced over its contents. "Nothing that we need to worry with. Let's move." The ball of paper dropped to the floor.

The radio called back, "Roger that. Over," Watts said.

Gus slung the radio from his hip, once more, holding down the receiver. "Going to keep the line closed. Don't want to draw any unnecessary attention. Over." Gus shoved the radio back on his hip, turning the volume knob until it clicked off.

Exiting the storage space, the two soldiers found themselves in a long hallway. From the looks of it, there had to be at least twenty or thirty rooms on this floor alone, including the bathrooms.

"This is going to take longer than I had hoped," Gus murmured. "We're going to need to pick up the pace if we plan to make it home in time."

"Home in time for what?" Clay asked.

Not giving a response, Gus moved forward to the first of several doors, side-stepping, rifle at the ready. All the lights were off in the building; the hall was dark, eerie, and quite. With Clay at the rear, Gus took the lead. Thus, leaving the younger of the two stuck covering their asses.

Checking the door with a quick turn of the knob, it was unlocked. Gus shoved the door open, quickly scanning the room from side to side. With light coming in from the handful of rather large office windows, the room was well lit. Scanning the hallway one last time before peeking into the room, Clay did likewise.

"This doesn't make any sense. The place looks freaking empty," Gus said, dropping his rifle at his hip.

The room looked like it had once been an office space. Four large desks sat against each of the four walls of the room, with three computer monitors on each desk. Each chair was neatly placed in its designated location, scooted under the desk in front of each monitor. Nothing looked out of the ordinary. There was no sign of struggle or forced entry. Papers and other office supplies lay neatly stacked and organized in selected bins.

The two soldiers moved on. Checking room after room, they made their way across the hall. In a matter of minutes, they managed to check every last room on the third floor. Nothing was out of the ordinary.

"I need a break from this thing," Gus said removing his gas mask and holding it under his arm. "Where the hell is everybody?" With his rifle set on a desk directly behind him, Gus looked out at the open field of sparsely spaced trees and brush from a third story window.

The room they now stood in was the last one to inspect. Just like all the rest, there wasn't a soul in sight; no one, infected or otherwise. Most of the office spaces in each room they came across were almost identical. Every other door they opened led into one of two types of rooms. The window that Gus currently peered out of, however, was in a room set up almost like a classroom. The only room of its kind on this floor. It reminded him of high school. There was a large desk toward the front of the room, by the main door, and twenty-some-odd student desks facing the same direction. Behind the desk, on the wall, lay a large, unfamiliar, map of a third world country, neither man knew much about.

"Let's move," Gus said. He pointed toward the door as he stepped away from the window, tossing his mask back over his head. Gus mumbled, "There has to be something here. It's up to us to find it."

Clay quickly agreed with a nod, finding his place behind the big man, covering the rear.

The two soldiers made their way stealthily down the second flight of stairs winding round to the second floor. With rifles at the ready, they crept swiftly down each step.

"Shh…" Clay tapped Gus on the shoulder, consequently, stopping them both dead in their tracks, halfway down the steps. With the silent signal, Clay tapped his ear and then pointed at both of his own eyes.

Gus double-checked his safety: clicking it back, then, opened it again. Simultaneously, he cocked the release, checking to make sure he had a live round in the chamber. The quick clinks of his weapon sounded loud in the enveloping silence.

Taking each step a little slower, they rounded the corner of the descent. In the back of Gus' mind, he was actually blown away by the younger man's readiness. The boy's training seemed to simply kick in, like second nature. Hidden beneath the glass of his protective visor, Gus grinned slightly. He decided he had started to take a liking to Clay. He might just be cut out for this yet.

Clay had heard something all right. As the two soldiers reached the lower part of the steps, they could see something and hear it too.

The door leading into the hall from the staircase was blocked.

A middle-aged female, covered in blood, lay against the door. Still holding onto the door handle, she was clinging to life too. There was blood everywhere. Smeared across the door and all over the handle, *her blood*. She lay in a pool of the stuff, red ooze pouring out around her. She sat against the door, draped to one side. She was weak, dying.

The noise that Clay had heard was her moaning in pain. She had been bitten, and recently. With the two men standing over her, guns pointed at her face, Gus crouched to get a closer look.

Her throat was torn out, blood bellowed out onto her chest. She had several deep bites on her left arm, massive chunks of flesh missing. The lab coat that she wore had red congealed mess covering it. She was missing a shoe, obviously lost in a chase.

She suddenly moved, and reached up to Gus, grabbing his arm. She tried to speak, but only gargling spray shot from her mouth and torn throat.

Gus stood.

Clay was eyeing the woman and the direction they had come from, just in case. "This was recent. Looks like things are about to get ugly."

Gus stepped aside, pulling up his radio.

Clay moved forward with his rifle, aiming it at point blank at the woman. The dying woman flinched, letting out a horrendous cough. Right as he was about to pull the trigger, Gus pushed Clay's M-4 aside.

Reaching for his own handgun, Gus cocked a round into the chamber and aimed it at the woman's face.

The loud shot rang out. The woman's head violently kicked back, sending even more blood against the door behind her. It sprayed a wet splat as she slumped over to one side, dead, releasing her grip on the door handle. A clean hole marked the center of her head.

The door shook abruptly with the bang of fists.

"In and out my ass," Gus grunted holstering the pistol.

The familiar sounds of dead hissing emanated behind the door. The two men stood there for a moment.

Clay reached down and pulled the dead woman away from the entrance. A thick trail of blood followed as he dragged her corpse across the ground.

"Hoorah!" Clay shouted with an obvious hint of sarcasm. Looking at Gus, he shrugged his shoulders and lifted his M-4 signaling that he was ready.

The door swung open with a forceful kick, sending several looming zombies off balance. Without stepping forward, the two soldiers lit up the hallway leading into the second floor. Zombies convulsed and shook rapidly as bullets tore into their rotting flesh.

With the M-4 rifles set on full auto, Gus and Clay watched as a jacketed lead barrage sent the ghouls falling back. Dark blood and gray pus shot in every direction as endless bullets ripped through rancid skin and tissue.

Clay's rifle clicked empty. He fell to one knee, disregarding the puddle of blood he had been standing in, and reached in his side pocket for a fresh magazine. After spitting out the spent magazine, he slammed the new one home cocking in a fresh round. Before he could stand, Gus found himself doing the same.

With a momentary lapse of rapid fire, the hallway cleared of dust and scattered drywall. The building was littered with holes. Several zombies still lingered forward toward the end of the hall, and many of those that fell in the onslaught began to rise again.

"Fuck!" Clay instantly stepped from the safety of the stairwell out into the hall, shifting to one side of the doorway. With the dust built up around them, wearing his mask made it hard to see. Clay pulled his up over his head and looked down at his rifle.

The zombies started closing in. Eight lay on the ground no longer moving, but five of them still pressed on. All were dressed in basic office worker attire. With bloodied ties and tucked in shirts, the dead, rot-infested pus bags crept onward. Their moans and raised hands were in one accord.

Clay quickly brought the M-4 to his shoulder, sighting one of the ghouls down the barrel. The three-round bursts rang out as Clay lit into the hallway toward his targets. One set of shots went wild. Blood sprayed from chest to shoulder and then down the hall into the wall, sending more dust out into the air. The zombie jerked slightly but wasn't slowed at all. It pressed on. Clay fired again sending two rounds into the same zombie's chest and one right in the center of the dead man's throat. Blood splattered out from behind the walking corpse as the lead zombie still moved forward.

A rapid succession of three round bursts erupted right beside Clay, sending him off guard for a moment. He jumped, startled by the unexpected fire.

Gus stood beside him, the doorway leading into the stairwell at his back. With more controlled accuracy, the first burst of shots sent the lead zombie to the ground. All three shots tore through its face, sending it to its final rest.

The staccato of gunfire poured out once more. This time with more intent to destroy than subdue, each burst of bullets rang out, hitting their targets. One by one, the zombies fell to the floor. Some limbs twitched here and there as the final ounce of animation slowly drained from their decaying bodies. Others just lay still, forever free from the torment of their horrendous existence.

With a stifled shout from behind his mask, Gus shoved his new partner on the shoulder and then pointed to the first of many doors to be checked on the floor. "Good shooting, kid."

Same as before, the two men made their way through each room clearing it in hopes of finding their target, Mr. Grech Vonhinkly. GCUR-TECH's facility looked nothing like what Gus had expected after what he was told in the debriefing. For some reason, he had anticipated more of a sci-fi high-tech place with tons of machines and labs. This place was everything but.

Very similar to the third floor, the second floor was filled with offices and an occasional classroom. The place came across as more of a training facility than anything else. Gus stood in the sixth cleared room on the floor wondering where all the mad scientists or the crazy lab equipment were that would be utilized to bring back Frankenstein.

The scenery had, however, changed just a bit, and not in a good way. Unlike upstairs, the second floor had seen a lot of action. The place was a wreck. Desks and chairs were tossed all about the rooms. Papers and office supplies cluttered the ground. So far, the only creatures they had come across were the ones at the stairwell.

Dead bodies, on the other hand, were another story. Mangled and mutilated, devoured corpses littered the building. They had been devoured almost to the bone, some even unrecognizable by gender. The place was a blood bath.

As they turned to exit the room, a piece of paper on the floor stuck to the bottom of Clay's shoe. The clotted blood and matted remains of flesh on his boot heel clung to the paper as he stepped away. Leaning down to remove it, he noticed that the header read something odd.

"New Panglobal Habitation Project," he read out loud scanning down the paper a bit farther. *"The changes in the behavior of the infected ants are very specific; giving rise to the term zombie ants... the dead ants are then repositioned in various other situations... abnormal reproductive structures.* What the hell is this?" He looked up suddenly, realizing he was alone in the room. He quickly rushed out into the hallway, catching up with Gus, who was already clearing another room.

"If we are going to stay alive, boy, you better stick close and cover my ass," Gus said.

"What were they doing here?" Clay asked.

"That's not our problem, and there are some things best kept in the dark. I've got enough to keep me up at night as it is. No need to go adding another one. Now stay behind me, or you're going to get yourself killed," Gus replied.

Moving on to the next room, the two men finished clearing the second floor. Both were starting to wonder if there would be anyone left alive. If the second floor was bad, then the first one couldn't be any better.

"Hey, we forgot the bathrooms on this level," Clay said as they made their way back to the stairwell, stepping over the dozen zombies they had brought down earlier in the main hall.

Without saying a word, Clay, his gun hanging at his waist, took two wide strides over a gunned-down zombie, grabbed the bathroom door handle, and hurled the door wide open.

A cowering ghoul leapt out, taking Clay by surprise, and when it fell upon him, Clay lost his footing and tripped over a body lying in the hall. Clay fell to his back, taking the attacker down with him, and his rifle fell from his grasp upon impact.

Gnashing and snarling, the zombie bit and tore at Clay's face. Saliva and blood poured from the foul creature's mouth as teeth came down on him. The zombie's hands clawed violently, ripping at his clothes. Unable to break through the thick plastic of the gas mask, Clay fought frantically as the zombie tried to meet flesh.

He searched for his weapon with a free hand, while using his other to pull the zombie off of him. Unable to find his gun, he reached down into his boot, pulling out a large blade. The sharpened steel instantly penetrated the zombie's skin. Clay instinctively went for the heart and jabbed quick and hard. It was a solid hit. As he pressed the knife in deep, he tried shoving the zombie to one side, hoping to get out from under it. However, as Clay jumped to his feet, the zombie did likewise. With the knife protruding from its chest, unhindered, it lunged forward.

Clay stepped back fleetingly, but unfortunately, his feet again became entangled with a lifeless corpse on the hallway floor, and he fell. Staring up at the undead thing as it approached him again, Clay froze.

From out of nowhere, Gus appeared over Clay, pistol drawn and at the ready. He fired two quick shots straight to the head of the ghoul sending it to the ground. Gus leaned in close over the young man. Expecting to be helped to his feet, Clay reached out a hand. Instead, Gus was already stepping away. Clay's blood-covered knife, unexpectedly, landed in his lap. As he staggered to his feet, Clay wiped the knife on his pant leg and shoved it away in the top of his boot.

Without looking over his shoulder as he spoke, Gus snapped, "Not going to say it again, kid! I'm the front man for a reason. Stay tight, live to see another flight! You got it?"

Clay caught the brash tone that Gus had intended. "Yeah, I got it," Clay said, wiping his facemask down with the sleeve of his shirt, thankful that he had put the mask back on. It saved his life and he knew it.

Having cleared the rest of the facility's second floor, Gus and Clay slowly made their way down the same stairwell once more. This time, a little more apprehensive, the two soldiers worked as a unit.

Unlike Gus, who only had a little blood and guts on his boots from traipsing around, Clay was a mess. He was covered in gore; having fallen twice from the mutilated attacker did a number on his appearance.

Gus hadn't told him yet, but the first day out of the epidemic, Willy had gotten covered like that too. When they got back to base, Willy had the luxury of sleeping in a holding cell for fear that he might turn overnight. With the infection being in the blood, Gus planned to stay as clear from it as possible.

As they rounded the corner, they noticed that the doorway leading into the hall of the first floor was wide open. Gus shot up a fist, halting them were they stood halfway down the flight of steps. Putting a finger against the lips of his mask, Gus took one slower step forward, peeking around the corner.

There were no moans or growling, but there were definitely zombies. Just from what Gus could see, the hallway was filled wall-to-wall with the undead. So far, the two soldiers had remained unnoticed. The looming ghouls just stood in place, swaying back and forth ever so slightly, taking hardly any steps in any direction. Even if they did have enough ammunition, they would easily be run down by the mob before their bullets did enough real damage.

Gus crept back a few steps, out of the undead hordes' line of sight, trying to come up with a game plan.

8

"Well, what's next?" Clay whispered as they both sat on the set of stairs out of sight from the undead in the hallway below. "There must be more than a couple dozen of those things hunkered down in there. Honestly, I am surprised they didn't hear us making all that racket upstairs."

Gus looked at the radio in his hand for a moment.

After waiting a while, Clay said, "Well?"

As if to answer him, Gus clicked the receiver on the radio, grinning up at the young man. "Blue Bravo, come in... Over." He paused for a second, and winked at Clay. "We create a diversion."

Despite the thick plastic of his mask and the darkness of the stairwell, Gus saw the young man's perplexed expression. "We send the chopper down to blow out the front door, sending the creeps out to investigate..."

*

"I hope you're calling to say *mission complete*," Watts said over the radio. He had spent the better part of an hour twiddling his thumbs. That is, up until recently. A few stragglers from out in the woods had finally managed to meander their way to the facility. The attention drawn by the chopper had sent them in from *who knows how far*. Trying to help pass the time, he pulled out his handgun for a little run with some target practice. He had already taken out three walkers when Gus radioed in and broke his focus on the fourth zombie in his sight.

"What's your status, Chief?"

*

Back on the stairwell, halfway between the first and second floor, the radio rang out with only a moment's delay.

Before Gus could answer, a gut-wrenching sound bellowed out from within the hallway on the first floor. Footsteps and moaning cried out in unison, the soldiers' presence detected. It only took a split second for the first of several putrid zombies to break from the hallway into the stairwell.

"Oh, well. New game plan," Gus said and grunted. He jumped to his feet tossing off the ammo pack from his shoulders. Anxiously, he sifted through it. "Hold them off," he shouted, not taking his eyes from the bag.

"Gus, come in… Gus, come in… Over," Watts chattered over the airwaves from the rooftop.

Clay darted several steps down, alerting the dead even further to their whereabouts. The zombies uncontrollably convulsed with excitement as the fresh meat appeared from around the corner several steps overhead.

Instantly, an onslaught of fire rang from Clay's rifle. The M-4 grew warm in his grip as each bullet ripped through decay. The vibration of the gun tightened his muscles as Clay shook in unison.

Looking over his shoulder and back up the steps, Gus was still fumbling with the bag and ignoring the persistent radio calls from Watts. "What the hell are you doing?" Clay shouted. He had stopped the constant blasts of ammo rocketing through the air just long enough for him to ask the question and instantly started back up again.

With a handful of zombies down, the front of the hallway had quickly begun to fill from all the excitement. What zombies didn't go down, did their best to press on through the rain of bullets. Waving his rifle from side to side, holes tore through chests and necks, chunks of flesh and bone ripped from arms and legs, but they just kept coming. Every few seconds seemed to gain the horde another inch in their ascent up the stairs leading to the two soldiers.

Clay started to tense, taking a step back up the stairs. Right as he turned to see what the delay was, Gus appeared beside him with a grin on his face.

Muffled beneath the protective gear, Gus mumbled, "Plan B, it is then?"

He quickly jogged down the six steps between them and the horde, and kicked the lead zombie square in the face as hard has he could. The creature's face caved in. With the large man's practice at taking down doors, it was no surprise that the instant the heel of his combat boot met its face, it collapsed. Red and gray splatter squished from the zombie's nose as it collided with the inside of its own head. One eye instantly erupted, sending the ghoul falling back with the spray of gore and grime from sudden impact.

Clay didn't see anything leave Gus' hand, but based on the arch that it was tossed, he had a good idea on what the man meant by Plan B. Still in mid-thought registering the event, Gus was already on top of him, pushing him back up the stairwell.

"Move! Move! Move!" he yelled, passing Clay up in the process, his big feet pounding up every other step in long strides.

Clay had taken a few steps before the grenade exploded, knocking him off his feet. The impact of the detonation was contained to the hallway. The stairwell shielded the blast from the worst of it.

*

On the rooftop, Watts heard the grenade go off. He knew what it was, having been in the field enough. Glass from a few windows on the first floor blew out, sending a cloud of smoke with it. Leaning over the edge of the building looking at the damage, Watts hoped all went as planned. Swiftly making his way back onto the chopper, he started gearing up for takeoff. "Gus... Come in, Gus... Over." A moment passed. "Gus, you have five minutes to report, or I am taking the fuck off without you. Over," Watts shouted over the radio.

*

In the stairwell, Gus stood to his feet, brushing the dust and debris from his uniform.

Clay still awkwardly leaned against the railing coughing up dust and drywall. His ears were ringing.

Gus, gladly, could not say the same and made the effort to cover his ears while he ran up the stairs. Grabbing up his gear as quickly as he could, Gus reached his stunned partner, who was off balance. Gus shoved an M-4 into Clay's arms, passing him up as he descended the steps to the first floor. He might have said something as he passed, but Clay couldn't tell.

Clay heard the very faint echoes of gunfire, but it was so muffled that it sounded more like the subs in the back of his car rattling off. Descending the steps to join Gus, Clay witnessed as the lead soldier lit up the floor around him. The man had his rifle on full and was aiming at the ground in front.

Gus was doubling over the fallen zombies with fire from point blank range. He swept the perimeter from side to side with bullets as he moved forward, slowly leading from the stairwell into the hallway of the first floor. Blood and guts danced around his feet as the hail of ammo ripped into the undead. He wanted to be sure none of them would be getting back up again.

Stepping over the uninviting mess that the other man had just made, Clay squished and slid through bile and filth. The puddle of grime and blood was unrecognizable for the most part. Nothing but parts littered the floor. Arms and legs and the occasional torso lay strewn and bullet-filled.

As they made their way into the hall, it was filled with smoke and dust.

"How the hell are we supposed to see through this shit?" Clay shouted, ears still a little shot.

"Slowly," Gus replied.

The two soldiers moved forward clearing the floor of possible threats. The lights strapped to their weaponry only made it harder to see, reflecting right back at them in the dust.

Unable to see more than a foot in front of them, Gus kept his head low, watching the floor as he moved forward. He moved down the hall doing what he could to clear it. Bodies and parts of bodies laid everywhere. It was hard to tell in the dust cloud, but it looked like parts of bodies had also managed to make their way onto the walls as well.

Not paying any attention to the front of the building, a large number of zombies not affected by the blast sifted through the dust and debris ahead of them. The two soldiers moved along, clueless to the sounds of their steps and moans as they continued to fire round after round, taking out the scattered remains of a once prevalent horde.

With Gus in the lead still sweeping back and forth with his rifle, his cleanup procedure suddenly became interrupted when a zombie appeared from the dust cloud only a foot in front of him. Startled, he stepped back, but it was too late. The creature was already on him.

He stepped once more wrestling with the ghoul. With one big shove, the creature flew back against the wall, giving time and space for Gus to raise his rifle. He aimed it right at the zombie's head and fired. The chamber clicked empty. "Hell!"

The lab coat wearing man leaped forward again, landing on Gus for the second time. Gus fumbled his weapon, dropping it to the floor. The creature's teeth gnashed violently as it spit and snarled over him. With the same half grunt of effort, Gus tossed the zombie against the wall. He reached down, yanking up his weapon, then fell back a few paces to where Clay stood.

"Shoot it," he screamed.

Clay frantically pulled back on the charging handle on his M-4. "It's jammed! I had to reload and it's jammed."

Gus flipped the ammo bag from around his shoulders and onto the blood-covered remains littering the hallway. He reached in to retrieve new rounds for the M-4, but after two attempts kept coming up with only nine-millimeter magazines.

Beside him, Clay stood, still feverishly trying to get his rifle un-jammed.

Only a few feet ahead of them, in the cloud of dust and drywall, came the moans and howls of more flesh hungry corpses, their bodies slowly coming into view from amidst the fog.

"Time to move," Gus said as he watched half a dozen zombies appear before him, more undoubtedly following in their wake.

"Over there," Clay pointed. A door a few paces behind them stood wide-open, leading into one of the office rooms.

The two soldiers backtracked, stepping into the room, slamming the door closed, and locking the bolt. Without passing any words, the two men grabbed the large desk and slid it in front of the door.

"That should hold," Gus said and huffed for air as he took off his gas mask and slung it to the floor.

Clay followed suit. Taking a small canteen from his hip, Clay took a deep pull before passing the bottle to Gus. "Man, you think they would make it a little easier to breathe in these things," Clay said heaving for air, both hands on his knees.

It didn't take long before the relentless banging began. The remaining ghouls in the hall found their way to the door.

"I can't help but feel like I've been here before," Gus said.

Ignoring the statement, Clay continued, "So, what are we supposed to do now?"

Gus leaned against the vibrating desk propped against the door, taking another drink from Clay's canteen. "Ahh..." Wiping his lips and propping up and off of the desk, he handed the bottle back to Clay. "We wait."

"Wait, what do you mean *we wait*?"

"For starters, if we're going to have any chance against those things, we need to give the dust some time to settle out there. No sense in trying to fight a battle with our eyes closed. Second, we need to reload and wipe down our face shields. Mine is already too hard to—"

Clay suddenly interrupted, "Watts! We need to radio him."

Gus brought the radio to his lips. "Blue Bravo, come in. Over."

Nothing came back but static. Then, "What's your status? Over."

"Man, you had us scared for a minute. Thought you left us high and dry. Over."

"Had you scared? I'm not the one blowing shit up. What the status? Over."

Gus smiled at Clay as he clicked the receiver on the handset. "Desperate times call for desperate measures. We cleared the second and third floors. One more to go, but it is crawling with hostiles. Already took out a dozen or so. Still doing what we can to clear it. Over."

After a moment, Watts clicked back on, "And the package?"

Gus sat waiting for him to continue, having not said *Over* at the end of his transmission. Both Clay and Gus made eye contact, and then shrugged simultaneously. Gus continued, "Not acquired. I'm beginning to think that we might not find this Grech guy. If we do, he's probably a walking pus bag by now. Over"

A moan shrieked out. Both soldiers realized they had not yet cleared the room. Both men jumped up with rifles at the ready, but not before giving one another quick glances. Totally forgetting that both rifles were currently out of commission, the two men spread out to check the room.

As Gus crept toward a row of smaller desks, the radio rang out startling him.

"Roger that," Watts said.

Gus jumped, grabbing the radio from his hip. "Check in later. Over and out."

Hidden behind one of the desks, Clay closed in on the sound. It couldn't be anything but a rotting corpse come back to life. They all sounded the same. The grunts and moans were unmistakable. Reaching over the edge of the desk as his head peered around its corner, Clay laid eyes on the monster. It was crunched up, obviously stuck in one place. He pulled the trigger. The rifle clicked. "Shit!"

The body moaned again, sounding more human than not.

Clay stared at the body for a few moments. "The skin... looks normal. Gus... Gus, we got a survivor over here!" Clay laid his M-4 on the desk and pulled out his pistol.

The woman was dressed in a lab coat like some of the others. The only difference with this one was that it wasn't covered in blood and gore. The woman's gaze met with Clay's. "She's in really bad shape."

Gus joined Clay's side, leaning over the defenseless woman. She was dehydrated and probably starving to death. Her lips were cracked and dry. She leaned forward trying to sit up, but was unable.

"It's okay, Miss. We're here to help," Gus said, motioning for Clay to hand over his canteen.

The woman's ID card clipped to her pocket read *Level 4 Administrator* and her name. Clay took the ID card and placed it in his pocket.

"Lilly, is that your name?" Gus asked as he wet her dry lips with water. "Is that your name, Lilly? I need you to try and sit up for me, okay?" With Clay's assistance, the two men maneuvered the young lady into a sitting position.

There was no telling how long Lilly had holed up in this office without food or water, just trying to stay alive. Her skin was wrinkly and her eyes sunk back deep into each socket. The dark rings under her eyes gave her a ghoulish appearance. Her bright green eyes, obviously once breathtaking, seemed hauntingly eerie. They danced frantically around the room and back at the soldiers standing before her as she observed her situation. She was lucid, at least.

"Lilly, we need your help. How long have you been locked in here?" Gus asked.

She moved her mouth trying to form the words, her muscles straining to work. "Fo... fo... fo..."

Clay interrupted her trying to help. "Four days?" he asked, nodding his head.

She shook her head. "Fo... Foive... Five... Five days."

"We need to get this one to a medic, and right away," Clay said, standing to his feet and holstering his handgun.

Gus ignored the remark and the woman's condition, making a clear point to stick to the mission. "Can you tell me, have you seen this man, Lilly?" He shoved a photo in front of her of Grech, the same photo that he had shown to Clay on the flight in. "This man. Have you seen this man? We need to find *Grech Vonhinkly*. Is he here?"

"Give it a rest, Gus. The woman is dying. Look at her," Clay said.

Gus leapt to his feet. Bumping chest to chest with Clay, he was sure as hell going to get his point across. "Don't ever talk to me in that tone, soldier. Don't forget who's in charge!" He peered over the younger man, breathing down the soldier's neck.

The woman reached up. Pointing at the wall with a map, she began to mumble. "Ground Zero…" The dying woman's voice barely broke past her own lips as she started to repeat herself once more, arm still raised.

"Wait, what's she saying?" Clay asked.

Her arm fell to her side. Her head kicked back against the wall they had placed her against. Her eyes slowly closed.

"She was trying to tell us something." Clay dropped to both knees by her side, palms on the carpet floor before him. "What? … Tell us again."

Nothing.

"Come on, Lilly," Clay leaned in close and put an ear to her mouth. "What, Lilly?" he said.

"Grechhh…" she said, and lifted her hand toward the map. She instantly slumped back over in the same position.

Clay leaned back and sat on his butt. "Hell, man. I think she just died."

"Ground Zero…" she whispered.

"She said *Ground Zero*," Clay said,

The two men's eyes instantly met with the map hanging on the wall from across the room.

As Clay staggered to his feet, his gaze locked on the withered woman. "Man, we have to do something for her," Clay said.

"You're right," Gus said. He took one long stride forward, pointing his 9mm, and pulling the trigger before Clay had a chance to react.

The shot rang out, sending a spray of blood against the wall behind the fallen woman. Her head hit the wall, then slowly slid down it to one side, leaving a blood-slicked trail behind. The woman finally stopped breathing as she came to rest on the floor.

Gus holstered the pistol like it was nothing and made his way toward the map.

"If I'm reading this correctly, Ground Zero is what they call the basement. There aren't any steps leading down to it. The only way down is by this elevator," Gus said in a mumble, mostly just thinking out loud as his hand pointed at a spot on the map.

"Then the elevator it is," Clay said.

DEFEND

1

Seated at the center of the well-lit lab, a short, chubby lab worker covered in the aroma of ripe cottage cheese sifted through the blood samples of the new arrivals. Examining the test results of each survivor one at a time, the lab assistant steadied his hand, pulling the plastic test tube from the Revco.

Each sample of blood held in the Revco was placed in small plastic tubes set upright in little cylinder racks. The ultra-low temperature freezer named Revco looked more like a small cooler than a refrigerator. These freezers always opened from the top and never from the side. This helped prevent any possible biohazard spills.

The particular blood sample he steadily pulled from the rack was sample number *12EM3*. The letters stood for the patient's initials. The first number was the sample number, then the tests administered, followed by test results received.

The frumpy little man eyed the sample number on the tube, jotting it down before setting the sample aside on the table, his white coat almost lost in the white room under the bright lights.

"This is all wrong," he said and grumbled.

Behind him, Stately Christopher was prepping the microscope and reading the test space. Today, the scientist's decided to see the effects in action. The idea was to place the blood from an uninfected host onto the tray and then introduce the blood of the later, that being the late Professor Taft's. Once the two samples made contact, the agenda was in timing the total transfer of pure samples to the fungus, then test the newly infected with anticoagulants, hoping to in turn reverse the effects at the same metabolic rate.

"What's not right this time, Benton?" Christopher huffed; he didn't bother to turn and face the man seated behind him.

"This blood sample. Who was the last person to document this?" Benton asked.

"I was, why?" He lifted his head from the microscope, irritated to be stuck working with *Captain Tight Ass*, the cheese factory, Benton. *It's something every day with this one*, he thought to himself dropping his face back toward the microscope, and then making slight adjustments on the spindle, bringing the contents below into focus.

Benton lifted a gloved hand, holding the frozen blood sample sealed away in the plastic test tube. "How can you have three possible test results on a sample that has only been tested on twice?"

"Let me see that," he said and turned from his station to take a closer look.

As the lab assistant took the tube from Benton eyeing the mismarked label, Benton continued his rant, "If you're the last one to have run the test, then I need to go over your entry for last night's log. We don't need to have you or anyone else mishandling or labeling these samples. What do you think this place is? A—"

Christopher shoved a finger in the smelly man's pudgy face. "Look, just because Gibbs hasn't made it in yet, doesn't make you the doctor; you're just another lab assistant, just like me."

Keeping calm and adding a grin, Benton continued, "That doesn't change the fact that I need to see last night's log entry for the sample tests. All of them!" Benton set the *12EM3* on the table, putting out his latex glove covered hand, empty. With a raised brow, Benton shot his other hand in a fist, shoving it under his other arm to support his extended limb, palm up. His posture and facial expression suggested that he intended to wait there as long as it took. "Well?" he said.

Christopher shook his head, breathing a heavy sigh. "Why does it seem like I always get stuck with this guy?" He tossed his hands up in defeat. He quickly turned and shuffled through a folder for his notes.

Benton raised his head back and looked down his nose at Christopher.

Christopher knew Benton was right. As he looked up from the folder, unable to place where he had set the log entry, he caught the dreaded Benton boast of a smile from across the table.

Trying to play it off, Christopher glanced around the room at the counter tops for what might be his unwritten report. "Hmm… Now where in the world did I set that—?"

"Don't play me for a fool, Christopher. We both know good and well that report never got filed. Which means that I'm going to have to backtrack over you and do everything myself. I just don't understand how some people manage to—"

The door to the lab room swung open.

"Oh, hello, Lieutenant," Christopher said and gave a polite smile and a wave, thankful for the sudden interruption on Benton's high-horse rant that never got anyone anywhere.

*

"Hello, gentlemen," Foster said as he stepped into the room, resting one hand on his hip holster.

From behind the desk, the two lab assistants looked up with eager eyes, curious about the unexpected visitor's arrival.

Behind them, off to the right in the far corner of the room, a very undead and decomposed Professor Taft stood chained to the wall. The blood that stained the area around him was no longer a dark red, but had more of the appearance of tar. The blood, now totally dried out, a dark, thick black-colored resin, stuck to the floor and walls around the bound corpse. Fresh chunks of bloodied tissue and muscle lay scattered around the creature's feet. The zombie had resorted to completely devouring a majority of its own arm. Its naturally carnal instinct to feed was so strong that it inevitably turned on itself for sustenance.

The thing that caught Foster as odd was that Taft seemed not at all concerned with the others in the room. It stood silently in the corner, occasionally shifting from one foot to the other and then back again. Other than that, nothing caught its interest, its gaze fixed on the floor below.

"What can we do for you, sir?" Benton asked, standing tall, but appearing to still be seated, his lower half hidden behind the table.

Finding it a little hard to take is eyes away from the pus-festering remains of a still-functioning Taft, Foster stumbled over his words, "I… I was just… just stopping by to speak with Dr. Gibbs," he said, not stepping a single foot farther into the room, hand still clenching his holstered pistol.

Benton said, "It's perfectly safe in here, Lieutenant."

Foster suddenly realized that he had not taken his eyes off of Taft since entering the small lab. Diverting his focus, he cocked his head away, catching Benton's gaze. Benton's bulging eyes were magnified behind his thick frames and that beady little grin and chubby cheeks did absolutely nothing to reassure the Lieutenant otherwise.

"We haven't seen her today, sir. She did have a meeting with the General first thing this morning. Something about the new arrivals, if I am correct. I would presume to believe that she is still in said meeting. You know how longwinded Baker can get," Benton said.

Foster lightly smiled in agreement, then turned to leave the lab and the two men standing behind the table. Pulling the door open, he turned back and caught Christopher's attention, addressing only him, "When she does come in, tell her that I came by, please."

"Sure thing," Christopher replied and gave another polite wave and smile as Foster exited.

*

Christopher quickly closed the folder and moved on to his appointed tasks, knowing good and well that the little man had the attention span of a gnat. It worked every time, the miscataloged blood sample test entry forgotten. He quickly learned from working with Benton, and others like him, that the really smart super nerds generally had way too much going on inside those heads of theirs to stay focused on the small details.

"You know... I heard that the Lieutenant and Dr. Gibbs were... well, you know." Christopher chuckled, his eye cupped around the lens of the microscope to double check the setting.

It was as he left it, in just the right spot.

He leaned up, retrieving a needled syringe from the workspace directly next to the microscope. He lifted it to the light to inspect it briefly, and then turned to face Benton, who sat back in his chair prepping the blood sample.

Having done it a dozen times, he walked up to the reanimated zombie and filled the cylinder of the syringe with a small portion of the dead man's blood and pus. He hadn't liked the man to begin with; Taft had been a prude, one of those people that were never wrong. Ever! Kind of like Benton.

Pulling the partly filled syringe away from the undead man, he examined it once more in the light, before stepping away. Right there where he stood, the zombie, Taft, could reach up and just take hold of him if it wanted to. But for some reason, it never did. Normally, it was excited during this exercise. The close-range activity got the creature wound up. Something in the monster was changing, and they weren't quite sure what that was. It was undoubtedly getting slower and the decomposition spread quicker through its body. But what?

"Oh, and where did you get that little slice of intel?" Benton inquired.

Walking back across the room to his test station, Christopher divulged his story about how one of the other assistants ran into them the other day in the hall. He explained how this individual mentioned a kiss and some touching. Besides that, wasn't it obvious? They ate together every day in the cafeteria.

While still telling the tale, he turned to Benton, retrieving the *12EM3* that was now ready for the microscope. The small splotch of blood sat centered on a thin glass tray that Christopher slid under the microscope.

He then turned away, taking off his latex gloves, tossed them in the proper receptacle, and then thoroughly washed his hands. "Yep. I also heard from Trish that she watched Gibbs leaving the Lieutenant's room in the barracks last night."

"Oh really? And why would Trish have been in the men's barracks? That seems highly unlikely," Benton said, now peering down the scope to view the *12EM3* in action.

The blood was rapidly deteriorating. The white cells almost entirely dissolved and replaced by the nasty gray matter. The fungus swiftly started killing the fortified structural foundation of the blood cells, one piece at a time. The parasitoid fungus continued to grow as its mycelia invaded the host sample. "The decomposition rate is incredible. I've never seen any parasitoid organism move so fast. It's moving at three times its normal speed."

Benton glanced up from the scope and looked at the timer. "Seriously, Christopher!" He slammed his hands on the table.

Christopher shot his head up from the sink, startled. "What now?"

"How are we supposed to study the natural decomposition rate in this sample if you continually forget to set the freaking timer after injecting the *Cordyceps Unilateralis*?" Benton said and glared.

"What are you talking about?" he replied, rinsing the soap from his hands. "I haven't done that yet. The syringe is right next to you, in front of the stupid timer."

"What?"

Christopher was correct. The injector was right there. Benton quickly peeked back down at the unwinnable war going on atop the thin piece of glass beneath the scope. "This can't be right."

"What do you mean?" Christopher asked, drying his hands and making his way back to the manila folder. "If I'm not mistaken, this sample is from the teenager that we have already established as a carrier. If that's the case, then perhaps the parasitoid is just, finally, at its crucial point. Hell, look at Taft. I'm surprised the boy hadn't turned already. Taft changed less than an hour after transfer."

"This is true, but Taft was practically eaten to death, so he received a much higher concentration of the fungus. The boy just had a scratch," Benton said. His eyes met with his lab partner revealing something Christopher had never seen in Benton, *concern*.

Christopher thumbed through his papers one more time, suddenly realizing that he hadn't been the last person to test the blood sample, which explained his lack of paperwork.

Whoever administered the last set of tests on the *12EM3* sample must have done something to increase the production rate of the *Cordyceps Unilateralis*. Whatever it was, he stood over his notes, hoping like hell that it hadn't also been administered to the patient.

Slamming the manila folder closed, he jerked his head up, locking gazes with the dead thing strapped to the wall at the corner of the room. Its milky-white eyes were lost somewhere between them. He stared right back, while trying with all he had, to remember what it was that Gibbs had given the boy for pain. Was it Demerol, a small dose of Morphine, or something else?

2

Gibbs sat quietly in the dark, damp room behind its thick steel-reinforced bars. Trying to make herself as comfortable as possible, she had removed her lab coat and shoes shortly after being thrown into the cell, placing them neatly on the bed. She squatted uncomfortably against a thin and rickety bench at one side of the cell, eyeing her watch and shaking her knees. It had been a few hours now and she was getting restless.

She had tried making small talk with the guard, hoping to help pass the time, but to no avail.

The Brig, as the General liked to call it, was nothing more than an old warehouse at the far side of the base, at the west end. Initially built to house large amounts of explosives, along with other things, the building was far away from most other buildings. Being one of the original buildings on the base, along with the fact that it was hardly ever used, left the Brig in bad shape.

The small holding area only consisted of three, ten-foot square cells, and a guard station. The walls in each cell, excluding that of the warehouse foundation, were comprised of steel bar. With each cell set side-by-side, you could see each toilet in the room from any cell, leaving no privacy when occupied by more one prisoner.

Each cell had a functional toilet, bed, bench, and sink. If and when, a fight broke out between the soldiers, or, someone decided to drink a little more than their fair share, they generally ended up in a cell for a day or two. Depending upon how the General was feeling had a lot to do with the length of the confinement.

The single guard, manning the small warehouse of cells, was only stationed when someone was in custody. The solo guard sat with legs propped up behind a desk, doing everything he could to ignore the captive. After deciding he was tired of the doctor disturbing his nap, the soldier got up and walked out of the room, closing the door behind him.

She sat there alone, and had been for close to an hour, imagining the guard passed out in a chair on the other side. Other than that, her mind raced with questions. Questions about the blood test results and what Baker planned to do with her played out in her head.

The sudden thought of Rob Foster, in all his gentleness, crashed in knocking the other ideas away from her mind. Had she been too irrational visiting him last night? Had they gone too far, and, what could sex really change about their relationship? She liked things the way they were, and, began to worry that maybe she had made a bad decision. But then again, who doesn't make bad decisions after having a few tall glasses of wine?

Thinking of his soft breath tickling her bare chest entered her head creating a bleak smile. *His gentle fingers rubbing down her belly in a slow and sensual—*

Her daydream was suddenly interrupted when in walked a tall soldier, thrusting the door open, letting it crash against the wall as it pivoted.

*

"Line 'em up over there!" the soldier grunted, stepping into the small warehouse.

Behind him another soldier entered, followed by another, and another. All three of the soldiers, excluding the one barking off the orders, wielded pistols. With their weapons drawn toward the open door, one after another of the civilian survivors entered the room, gazes down, hands on top of their heads. Filing in as a straight line, the five captives stood in single file against the wall, a state of disbelief etched on each face.

"What's the meaning of this?" George asked, instantly getting struck with the butt of a 9mm on the back of the skull.

"Shut up and stay in line," the soldier that delivered the sudden blow shouted.

George staggered to the side, off-balance for a moment, his sight fading in and out briefly in a white blur, but it quickly returned as he caught himself before falling to the floor.

"Back in line I said," the soldier shouted once more.

The tall, commanding soldier produced a clip of keys from his person, tossing them across the room and into the hands of a shorter, yet still very tall, man wearing the same military attire.

"Open 'em up," the lead soldier said, the keys clinking in the silence between his words.

The man, now holding the keys, made his way to each cell and unlocked them, including the cell that held the Dr.

"You!" the man said, giving orders and pointing to Cynthia, who was obviously scared out of her mind. "In there!" the soldier said, pointing at the first open cell currently occupied.

Eric and Kent were placed in the middle cell, leaving George and Billy at the far end of the warehouse in the last cell.

With the cells locked down and the small squad of soldiers getting ready to leave, Kent burst out into a fit. With both fists gripping the steel, he violently convulsed as he shook at the bars, yelling, "You can't do this! Why, tell me why? I want an answer!" His face had turned a deep shade of crimson.

"Who gets to stay and watch guard?" one soldier asked, totally ignoring the civilian's demands. The lead soldier walked over to Kent and pulled a large pair of aviator sunglasses from his front pant pocket. "You forgot these," the soldier said, handing them over.

Before Kent had a chance to grab them, the soldier let them fall to the floor, and then smashed them under his boot.

"Oops," the soldier said and smirked.

"Fuck 'em! Let's go. They aren't going anywhere." The soldiers' holstered their handguns simultaneously before leaving. The door slammed shut with a loud crash, but not before the last soldier reached in and flipped off the main light switch. His hand disappeared before the door hand a chance to close on it.

Kent knelt and snatched up the crushed glasses. With one lens missing and the other cracked, Kent let out a large sigh and threw them on the floor in his new cell.

He sat on the edge of the bed trying to play it cool. Those shades were the last bit of tangible memory he had of his grandfather. They meant a lot to him, which was why he wore them so much.

Not actually knowing his real parents, Kent had been raised by his grandparents after his real ones died in a house fire, while he was still too young to remember. To him, his grandfather meant everything. Being in the Air Force all the way through retirement,

Kent always wanted to follow in his grandfather's footsteps. Having dropped out of high school and with the added minor drug charges as a teen, he wasn't able to. Now that he was older, what was the point? Sitting on the edge of the rickety bed, Kent thought these things, his eyes slowly adjusting to the sudden darkness.

With the lights unexpectedly shut off, the only light in the small warehouse building was that of a poorly-painted-over window in one corner. Small hints of light peeked in, keeping the room from going into total darkness.

"Are you all right?" Eric asked, standing beside Kent, but looking past him into the next cell at George, who was still rubbing the back of his head.

"Yeah, I should be all right. My head is throbbing," George replied. He and Billy were both sitting on the bed in their cell wondering, like all the rest, what the hell was going on.

Eric nodded and turned to face Cynthia. Expecting the lady to be sitting in her cell alone, he was slightly startled to see that she wasn't. So focused on the situation and the guards, he hadn't been paying that much attention to his surroundings. Intending to ask Cynthia if she was okay, his thought process in midsentence changed. Seeing Dr. Gibbs out of the blue made him stumble over his words, "How a... who... what are you doing in here?"

With her eyes still fixed on the door that the soldiers had just exited, Gibbs stood at the edge of the locked cell in deep thought.

Cynthia sat on the bed behind her, already looking up at Eric.

"Hey, science lady, what the heck are you doing in here?" he asked again, true curiosity inflecting in each word.

"It's complicated," she said, not taking her gaze from the warehouse entrance.

"Hey, you're Dr. Gibbs, right?" Kent shuffled about on the bed mat. He easily remembered her name, because man, was she fine.

Behind him, George and the little boy both stood to their feet trying to get a better look from the far end of the room while listening in.

"Yeah," Cynthia said to emphasize Eric's question once more. "What gives? One minute we're getting the royal treatment, and then thrown in the dungeon the next." She crossed her arms kicking both feet up onto the bed.

"And what did they do with all of our stuff?" Kent said. "They took my shotgun. Hell, they took all of our weapons."

"Like I said, it's complicated." Gibbs turned to face Eric and Kent, and leaned against the wall where she stood.

"It's not like we don't have time on our hands," Kent said. "So if you have something to say, then let's hear it."

*

Sighing a deep breath, Gibbs looked around the room at her new fellow captives. Eyeing each one individually for a moment or two, she recalled her notes and the files of each patient. Cynthia, the danger to herself. Kent, the slacker from Mars. George, the retired widower. Billy, well there wasn't much on him. And then there was Eric, the straight A student, all-American teenager. She had stayed late again in the lab last night running tests on Eric's blood samples, the log report still sat on her desk in her office. She removed her glasses and wiped them on her shirt.

Well, if I can't get to the lab and study the test results of last night's blood tests, at least I can monitor the patient in here, she thought.

Pulling her glasses back to her face, Gibbs looked across at Eric once more. "How are you doing, Eric?" she asked.

"I'm fine," he said, unconsciously reaching up and scratched at the cut beneath his bandaged hand. The wound felt like it was on fire.

3

The two soldiers had been sitting tight for quite a while now, just waiting for the dust and smoke from the grenade to settle. Shortly after going over the map displayed on the wall in the center of the room, Gus and Clay came up with a game plan.

Clay lay against the floor on his back, looking up at the ceiling. With both hands tucked under his head for support, he found himself lost in thought. He imagined what he would have been doing right now, had he not actually joined the military, and assuming that the apocalypse of the dead hadn't struck. He liked to think that he would have finally gotten out of that dingy, little trailer and locked down a solid job that he enjoyed, and found a good-looking girl. He never had problems finding ladies; it was keeping them that he had trouble with. That must have had something to do with the lack of effort put into his home life and a lack of job security. He laid quietly on his back, thinking and doing his best not to notice the dead woman on the floor across from him, eyes fixed on the ceiling.

*

Gus, on the other hand, could not so easily block out their current set of circumstances. It was his job to keep the two alive. Running over the plan, time and time again, he sat with his back to the wall, across for the main doorway. He intently tried to relax. With one hand, he held his other extremity out. It throbbed with pain. The shot of painkillers the doc had given him for his fractured hand was starting to wear down. His focus consistently jumped from the bandaged fist and the blocked doorway in front of him. The sounds of the living dead, relentlessly trying to get in, pressed on. Their pounding and moans had given away the two soldiers' location and had only reassured Gus that they knew the two men were in that room.

Flexing his fingers from outstretched and into a balled fist repeatedly, Gus held out the throbbing limb, hoping like hell that it wasn't going to slow him down. So far, he hadn't even noticed the fractured appendage. That meant that the painkillers had been doing their job. Sure, handling his M-4 with the bandages was a little awkward at first, but it was nothing that held him back. With the drugs starting to wear off, that was, however, going to be another story. Looking up at the door covered with a large desk and a few smaller student chairs, Gus was at least a little worried and wished that he had talked Gibbs into packing him a few extra pills to take for the trip.

"You think the smoke is cleared up by now? It's been fifteen already," Clay said, pulling one of his head supporting hands away to glance at the wristwatch strapped on the outside of his suit.

Gus replied, "Eh... another five wouldn't hurt." Upon pronouncing the word *hurt*, a sharp stabbing sensation erupted in the man's bandaged hand. He had taken attention away from the flexing limb to reply to Clay and suddenly bent his fingers up too high. The pain was unbearable, causing the soldier to wince.

"You all right?" Clay asked, sitting up and pulling his rifle from the floor beside him and into his lap.

He pressed the release, dropping out the magazine, then dispensed the chambered round all in one fluid motion. He then sighted down the barrel right before disassembling the rifle. If they planned to sit tight for another five minutes, he had time to take apart his M-4 and give it a quick cleaning.

"Yeah, I will be fine. Just bent it back too far," Gus said.

"You would think with your hand being like that, they would have sent someone else out to do this mission, don't you think?"

"Hell, if you want to look at it like that, what in the world was the General thinking when he decided to send you with me?" Gus said. "No offense, but an OP like this should never have been your first. You got to build up to this sort of thing, you know. At the end of it all, this outbreak has us all running like chickens with our heads cut off. We just have to do what we have to do, I guess," Gus said.

"If I had to guess, having me tag along wasn't the General's idea."

"Foster?"

"Yeah, he has this big idea in his head that I'm going to be promoted soon, once I get my act together and stop shitting away my potential. I hate to break it to the guy, but I'm out in two and that's that," Clay said.

The two men sat for a while longer, waiting for the time to pass. Clay finished reassembling his rifle and slammed the magazine back into the chamber locking a fresh round into position. Standing to his feet, he slung the rifle around his shoulder and across his back, retrieving the handgun from his hip.

"Well, you ready, then?" Clay asked, taking Gus' attention away from his wounded fist. The man nodded, standing to his feet as well.

With the set of smaller study desks spread out in what must have been the makeshift classroom, the two soldiers had already piled them up high enough for Clay to reach the ceiling grate. He climbed them with Gus' assistance and reached the top, popping the grate out of place, and tossing it to the floor.

*

With one big heave, Clay pulled himself up and into the ventilation system that ran above them and through the entire first floor. It took a minute, but once he got situated, he turned around, facing Gus to give a thumb-up from inside the vent. He was ready. The space to move around was narrow and definitely a tight fit. Clay was, however, able to maneuver well considering his weapons and bulky suit.

Setting the timer on his watch, Clay took off down the ventilation shaft. Crawling on all fours, he shimmied forward, attempting to make as little noise as he could. Periodically, the clink and clang of aluminum would pop and bend around him as his weight shifted with each moment he inched forward. It was hot, and luckily, he wasn't claustrophobic. Otherwise, he might have already started to panic, having only made it a few feet.

Ahead of him, a small gleam of light peeked from a square grate. It was the hallway littered with infected. As he came up to it, the moans and pounding of their relentless pursuit echoed louder and louder against the aluminum.

Trying to get a clear view of the hall, he tilted his head at an angle trying to get a better look. He couldn't see them, but he knew they were there. And from what he could tell, he was in the right place. Blood and tattered body parts littered the floor, undoubtedly, from the grenade, as well as the barrage of fire they laid down earlier. The smoke and dust had settled quite a bit. He was still having a little trouble seeing down the hall as far as he wanted to. The dust and debris still taking its time to settle didn't help his efforts much.

"Well, here goes nothing," he said to himself hoping like hell that this little idea was going to do the trick.

He reached down to remove the grate, but it was screwed down. It was obviously not going to give as easily as the other one had in the classroom. It didn't move. He pulled and pushed to no avail.

Reaching back, he retrieved the 9mm from its holster, struggling to bring it forward in the tight little space. After a moment of fighting with it, he finally got his arm and the weapon out in front of him.

"So much for stealth." He took a breath, already breaking out into a sweat from the cramped duct.

He forcefully brought the butt of his pistol down on the grate. With the first hit, the grate bent in, almost entirely giving way. He came down on it again, with one more violent knock of the butt of his weapon, sending the mangled metal falling to the floor in the hallway.

The sudden clang of metal crashing to the floor echoed in Clay's ears. The instant sound of dead footsteps followed. They were on him in a flash.

Drawn by the unexpected clatter, the horde of zombies shambled down the hallway and across the already-fallen remnants of their forever-dead comrades. Their moans grew louder as they drew closer to Clay's location. The echo of their cries was magnified in the confines of Clay's fortified position.

After only a few seconds, the first of several dozen shamblers appeared in Clay's sight, stopping right underneath him. It didn't look up but rather looked around for what had drawn its attention.

It was totally clueless, Clay thought as he reached his pistol out past the opening in the ventilation system. Aiming the 9mm at the unsuspecting creature, Clay opened fire. The first shot echoed out into the vent scaring the hell out of him. It was a direct hit, landing straight down on the center zombie's scalp, not exiting. The shot sent the zombie to its knees for a moment, then to the ground for good.

Before the creature had time to drain its final bit of life, Clay had his sights on another of the undead. He tightened down on the trigger sending another bullet down upon the unsuspecting mob. With his gun at more of an angle, the zombie hadn't been given enough time to make it directly under Clay. The shot penetrated the corpse's face right above the nose, off center in the right eye socket. The eye exploded, sending gore out into the air. The bullet instantly exited the back of the creature's upper neck, sending blood and brain out with it, the bullet ripping into the carpet at the zombie's feet. Only a moment later, the zombie collapsed, lifeless.

With the mass of zombies finally coming into view, Clay decided to change it up. Shooting them one at a time was going to take way too long, and he had already taken enough time. Clay set the pistol down in front of him and reached over his back for the M-4. As he did, he glanced at the wristwatch. Three minutes. He needed to dispatch as many of those things down there as he possibly could in the next three minutes.

Gus would be busting out of that office space with a surprise attack, flanking them from the rear. The goal was to distract the mob away from the door, allowing them more time to have selective fire. With the number that had gathered in the hall after the explosion, Gus felt that facing them in that large of a number with no real exit was not the best of ideas. Even with the good supply of ammunition, the last thing he wanted was to get run down simply by their numbers. He had already experienced that in a confined space once before and knew that it was suicide.

*

Having removed the makeshift blockage from the doorway, Gus stood weapon at the ready. He listened intently as he heard the fire of Clay's rifle. He glanced down at his watch. *Only a few more minutes*, he thought.

With the small horde of zombies fixed on Clay's location, the attention at the door was minimal, but still present. Gus leaned against it, guessing two, maybe three at the most. He leaned there, feeling the door bounce and shake as they tried to get in.

Gus suddenly no longer heard the sound of gunfire. Clay must have been reloading. Gus glanced at the watch again. Two minutes.

*

Clay reached back, trying to get at a fresh magazine, having already unloaded one on the mob below. The entire horde now centered themselves around Clay's location, reaching up toward the vent. They reached with arms stretched out, their heads and necks cocked back. Their milky-white eyes locked on his sight as they watched him fumbling about in the vent. Most of his head and shoulders poked out into view as he looked back, trying to reach a magazine for the M-4. The moans and screams grew with excitement having their prey in sight. One false move, causing him to slip down and into the hallway, and he would be theirs.

Fumbling forward, still trying to get his hands around in the tight space, his shoulder knocked his 9mm that had been sitting in front of him. It bumped forward, falling. He instantly reacted, trying to catch it as it fell. Reaching out an arm, he leapt forward and out, half coming into the mob's full view. Their arms frantically stretched out, coming within inches away from reaching Clay as he started to lose his balance. Recoiling, he doubled his effort to retreat back into the safety of the ventilation system. The pistol was gone. It landed on the floor, lost beneath the steps of the looming crowd.

*

Gus sat waiting for the gunfire to kick back into gear before pushing the door open. It never came. He looked at his watch again. The time was up and it had been for a few seconds. Each of those seconds seemed like minutes.

Abruptly, a barrage of fire echoed out in the hall. It was Clay and that was his cue. Gus stepped back, kicking out the door with one big push. The door burst open, sending back two lingering zombies. Gus brought his rifle up against his chest, sighting the first ghoul down the barrel.

The volley of bullets fired smashed through the thing's face. The creature jerked violently as its face splattered into a mesh of unrecognizable goo. Blood and grey matter splashed and sprayed everywhere. His hand throbbed with each pull of the trigger.

Gus stepped back into the room a few paces, ignoring the pain, allowing his eyes to catch a wider view of the battlefield. Only one more zombie stood in the way between him and the horde that lingered beneath Clay, who was already doing a hell of a job.

To Gus' right, a hail of fire fell from the ventilation system right above the mass of undead. Clay's rifle peeked out from the ceiling as endless bullets tore through reanimated flesh and bone. Bodies shook and jolted, sending one to the ground for good every second.

The lone zombie staggered forward, wobbling left and right with each step. Gus took another step back as the zombie made its way into the room with him. With arms outstretched and its teeth gritting at the sight of fresh flesh, Gus lifted the rifle.

Dried blood and small chunks of meat caked the zombie's mouth and lips. Its outstretched hands were covered in the same dried blood and grime clear to the elbows. What Gus found odd about this particular zombie wasn't that its shirt was removed, but that it had no identifying marks that he recognized. Most of the undead that he had come across had something that identified the cause of death. A bite to the shoulder or throat, ripped out intestines, or a missing limb generally told the ghoul's story. This one, however, had none of these markings. Even with its shirt off, Gus only saw what looked like little rash marks that resembled small bug bites. Whatever they were, the creature's stomach was covered with them.

Gus took a deep breath then fixed his sights and pulled the trigger. The single shot cleanly entered and exited the zombie's forehead right between the eyes, instantly sending the ghoul to the floor. Before exiting the room, Gus looked up, glancing at the large map on the wall. It was *do or die* for them to make it to the elevator.

He turned the corner to find that the onslaught of fire had ceased. Clay was standing over the mass of bodies in the hall with one hand on his head, a look of confusion over his masked face.

"What is it, Clay?" Gus asked, catching up to him.

"My handgun. I freaking dropped it," he said while looking down at the mound of bodies burying him almost up to his knees.

"Ha! If it's in there somewhere, you can forget about it. Let's go. We still have a few rooms to clear."

4

Ashley Fox led the four Sears survivors in single file, through the darkness of what was once a booming place of business this time of the afternoon on a Friday. As they slid down the aisles, past a handful of home appliances, Phillip followed behind Ashley, who was in the lead. Behind him, Kieta and Jenny scurried along, leaving Victor in the rear, sporting the same gun that took down Chadwick, Ashley Fox's partner. The group had left the security of their hiding spot in the store less than ten minutes earlier and had yet to come across any unfriendlies.

Before leaving the room where Ashley had met the restless and weary group, they came up with the game plan. The goal was to stay alive. The way they planned to achieve that was by staying close, staying quiet, and being alert.

Making their way from the office and around to the back of the store, then up two flights of steps to the roof, should have taken less than a few minutes in a full-out sprint, but that just couldn't happen. The young girl and the pregnant teenager held them back.

So far, they had only made it halfway across the building. The office they had been held up in was toward the front of the store and they needed to make their way to the back. They had to make it to receiving and shipping, according to Victor.

Moving forward at a very steady crawl with bodies low, the line of five inched along.

Ashley kept playing the previous series of instances back and forth in her head. Where did she go wrong as a leader? She had been doing this job for a long time now and had not once lost a teammate. All she could think about was the milky gaze that Chadwick grimaced at her when he reanimated. Lunging at her, those snarling teeth and the blood all over his hands, really shook her up.

With her M-4 rifle at the ready, she sighted down the barrel, quietly waving it back and forth while using the attached lighting as a guide in the dark. She intently listened for any sudden noise that might break in any direction. The only sound she heard was that of their own muffled footsteps. She would periodically look over her shoulder and count heads, *all accounted for*.

Behind her, Phillip kept a close proximity. He frantically kept glancing over his shoulder in all directions, sweat beading down his brow. His eyes so wide they looked like they might pop out of the sockets. He did his best to look calm when Ashley would look back at him, suddenly throwing up a smile and nod in her direction. Being pregnant, Kieta was the only one not hunched over as they slid forward in the looming darkness. She tried to at first, but the awkward posture quickly started giving her cramps. With her oversized belly protruding from her maternity clothes, there was no doubt that Victor Jr. would be coming any day now. With one hand against her cramped back, pushing against it for support, her other hand attempted to support her unborn son. With her hand rested under her massive bulge, hidden beneath her shirt, she rubbed her stomach occasionally. Even in the devastating circumstances, a small smile would occasionally climb across those cheeks of hers. Following a little too close behind her, Jenny held one hand out, clinching her index and pointer finger tightly around one of the loops in Kieta's pants. The other hand slung freely and wildly about in the air beside her. Her bare feet slapped against the cold white tile. Her little, pink dress was covered in dried blood on one side, and her eyes were glazed over with uncertainty. She was clueless, in a child-like way. Holding tight to Kieta, all she knew was that her mommy and daddy would be wherever it was that this scary lady up front was taking them and that those bad people who hurt her friends would go away too. There was no reason this little child couldn't comprehend the situation, but on the first day of the outbreak, when she watched her neighbor and two other people attack and kill the mailman and then chase after her, something snapped. She reverted inside somehow, shocked. The bad people chased her from the front yard back into her house and into her bedroom. After closing the door, she sat there screaming hysterically. Her young mind just couldn't, or wouldn't wrap around the tranquil, suburban landscape imploding into the ravenous siege of rotting pestilence. In her mind's eye, all she could see was her parents waiting for her in a safe place, and Ashley Fox was going to take her there.

Behind the little girl and at the rear of the line, Victor focused on the task at hand, getting to the chopper. With his eyes wide and his mind sharp, Victor took each step forward with determination. He was going to make it out alive, and by God, so was his unborn son. Sure, he was quite a bit older than Kieta and they weren't married, but none of that mattered anymore. Her spiteful parents weren't alive anymore to tell him off, or to say other terrible things to him. They hated Victor and definitely didn't approve of the situation, but who were they to get in his business? He was a grown-ass man and could very well take care of a kid and his girl. She could finish high school after the baby arrived. Her parents didn't know anything and why should they? They were dead now, anyhow. With his pistol raised high, Victor did his best to push his thoughts aside and focus on the noises around him, or the lack there of.

Suddenly, Victor collided with Jenny. The instant thud shook him slightly. He almost lost the grip on his gun and nearly dropped it to the floor. He looked up, noticing that the line had stopped. Ashley was standing upright with one hand fist up. She was signaling them to halt. He had been so lost in thought that he hadn't noticed.

Ashley stood at the edge of a small row of aisles filled with tools and hardware accessories. They had finally hit a solid wall of the building plastered with huge flat screen televisions.

"We take a right," Victor whispered, pointing his finger.

Not making a single sound, Ashley instantly turned to face him with a finger over her lips. What had made her stop wasn't the sudden need to make a directional choice, but something else.

Around the corner, only one aisle over, a single zombie stood just shifting back and forth in the same spot. After peeking around the corner, the light quickly catching a glimpse of the creature's leg, she instinctively shut off the light and stepped back signaling the group to halt.

With the four civilians finally heeding the warning to quiet down and stay still, she poked her head back around the edge of the aisle to take a better look. Unless there was another zombie on the aisle right beside theirs, then this thing was definitely alone. She reached down, removing the large blade from its sheath which was attached to her ankle.

The four survivors watched as she crept forward toward the creature. Her intentions were clear, as she set her rifle aside. The idea was to keep quiet and stay close. If they did that, they just might stay alive.

The zombie was wearing a pair of light brown steel-toe boots and navy blue pants. The red vest he wore, with the large Sears emblem on the back of it, indicated the individual once worked at this store. Its hair was a mess, and its rather large beard was caked in dry blood. Chunks of muck and gore festered in its facial hair. The stench of urine and feces filled the air around the zombie as it swayed.

As Ashley moved in, she could tell that the creature had either soiled itself before death or had released its bowels after. The back of the ghoul's pants were stained with its putrid waste. The tribal tattoo on the dead man's upper arm peeked out beneath a blood-soaked shirt. The black ink popped against the pale, lifeless skin.

As quietly as she could, Ashley leapt from behind the creature with her blade in hand, the zombie unsuspectingly swayed away in place. Something caught under her foot and kicked away as she stepped, gliding across the cold floor; bouncing off of the corner of the shelf in front of her, it *tinked*, metal meeting metal.

The zombie flinched, then wildly slung itself around, meeting eye-to-eye with a startled Ashley Fox. Momentarily paralyzed, Ashley hesitated. The creature's mouth and eyes went wide as its hands darted forward. Before she was able to make the blade collide with the zombie's throat, it was too late; the zombie belched out a feverish moan. In mid-cry, before the ghoul had time to finish its howl, Ashley reached up, slicing deep and hard into its jugular. The moan instantly turned into a gurgling bubble as blood poured out from the open wound sliced across its neck.

Other than that silenced cry, the creature was unfazed. It lunged forward, pouncing down on her. Feeling her position already compromised, Ashley reached down pulling out her 9mm. With the zombie's dead cold fingers gripping her arm and its mouth closing in, she pulled the trigger. A single loud crack echoed through the store alerting anything and everything within of their location. If the zombie's outburst hadn't given them away, the gunshot surely had.

The ghoul's grip quickly loosened on Ashley. Blood poured from the side of its head. A large hole with brain and rancid matter violently exited the bullet wound as the gun went off at point blank range.

Wailing moans instantly filled the store from all directions. Howls and groans echoed throughout. Something fell from a shelf and skidded across the floor, something heavy. It was time to move.

"Let's go," Ashley shouted as she appeared back in sight of the four panic-filled civilians. She reached down, snatched up her rifle, and holstered her handgun all in one solid motion.

The four startled onlookers stood frozen and silent just looking at Ashley.

"Did you not hear me? I said let's Move! Move... move... move..."

She grabbed Phillip by the shoulder, pushing him out of the aisle and over the zombie she had just executed. One by one, she shoved each of them on the shoulder shouting, "Move!"

Grabbing a hold of Victor last, she reached up with both hands, one of which still held her rifle. Shaking him on the shoulders, she looked deep into his eyes and calmly said in a slow and assertive tone, "You know the way. I need you up front. Move fast and just get us to the roof. I will do the covering… To the roof! Got it?"

Victor nodded and took off running past the others to get to the front.

With the idea of stealth thrown completely out the window at this point, Victor took the lead. In full sprint, he veered around a corner leading into the back of the building behind two large swinging doors. "This way, we're real close," he shouted, not looking back.

The others followed.

At the back of the group, Ashley had her rifle locked and loaded. A handful of zombies crept and shuffled from corners of aisles and refrigerators. Each of them with their own distinct flesh wound that painted the brutal way they met death. Ashley counted seven of them so far as she shimmied backward toward the double doors, the others already past them and hopefully well on their way up the staircase to the roof.

Ten, then thirteen, then eighteen. Zombie after zombie filled the large opening that led to where Ashley stood. With outstretched arms and mouths wide, she instantly thought of Chadwick, and a gut-wrenching pain of guilt and anguish flooded her stomach. She was going to be sick. She opened fire, the rifle jerking in her grip. With a wide birth of fire, she lit up the store. Bullets ripped through merchandise and zombies. Her shots were wild and unfocused.

Blood and gray fluids poured out in every direction. The dozen or so zombies shook upon being struck, but still pressed on. There were too many of them and they were closing in fast. She had to act, and quickly. She lowered the rifle, pulling out the pistol, aiming it at the nearest zombie. As it scrambled in her direction only a few paces away, she aimed and fired. The creature went down instantly. It was a clear and clean shot, taking off most of its ear and enough of its head to count.

As the one-eared zombie stumbled to the ground, Ashley Fox took two quick steps back and turned, breaking for the double doors. They swung open with ease.

Off in the not-so-distant path ahead of her, Victor stood, waving the others to follow him up the staircase. Ashley's eyes followed his hand gesture and saw that Kieta and Jenny were steadily climbing the metal staircase leading up to where she and Chadwick had originally entered the building.

Phillip, where was Phillip? He wasn't up at the top with Victor, and he wasn't climbing the staircase with the girls. Ashley's gaze went even wider trying to place the man's whereabouts.

Nothing.

The large black double doors swung open shaking her out of her thoughts. A small mob of zombies followed behind her.

"Shit," she said under her breath, looking back up at the people climbing the steps.

As she jogged across the room past the unopened boxes of merchandise nicely stacked in stalls and racks, she looked up, seeing that Victor's gun was drawn and he was aiming it in her direction. She looked back and the doors were still wide open. A large cluster of zombies was making their way into the back of the store. There must have been over thirty of them.

A loud bang rang out from in front of her and a bullet whizzed past her ear. Victor was firing over her head! Not wanting to get killed by an idiot, she kicked into high gear, and reached the bottom of the steps in a matter of moments.

Climbing the first several steps, three steps per stride, she quickly caught up with the two girls. "What's the hold up? Let's go," Ashley said.

Kieta was having contractions. The pain was too great, and she was stuck in her tracks. Halfway up the stairs, she just froze, holding her stomach and heaving heavily in pain. Wincing and gritting her teeth, a loud and long grunt exited her mouth. Still, gripping her belt loop, Jenny stood behind her one step lower waiting to move along.

"What's the holdup here?" Ashley shouted shoving the two girls.

"The...ba...bby..." Kieta's words came crashing out in one long breath between closed teeth and closed eyes.

"You've got to be kidding me. Now?" Ashley looked up to see the worried look on Victor's face as he looked down from the rooftop exit, gun still drawn. She took a deep breath while in disbelief, then turned to face the horde that headed toward them. Pulling up her rifle, she sighted the closest zombie lurching its way across the shipping area.

Dried blood filled the open fissures on the skin of the creature's cracking face. As it opened its mouth, most of its bottom teeth were missing, and blood poured out and down its pale chin. It's ragged and tattered clothes were dust and dirt caked.

She pulled the trigger. Four or five shots littered the creature's head before she panned the rifle out and into the rest of the oncoming crowd.

Many of the zombies instantly fell with fatal headshots, but most of them keep their persistent pursuit. Victor followed Ashley's initiative with a steady flow of single shot after single shot. He was no expert marksmen, but a damn good shot at least. Every other shot that rang out hit a zombie in the head, sending it to the floor for good. Still, it wasn't enough to turn the odds. The zombies crept closer, too close.

Ashley broke her concentration away from the horde below for a second toward Kieta. She was still gripping the railing, knuckles pressed white. With that same pain-filled expression, she kept heaving and huffing.

"Pull it together, Kieta! We need to move," Ashley said, who instantly went back to rifle fire.

The weapon looked large in her feminine grip, shaking the woman up and down as an onslaught of fire exited the barrel tearing into chests and necks. Above her, the single rifle ceased. Over the loud bursts, she thought she heard something. Then suddenly, she watched as a handgun flew across the room into the crowd below, hitting one of the undead in the chest. The creature shuffled back for a moment, but it did no real damage. They were only feet away from the bottom of the steps now and more were still entering the room from the large open doors.

"I'm out of ammo," Victor shouted, holding both hands in the air empty.

Ashley decided to make a choice and sure as shit hoped that Kieta would comply. She threw her hot rifle around one shoulder and started up the steps, grabbing Jenny with one hand, lifting the girl up off of her feet.

"It's time to move whether you're ready or not," Ashley grunted, heaving the little girl in one arm.

She reached up with a free hand and shoved Kieta forward. The very pregnant woman fell landing on one knee, catching herself with one hand on the step ahead of her.

"Get up!"

Ashley passed the woman by, jogging up the steps to the top. She dropped Jenny to her feet, then turned to get Kieta, who was still on one knee as Ashley had left her. Eyeing Victor with a nonverbal agreement, the two made it down the steps after her. They both lifted the pregnant woman to her feet, one person under each arm with a shoulder. The width of the staircase was confining, but the two steadied the soon-to-be mother, working to get her up each step.

It wasn't easy, and she wasn't the lightest of people to be toting around. *Definitely not Jenny*, Ashley thought as they made it up one step at a time. Below them, the first of several zombies broke the second step, making their way up. With the weight of the pregnant woman and the lack of space to move, the zombies made their way up each step with more ease than that of the rescuers trying to get Kieta to safety.

Suddenly, Kieta kicked into gear. The debilitating contractions had stopped, and she was back in action. They started to make some solid ground. At the top of the steps, Ashley opened the door leading to the roof, and with a large grin, could see that the pilot was ready to go. The large blades were alive and the engine in full swing. Just from the quick glance before sending Jenny out, then turning to help Victor with his girlfriend, she thought she could see someone else out there with the pilot.

Jenny ran off toward the chopper. Ashley and Victor followed, still helping Kieta along, one person under each arm.

Ahead of them, she looked up seeing the pilot and Phillip both with weapons drawn and pointed in the direction they had just come from. Ashley looked back to see that she had made one fatal flaw in the escape plan. She left the rooftop door wide open. She was so focused on getting people out that she overlooked the most important detail.

Zombies poured out onto the rooftop behind her. The pilot motioned for them to get onboard, and as she passed, the pilot and Phillip opened up a torrent of fire on the relentless undead that followed in their wake.

Victor and Ashley helped Kieta get into the helicopter. Jenny was nowhere to be found. As Victor jumped into the bird, checking on his woman and comforting her, Ashley stepped down to one knee of the rooftop scanning the grounds for the little girl.

There she was! The girl was off to the corner, crouched down in fear. A small cluster of the large mob approached her, breaking away from the main group that still seemed focused on the two men shooting in on them.

Ashley screamed for Jenny to run to the chopper. It didn't work. The girl couldn't hear her. Ashley watched as the little girl's dress danced in the violent helicopter wind. Ashley broke away from the chopper and ran for the child. With each of her steps more than twice the pace of any of the living dead, she reached Jenny well before the small mob descended upon her.

Ashley yanked her up with both arms, turning to make it back to the chopper. What her eyes instantly witnessed almost made her drop to her knees.

The helicopter had been breached. The mob of zombies made it past the fire that the pilot and Phillip had been laying down. As she watched them descend upon the only way out, Phillip lay dead. Several zombies hovered over his remains, feasting on his bones. The pilot was missing, obviously fallen to the same fate.

Something caught Ashley's peripheral to the right. She quickly glanced over and was relieved to see Victor helping Kieta down a fire escape ladder. Ashley quickly followed suit and made her way to their side, passing the little girl down the ladder to Victor.

Behind her, Ashley took one last look at the helicopter. Over thirty or forty of those things had fallen upon the bird and were now devouring the remains of her pilot and a man who she was sent to save. First Chadwick, and now this. She had failed.

Several zombies headed for Ashley. She turned and began to climb down the fire escape before they had a chance to get her.

Ashley pulled free her handgun aiming it up at the zombies. After two quick shots, one zombie fell.

Once Ashley's feet met the cement, her head went heavy and unfocused. The ladder reached down from the left side of the building and overlooked the employee parking. As she tried to focus, she felt one foot stepping in front of another. Ahead of her, she could barely make out Victor getting into what looked like a truck. The girls looked like they were already inside.

Her focus began to fade even more as she reached the truck. She was losing it.

"Get in, get in," Victor's shout seemed muffled and cloudy in Ashley's head. Her vision started to blur. The events unfolding before her were too unreal to grasp. So much loss. So much chaos and confusion.

As she reached up and climbed into the bed of the truck, a rancid face filled with maggots and dried blood lunged forward, grabbing her by the throat. It's green and black-stained teeth reared open, and a putrid stench of rot and festering flesh puffed out into the air. Ashley's stomach recoiled.

As the creature's teeth bit down into her cheek, tearing out a large chunk of her eye, beyond the pain Ashley imagined it was Chadwick. The blood sprayed from her face as the creature tore the flesh away. Then came the pain and warm sensation of blood spilling forth.

She reached up to cover her wound, everything coming into focus now. With a loud scream, she leaped back, jerking wildly.

As she opened her eyes with one hand covering her hot cheek, she realized where she was. In the truck's cab, with Victor in the driver's seat, heading down the road.

"Ashley? You zoned out and dozed off after you climbed in. Bad dreams?" Victor asked, not taking his eyes off of the road.

Still a little out of it and caught up in her delusion, Ashley jumped up in her seat, looking back at the truck bed. The girls were safe. Kieta sat leaning against the tailgate with the wind in her hair. And Jenny was dead asleep sprawled out on the bed of the truck.

Ashley's cheek was fine. It had all been in her head.

5

The piece of junk for a truck sped down the highway headed east from Lake City, Florida. With plenty of miles already behind them, Ashley and the others simply waited. The white lines as they passed could seem like seconds and hours all in one. The Chevy zipped along at a steady 80 mph, passing abandoned cars, vans, and trucks of every make and model. The highway was nothing more than a remnant of the last lingering few days that had just ravaged the coastlands of the southeastern state. How far had it spread?

"How long was I out?" Ashley asked.

"Eh...not long really. Maybe twenty minutes give or take," Victor said.

Ashley sat up, back cramping and head still in a bit of a fog. Way too much had happened way too fast. Her mind struggled to catch up. Processing her thoughts, she brushed her hair aside and out of her eyes. In the passenger side mirror, she could see herself and part of Kieta's hair flapping in the wind. She looked like hell. She had just been through it too. She lost a pilot, a civilian, and her partner all within the same twenty-four hours. It had been rough on her, and her mind was careworn with stress and disbelief. How could any of this be real?

"So let me get this straight. Before you dozed off on me again, you mentioned that the coastline was quarantined and that the rest of the planet was okay. If that's true, then where do you think they are going to send us once we get cleared by the base?" Victor asked.

"What?" Ashley asked, still focusing on the road as it moved away from her in the side mirror. She hadn't caught half of what Victor had said.

"Where do you think we are going to get shipped once this is all said and done?" Victor restated from behind the wheel, only taking his eyes from the road for a second. "You know... *us*," he said pointing with his thumb at the passengers in the bed of the truck.

"No idea. I just do the field work. There haven't been many survivors, and that was what we expected. So hypothetically, you three are a miracle. Probably get the same basic treatment we've been getting. Once we get to the base, they will end up running half a day worth of tests on us just to ensure we didn't catch the death-walk thing, and then who knows? A fresh set of clothes and a meal, for sure."

Victor's reached up with one hand, cupping his belly, giving it two good slaps with a smile. "One thing at a time, I guess."

*

In the back of the truck, Jenny had finally awakened from her little nap. It was hard to actually fall to sleep in the bed of the truck, with the wind blowing so hard overhead and the engine roaring so loud. Squinting into the daylight, in an attempt to take a nap, Jenny leaned against the back of the cab facing Kieta. Her golden-brown hair danced about out in front of her, the shorter strands occasionally popping her in the eye. She was tranquil and quiet, too quiet.

Kieta was worried, worried about Jenny in a bad way. She was acting odd when they had found her screaming her head off. Victor was her neighbor and could hear her screaming from the driveway. She had been locked in her house and he rushed over to help. Her parents were nowhere to be found, which was odd to leave a child that age alone. But after Victor broke a window and rescued Jenny, they spotted a half-eaten woman in the garden. Thank goodness Jenny hadn't noticed it too.

It was then the three of them made for Victor's work, feeling that it would be a secure place to hide. They had met up with Phillip along the way, but that didn't matter anymore. He was gone.

It took Jenny almost the entire day to quit heaving and crying before she calmed down and passed out. After she awoke, locked away with the others in the office of Victor's work, she never came to her total senses. Kieta had known the girl well enough with her soon-to-be husband living next to the kid's parents. Needless to say, Jenny was once a vibrant child filled with laughs and love. And now, every bit of that was gone. All that was left was dried up to dust. The girl looked as if she had aged rapidly. Across from her, Kieta watched as the girl blankly stared off at nothing. A somber expression plastered to the child's face.

Behind Jenny, in the cab, Victor and Ashley were talking and pointing at something out ahead of them.

Looking over the roof of the truck without taking her butt off of the rusty bed, Kieta saw what they were pointing at. The sky was graying, with thick, dark clouds some ways out. Kieta scooted up, tapping on the glass to get the front passengers' attention.

Ashley reached and slid the back window glass of the truck open.

"Looks like it's going to rain pretty hard," Kieta yelled, holding one hand on top of her head to keep her hair from getting too out of control.

"Yeah," Ashley shouted in response. "But, that is the least of our worries." Ashley pointed out past the light drops of rain already hitting against the windshield to the road ahead.

It was then that Kieta noticed the truck had been slowing down. Looking out at the winding interstate ahead of them, she could see the worries Ashley had referred to.

The road a few miles up was congested with cars, and the small overpass was utterly impassable.

As the truck moved closer to the mountainous wreckage blocking their path, the raindrops turned into rainfall. The steady sheets of rain became heavy within moments, the clouds finally deciding to open up right on top of the Chevy and the passengers within and without.

"What do you want to do?" Victor asked leaning forward and looking up at the dark clouds overhead, the rain steadily falling.

Not even the slightest bit concerned with the rain, Ashley scanned the surrounding road filled with parked cars. There was no way around them. They were four and five cars deep, wall-to-wall leading up to the overpass. And from there, who knew? Ashley couldn't see that far. A large semi blocked the view. It wasn't like that really mattered anyhow. It was too bad for them to care about making it across.

Ashley glanced over at the truck gauges. "How are we looking on fuel?"

"We have half a tank. There's no reason we can't get there on that. We might cut it close, but it will get us there for sure."

"I hate to interrupt your little chat, but I'm getting drenched back here!" Kieta grimaced and pulled the back part of her shirt over her head. The rain fell a little harder now than it had when they stopped.

Jenny seemed to enjoy the rain. With that same blank stare and an awkward smile like something sinister, she stared into the clouds. With her neck cocked back at a 90-degree angle, the girl just looked up, eyes wide and not blinking. The heavy rain fell on her face, soaking into her hair and dress. The little beads of loose droplets ran down her cheeks and forehead onto her shoulders.

Ahead of them, less than a quarter mile, the pile up of vehicles stared back at them.

"I think I saw an off-ramp a couple miles back," Victor said.

Glancing at the gas gauge again, Ashley shrugged. "Not like we have much of a choice. If we feel like gas is going to be an issue, we'll just stop and fill up on the way. If it comes to that, I want to fill up before we get into Tallahassee and the more congested areas. We can handle a few of those things here and there, but it's the massive crowds that are going to be the death of us."

Victor agreed.

"Look," Kieta said shifting more into the cab from the window pointing out past the first few parked cars ahead of them. Her wet head dripped into the cab, and no one seemed to notice or care. What she was pointing at definitely took precedence.

Amongst the wall-to-wall automotive blockade, scattered and spread, ghastly figures started to appear. First, it was one, then three, and then a dozen. Ghoulish faces popped out from behind abandoned cars and open truck doors looking right at the passengers of the idling Chevy. The rain beating down on their rancid flesh bounced off the shoulders and heads of the approaching undead as they made themselves known. One by one, each zombie sluggishly crept out from the parked cars, trucks, and vans pressing forward. Several of the walking dead quickly broke past the cars out into the open street. With heads up high and arms out, their fingers reached with the intent of digging and tearing away at fresh tissue. The highway street at their feet instantly ran red and gray from the beating rain. Blood and chunks of rot, decay, and grey matter washed away from their putrid skin and bones onto the pavement.

"About that exit a few miles back, any time would be good," Ashley calmly said as she pulled up the M-4 into her lap, mostly just for comfort's sake.

"I hear you," Victor replied. "Sit back, Kieta." Victor looked over his shoulder and popped the truck into reverse.

After making an impromptu U-turn, the truck and its passengers made for Tallahassee and the military base. Ashley Fox sat back watching the rain slowly get a little worse. *How was she going to explain losing her partner, the pilot, and the chopper?* The closer the truckload of survivors got to Tallahassee, the more her stomach began to turn.

6

The song playing was familiar, yet Clay was having trouble placing what it was. It wasn't the actual song in its original form, but a softer version with wood flutes and chimes. He stood there humming along in irritation, trying like hell to recall the song's actual name.

After clearing each of the rooms on the first floor, which went off without a hitch, the hallway was a mess. But other than that, the soldiers had no luck in finding any more infected or unexpected surprises. Clay and Gus stood in the elevator as it descended to the zero level security clearance basement floor. The elevator was larger than normal and had a futuristic glimmer of silver and LED buttons. After it stopped, the doors failed to open. Clay smirked and pointed at the key card slot positioned above the small screen to the right of the metal doors.

Clay said, "I pulled the woman's ID back up there in so we could identify her when we got back. But I bet we'll need this to get the door open."

With a *told you so* grin, Clay inserted the ID.

"What the heck is that tune?" Clay said, under his breath.

Gus paid him no mind. He eyed the double doors, ready for whatever awaited them on the other side.

Clay readied his weapon and focused his eyes. He knew good and well that not knowing that elevator song would probably bug him for a couple of days, at best.

The elevator doors slid open up to a massive room. The two men quickly darted from the elevator, allowing the doors to close behind them. With weapons at the ready, the two soldiers panned their rifles, scanning the room for any threat. They were half expecting a zombie to leap out from a corner of the room or for someone to start shooting on them. But none of the expected threats existed.

The room was filled with scientific laboratory equipment and unfamiliar things that Dr. Gibbs would have probably drooled over. Some of the equipment Gus recognized as being something he might imagine being in the lab on base. There were several tables lined up in rows at one corner, with stacks of papers and boxes atop them.

Farther up, they could see what looked like hospital equipment. Gurneys and respiratory monitors lay stacked to one side along with surgical tools and protective gear. Next to the monitors, a large green sheet draped from the ceiling blocked off a section of the room.

Gus and Clay quietly inched forward toward the sheet. There was something hidden behind it, and Gus had the innate feeling that maybe, just maybe, he didn't really want to know what was behind it. His imagination gave him chills. The sound of heavy breathing came from behind it. The mechanical sounds clicked and pulsed rhythmically from behind the shrouded space.

Reaching out, Gus grabbed the sheet and pulled it back, instantly bringing his rifle up into position. The loud, steady, sound of metal rings sliding across the metal pole filled the room as the sheet slid open revealing what lay hidden away.

With his back turned to the two armed men, an old, frail-looking man stood over what appeared to be an operating table. On the table, laid a pale-skinned woman who looked just as old, if not a bit older, than him. She was unconscious and hooked up to monitoring equipment. A respiratory mask covered her mouth and tubes ran down her throat. Part of her head was shaved down to the scalp. Lines had been marked upon her skull, as if she was being prepared to be cut into.

The old man, facing away from Clay and Gus, pulled up a scalpel in one hand, and without turning, called out to the soldiers, "Took you two long enough."

"Turn around and face me. Hands up over your head!" Gus bellowed.

"You boys sure did a number on my employees up there," the old man replied, not the least bit interested in what Gus had barked at him.

"I said *turn around*, old man!" Gus stepped forward, clearing the chamber and setting a fresh round into place. The dispensed shell clanged on the floor.

The man obliged, turning around with both hands over his head. Gus reached into his chest pocket, pulling out the photo. And he put it back just as quickly. He then glanced back at Clay, who hadn't moved a foot since the sheet slid open revealing the old man.

"This is our guy," Gus said as he eyed Clay. He addressed the old man once more, "Drop it, old timer." Gus shifted the barrel of his rifle from the old man to the ground.

Slowly setting scalpel down, the man said, "No need to be so on edge, Mr. Stanford. That is your name, right? I've been expecting you both. I mean you no harm. Please, please, take it easy and lower that weapon," the old man requested.

"How the hell do you know my name?"

"I know a lot of things, Gus, but none of that is important right now." The old man slowly lowered his hands and stepped forward with his right hand outstretched. "Pleased to make your acquaintance. My name is Grech Vonhinkly, as you already know. But you can call me Grech. I own this facility, along with several others like it. And this is my wife. Her time has, unfortunately, passed. It was her time, as it will be mine, before long. You can just sense those kinds of things with old age."

Gus looked over the old gray-headed man's shoulder at the frail woman lying on the table. She looked peaceful.

Clay had made his way up next to the two men, handshake still lingering. "Hello, sir. My name is Jared Clay. I'm sorry to hear about your loss. What happened to her, sir?"

"It was just her time, my boy. I merely did my best to comfort her during the journey. She had cancer. It was a long time coming."

The two soldiers could see the age and pain in this little old man's bright blue eyes. He was holding back his sorrow. Gus was baffled as to what he should do next. The mission was to come in, get the old geezer and get out. But how could he be that heartless? With the monitors going and the respiratory stuff still functioning, it must have meant that she had just passed.

After a few moments of silence, the old man turned off the equipment and covered his departed companion's body with a white sheet.

"So, how did you know we were coming?" Clay asked.

"Well, my good boy, that is a fine question, indeed. I'm linked into every broadcasted signal, from here to Japan and back, all on this little device over here," Grech said.

Grech walked from the makeshift hospital quarters to another part of the facility. He moved slowly, like an old man that might be in his late 70's, and with a limp, at that. After a few moments, and with quite a few hobbling steps, the old man was seated at a large desk.

The two soldiers cautiously followed him to his desk. The desk had one big microphone and several buttons and knobs, all lit up. After sitting down, Grech reached up pressing a knob or two, then clicked the single button attached to his microphone, holding it in place.

"Go ahead," Grech said, motioning for Gus to lean over him and speak into the mic.

Gus shrugged, and feeling silly, did so, "Hello, come in!" he said.

The radio on his hip along with the speakers on the large table chimed in simultaneously. Watts' voice came back, "What's your status, Gus? Been on hold for a while. Started to think you might be dead. Over."

As Gus looked down at the old man, puzzled, he leaned in closer to the microphone to reply. As he did so, Grech got his attention by tapping on a set of monitors to his right. There were probably twenty screens in all. Each one showed live footage from a different part of the facility. One of the monitors showed the rooftop and a large portion of the chopper. The pilot was nowhere in sight, but that didn't mean he wasn't up there.

"Well, look at that. You've got this place on lockdown, for sure," Clay said, obviously impressed.

The old man liked that and let him know, with a smile and a nod of agreement.

"Still doesn't explain how you know who we are," Gus said. He leaned down, pressing the button on the mic one more time, and replied to Watts, the pilot, who suddenly came into view on the small screen, "Subject acquired. Facility cleared. Headed your way shortly. Over."

"Roger that," the pilot said. They watched as his handset clipped back to his hip and his rifle came out. Standing at the ledge of the rooftop, his rifle rested against the cement railing. He sighted something down the barrel.

"What's he shooting at?" Clay asked.

Grech reached up, clicking a few buttons. The monitors changed from many small images to two larger images spreading across all of the smaller screens. One image was of the shooter, still perched on the roof's ledge, and another was that of the fields beyond the shooter's sights. Although the screen was mostly brush and the surrounding tree line, several approaching zombies peeked out past them. Instantly, one ghoul dropped to the ground from a headshot. In the other set of screens, they could see the pilot adjusting his weight and resetting his aim on another of the undead creatures. It went down.

Gus said, "Hate to rush you after losing your wife, but we're here to bring you back to base. So, if there is anything you need to get together before we go, I suggest you get to it."

"And what will we do when we get there, Mr. Stanford?" the little old man asked, looking up at Gus from his seat, with squinted brow.

Before the soldier had time to respond, Grech continued, "You don't get it, do you? I have done the calculating and, realistically, it won't be safe to go up for close to another ten years, give or take. It's over! And, the sooner you come to that conclusion, the safer you will be."

"What the hell are you getting at, old man?"

"Let me spell it out for the two of you," Grech said, as he got up from the desk. "Five general stages are used to describe the process of decomposition: Fresh, Bloat, Active and Advanced Decay, and Dry/Remains. The general stages of decomposition are coupled with two stages of chemical decomposition: autolysis and putrefaction. These two stages contribute to the chemical process of decomposition, which breaks down the main components of the body."

Grech scooted along as he spoke, taking his sweet time, as he crossed from one part of the large lab to another section, all the way across the underground facility. As the two soldiers followed him, they passed hospital bays, similar to the one that Grech's wife was in. Others looked like testing stations, for God knows what, and others were decked out with computers and other test equipment. Slightly hidden away in the corner, something was broken; glass and dirt lay strewn all along the floor. It looked like someone had gone behind the mess and tried to clean it up.

Gus knew that they needed to be on their way, but he was just as curious and intrigued as his counterpart.

Clay followed along beside him, wide-eyed and full of childlike excitement.

At least, Gus felt at ease. There weren't any infected creatures in the room, and it wasn't like that little old man could do much damage if he did decide to flip out.

"Once the heart stops, chemical changes occur within the body causing cells to lose their structural integrity. The loss of cell structure brings about the release of cellular enzymes capable of initiating the breakdown of surrounding cells and tissues," Grech said, his voice swelling in excitement. "This process is known as *autolysis*. Visible changes caused by decomposition are limited during the fresh stage, although autolysis may cause blisters to appear at the surface of the skin. This is where our fungus, *Cordyceps Unilateralis*, comes into play, changing everything. I haven't had the chance to study the long-term effects in person, but I have a rough idea. Consuming the non-vital soft tissues, such as things like the *skin and blood cells*, causes the decomposition rate to rapidly occur."

Grech and the two soldiers finally reached their destination, clear across to the far end, where the elevator waited. In front of them, there was a small table, and setting atop it were three different containers filled to the brim with some type of liquid. Inside the liquid were human body parts. One container had the bottom part of a leg and most of the foot. Another held a heart, and the last had someone's head in it.

"Look, Mister, we don't have time to play *freak show* with you. Our pilot is up on the roof, expecting us any minute. I need you to get your things together so we—"

Grech interrupted Gus and continued his speech, "This you will want to see and hear, I promise."

Grech leaned up, pointing at the individual containers and their contents. "In each of these containers, we have major chunks of, what our fungus would consider, non-vital meat, if you will. The first container has not been introduced to the fungus, but the second and third containers have. The container in the middle has been given a very moderate dose in comparison to the other one."

The two men examined the containers for a moment, immediately seeing what the old man was trying to get at.

"So what? The fungus, or whatever it is, is breaking the flesh down a lot faster, which explains the disfigured bag of bones that are walking around," Clay said.

The leg and foot were normal, and the two other contained body parts appeared to be falling apart with rot and decay.

"What I am getting at, gentlemen, is that the decomposition process of someone who has come into contact with *Cordyceps Unilateralis* quickly jumps from the first stage of decomposing to the last stage within days. This is something that, at times, could take months or even years, considering the corpse's location.

Decomposition is largely inhibited during advanced decay due to the loss of readily available cadaveric material, or in our case, non-vital tissue. With how fast these things are decomposing, if denied new non-vital tissue, they could shut down altogether within a couple of years."

"So that explains their need to feed," Clay said.

"Exactly."

"Let me get this straight. So you are saying that as long as they have something to eat, they aren't going to die?"

"Right, and if we deny them sustenance, it is only a matter of time before the fungus turns on itself, slowing down the body's natural system. Once it does that, it will feed on itself and it slows down rapidly."

"Yeah, but if it only would take a few years to get rid of them, then, what is all of this ten years' crap all about?" Gus bristled, while he crossed both arms, puffing out his chest.

"*Ten years* is right, Gus. I have estimated that it will only take six years, or so, for them to actually run out of food. Add a few more years for good measure and we have ten," Grech replied, leaning against the table.

"So you got that figured out, do you? What about how this all started, then?"

"Now Clay, do you really think they would have you come all this way if I didn't have that bit of information?" Grech said. "Your government has sent you in here, with the pretense that they want to figure out what's going on, and that means they lied to you. They know what's going on. They are the ones that have funded my research for the last decade. Leave it up to the Americans." Grech huffed.

"If we're going to waste time down here talking answers and pointing blame, then explain that broken glass back there that we passed. All that dirt." Gus broke away from the table and swiftly made his way back toward the hidden mishap.

Gus ripped away the covering to find what looked like a massive, broken ant farm. It had to have been at least twenty feet wide and fifteen feet tall. A huge crack in the center of the structure had released its contents onto the floor. Dirt, gray specks of dust, and not much of anything else, still lay exposed. As Gus stood there, looking over it, Grech and Clay made their way beside him.

"Yes, we had a large shipment of infected ants carrying the fungus and they got out. That's what spread the plague out onto the streets. There's nothing we can do about it now and pointing blame isn't going to help. If it was anyone's fault, I blame your government for pushing my company, pushing me. They demanded too much and in too little time. When things are rushed, accidents happen."

The three men stood over the mess for a moment in silence, then, Grech continued again. "We contained the spill and killed all of the specimens before the outbreak could get out of control. Several people got bitten by the ants and they were taken care of. The breach occurred, when one of the lab workers that denied getting bitten, was infected and took a leave of absence. Three days later, the coast was hit. How was I supposed to know something like this would happen? We didn't invent the disease— it is in nature. We were just studying it."

"Something like this is fixable," Clay said. He stepped between Gus and the old man, hoping that Gus would keep his cool. "We have blockades covering the entire East Coast. We keep it from spreading and in a few years it dies out on its own. Right?"

"Wrong," Grech said in a bitter reprimand. "Like I said before, I have all radio frequencies, from here to the end of the Earth and back, and what I have heard over those waves, in the last twenty-four hours, have been anything but good."

"What do you mean?" demanded Gus.

"Follow me, and I will show you."

After walking clear across the room once again, they made it back to the table filled with surveillance monitors and the highly technical and overpowered radio transmitter. With Grech seated at the head chair in front of the microphone, Clay and Gus took seats behind him, in similar chairs. Next to them, Grech turned the monitors back to normal, but not before showing the pilot still on the rooftop shooting to help pass the time.

The large section of small monitors changed from various shots from the above ground facility to the sight of a fallen warzone. The living dead, thousands of them, walked the streets.

"So what? We saw plenty of that on our way in here. We are a good ways off from the quarantine borders. What's your point?" Gus asked.

"My point is this…" Grech sighed. "This is footage of Atlanta, Georgia. There are also other feeds I could show you in other states as well."

"That is way outside of the Q-zone!" Clay gasped.

"That can't be possible." Gus grimaced. "You're a liar!"

"That isn't even the bad news, son," Grech said. "The clean sweep they had scheduled for Monday officially got pushed to sunup tomorrow. They are blowing up everybody and everything before it gets any more out of hand, and there is nothing anybody can do about it."

"All the more reason to be on our way!" Gus said.

"No reason to rush. You, of all people, should know that they aren't going to just let you up and walk out of the dead zone like that," Grech said.

Gus stated, "But General Baker wouldn't let—"

"Your General is in the dark. They all are. I know, because I have been listening in. The Tallahassee area will be bombed too. If you want to stay alive, you could do what's right and bunker down with me until it's all over."

Gus yanked his M-4 up. His eyes caught one last glimpse of the footage displayed in the set of screens. "You're right about one thing, old man. Someone has to do what's right."

7

"Hurry up with it already. I got to take a piss," Stately Christopher said.

It was well past lunchtime, and Benton insisted on running the final phase of tests on a few of the blood samples before taking their break. That chubby little prick always wanted to stay ahead of schedule, not for any other reason than to possibly have the opportunity to impress, if and when it presented itself.

Benton readied the injection of anti-coagulant, while Christopher stood there, dancing in place. "Hell, if you need to go that bad, then just go. Come back before heading to the cafeteria.

We need to both log out of the computer systems at the same time."

"Log out at the same time…" Christopher said with a sarcastic tone, mimicking Benton. He stepped away from the table and headed toward the door and out into the hall to relieve himself.

Benton finished getting things ready for the shot. He wanted to see what the result would be on Professor Taft when introducing the chemical compounds to the already clotted, rotting tissue. The effects on each of the blood samples seemed to vary from sample to sample.

Standing over Taft's rotting corpse, Benton began to administer the shot into the dead man's neck. The thick silver needle slid in with ease, the flesh softening from rot and pus. It made a squishing sound as it penetrated the graying flesh. Taft didn't seem to mind one bit. Although upright and moving about, Taft was dead. It wasn't as if he could feel the pain. As Benton pressed the thick fluids into Taft's neck, the bright red liquid left the syringe and entered the creature's blood stream, or what was left of it.

Taft reacted in a way that Benton was not prepared for. The zombie, that had once been his fellow lab associate, lunged forward, grabbing hold of Benton's arm, the one that had been administering the shot. Other than grabbing him, the zombie remained still, staring at the captured limb, with its fogged eyes and drooling mouth.

Benton froze in fear, not exactly sure what he should do. When they first tied Taft up, he was thriving with life and aggressive, but that quickly died down after a day. He had drawn blood from the dead man numerous times before, and not once had the thing leaped out like that. Benton was shocked, letting go of the syringe. It hung there, half hanging from the creature's neck. Black and gray liquids ran down from the needle as the weight of the cylinder pulled down on the putrid skin.

Benton slowly pulled away, but the monster's grip quickly tightened. Benton frantically looked over his shoulder at the table behind him. It seemed to be so far away.

Before he had time to turn back and look Taft in the eyes, he knew what had happened. A sudden, unbelievable pain shot through his forearm causing him to let out a scream. He was afraid to look, but the pain made him jerk his head around.

Taft was pulling his head away from the stout little man's upper arm. Blood, chunks of red meat, and white flesh came away with one massive tear. It peeled away like an orange skin. Blood poured out from the cavernous chunk of missing skin and muscle. The blood splashed as it poured out onto the cold white tiles below.

As Benton looked on in horrifying shock, unable to pull himself away from the zombie's grip, the ghoulish figure came down for another bite. His rotting and germ-infested teeth fell upon Benton again, tearing into the same spot on his arm. This time, the bite went so deep, that as Taft pulled away, portions of the bald little man's bone became visible. He screamed, almost passing out from the pain.

The door swung open, and Christopher dashed into the room. He ran around the table and landed on top of Benton, grabbing him by the shoulders. Trying to help pull him free, he pushed against Taft with his right foot.

In the same instant that Benton came free, crashing to the ground with one hand covered in blood as he held his open wound, Christopher lost his balance, falling forward. He caught his footing and kept from crashing into the chained zombie, but not before getting too close. His right hand grazed right past the creature's face as he caught his balance. The abrupt pain caught him off guard. The ghoul's putrid rot-filled teeth chomped down hard and landed a clean bite right down on Christopher's hand, between the thumb and his index finger. He pulled away, instantly covering his pained hand with his other, and stared in shock and disgust at the foul creature that had just taken a large chunk from him. "You stupid fuck!" Christopher shouted, as he spit into the zombie's face.

He instantly thought of Benton and looked back, but didn't see him. Only a thick trail of blood littered across the tile floor suggested his whereabouts. The door to the lab was wide open. The bloody trail disappeared out of the room and around the corner into the hall. "You have got to be fucking kidding me, Benton," he said whispering to himself. "There's no way in hell I'm going to turn into one of those things!"

Christopher calmly sat at the table doing what he could to stop the bleeding on his hand and began to gather up the materials he needed to give himself a shot. He sure as hell hoped it would do the trick. It just had to.

8

"What the hell do you mean she committed treason?" Rob Foster said.

"That is exactly what I said. You better watch your mouth, boy. Remember who you're speaking to," General Baker said.

The two men had been going at it in the General's office for several minutes now and Foster was having enough of it. The General had lost it and there was no getting through to him. "I'm sure she had her reasons for doing what she did, sir, but that's no grounds for throwing her in a cell. And the civilians are there with her, I take it?"

"They are. They are going to stay there until the bombers come in and clear up on Monday. As far as your little girlfriend, you can just forget about her. She isn't going anywhere either," General Baker argued.

"The bombers aren't going to destroy the base," Foster said.

"I've learned different. Of course, the officers will leave before it happens. Consider yourself lucky."

"That's murder! I can't believe you'd go along with this." Foster's face was getting redder by the minute.

The intrusive chime of Foster's radio caught both men by surprise.

"Lieutenant, come in. Over," the voice said, echoing with static, clipped to Foster's hip.

Foster eyed General Baker with a glare of frustrated rage. Removing the large handset, he took gaze away from Baker, looking out between the blinds of the office window. "Go ahead. Over."

"We have some activity at the main gate, sir, thought you might like to be informed. Over," came the voice from the other end.

"What kind of activity? Over." The two disgruntled men eyed one another again, but this time with curious glances.

"A small truck, sir. Civilian. Over."

"What's it doing? Over."

"That's just it, sir, nothing at the moment. They're just sitting out there in plain view. I think they want us to see them. Over."

*

The small Chevy sat quietly idling in the middle of the street about a mile and a half from the main gate. The front of the military base was overrun with the walking dead. The entire fence line was crawling with them, especially so at the gate's entrance. The rotting corpses shambled forward, ten and fifteen bodies deep, right where the survivors planned to get into the safe zone. The entrance was blocked. A few straggler ghouls lingered farther out into the streets and the surrounding fence line, but for the most part, they were heavily concentrated on getting past that gate to the fresh meat. The stench was unbearable. It wafted into the air, replacing the breeze's summer aroma with something foul and decaying. From as far off as the truck sat, they could see the buzzing of flies over the heads of the dead.

*

"Holy hell, there are so many of them," Victor said, sitting in the driver's seat, with Ashley seated next to him.

"It must be all of the activity that excites them. The outgoing and incoming helicopters generally pass over this part of the fence line every day. It must be drawing them in," Ashley said, eyes fixed on the obstacle ahead.

"So, what's the plan exactly? I don't imagine we're going to be able to just mosey on up there and ring the bell to get in," Victor said, throwing a hand up from the steering wheel in defeat. "I vote we just plow through the son-of-a bitches and hit the fence."

"Are you insane? Like that is going to work!" Ashley said.

"Do you have a better idea, lady?"

"If I had my radio, we could call in and get them to let us in and—"

Victor said, "But you don't and you can't just shit one."

*

Back at the gate, General Baker and Lieutenant Rob Foster rolled up in a small base truck. Its framework was very similar to a golf cart but with a lot of upgraded modifications and off-road abilities.

Parking the cart a good distance away from the actual entrance, the two men hopped out. They briskly walked toward the gate. On the opposite side stood hundreds of the undead. They clawed, moaned, gnashed, and spit, violently shaking the chain link as the two men drew closer.

Baker pulled a hanky from his front pocket and used it to cover his mouth and nose with one hand.

Foster followed suit, using the crevice of his elbow to cover his nose and mouth as they moved forward.

Haunting dread overcame Foster with each step toward the small spiral staircase. All eyes were on him and that made him uneasy. The idea that the only thing keeping a massive mob of cannibals from tearing into him and taking him apart to the bone was nothing more than some wire and hollow pipe. He did his best to keep his head down. Focused on his boots, one foot in front of the other, he still couldn't help but feel the ghostly stare of an endless sea of eyes piercing at him. He didn't like it one bit.

Before he realized it, he was right beside Baker at the top of the guard tower overhanging the gate's entrance. The view was terrifying. Their numbers had almost tripled since the last time he had to stand on this very ledge. Most towers were manned by three guards at all times, surrounding the entire base. With this being the most active, and most importantly, weak point of their military compound, there was always at least five people on watch at a time. This was something Baker insisted on for safety measures, once the crowd became too large. The guards on duty had only two jobs when on watch. One was to thin things out when needed and to sound the alarm if something were ever to go wrong. Roughly once a day, the guards would flip a coin. The winner of this toss was given the honor of stepping behind the mounted .50 caliber machine gun. This massive gun ripped six-inch bullets in rapid succession of pure power, a true man's toy.

Overlooking the fence line of walkers and death beyond death, a sea of carnage and revulsion overcame the naked eye. Severed limbs and puddles of dried blood littered the street. The horrific damage that the .50-cal. had bestowed upon the lingering creatures over the course of a few days beset the pavement below.

Foster looked up from his boots, not wanting to look out at the putrid sight. Beside him, Baker stood, already wielding a pair of binoculars. With both hands up to his face, Baker silently looked out past the massive horde of undead. After a moment, he jerked them from his face and looked at the guard closest to him.

With a stern voice and stiff posture, he said, "How long have they been sitting here, Private?"

"I don't know, sir. Not long, sir." The young man stood beside him at parade rest, looking out past the hungry mob, both hands behind his back.

Baker tossed the binoculars back up for a second. "Nothing to see here. Whoever's in there is probably infected."

"How are we going to let them in? That truck would flip before it got halfway to the gate trying to get past that many bodies," Foster said sounding concerned.

"The hell with them!" General Baker said. He spit over the edge of the tower's ledge before pulling away from the railing. The spit slid across the wind on its descent, landing over a small cluster of the undead trying to get in. They didn't notice when the slime misted them from above. They just pressed on with their moans and howling, wanting to get to what lay beyond the blockade.

"What? You can't just leave them out there to die," Foster argued.

Baker pushed passed the Lieutenant toward the stairs. As he started to descend the first set of steps, he shouted out one last order before disappearing below, "If they try anything stupid, gun them down!"

Foster stood atop the guard tower, watching as the General drove away without him, most likely headed back to the peace and quiet of his tranquil little office.

"Fuck dude, I would take a bullet, sure as shit, before I risked getting eaten the fuck alive," one of the guards said leaning against the .50 caliber machinegun.

Suddenly, one of the other guards with a thick dark mustache pointed out past the mob at the truck. "Look, they're moving!"

*

"We're going to die right here, right now..." Victor said in a low voice. His bottom lip began to quiver, and a tear formed in his left eye and slowly trailed down his cheek. Abruptly, he shouted, "No!"

With the Chevy in reverse, Victor stepped on the gas taking off down the street. Kieta had been sitting up when he took off, sending her off-balance and almost tumbling out the bed onto the street.

"What are you doing, Victor?" Ashley asked.

"What else is there to do, woman? We don't have much gas left as it is, and there is nowhere else to go. You said so yourself, that we've been quarantined. We're out of options, and I'm getting us onto that base!"

Victor instantly hit the brakes causing the truck to shake violently.

Kieta screamed, banging on the sliding glass window, and trying to keep her balance. Next to her, Jenny, was still just as out of it as ever. She wasn't sure that the little girl was ever going to come back. With that stupid grin, the girl just stared off at the road behind them, dead to the world around her.

Without giving an answer, and ignoring both Kieta and his passenger, Victor slammed his foot on the gas to the floorboard. The vehicle quickly picked up speed heading straight for the massive crowd of dead walkers and the gate's entrance.

*

"Holy shit, they're actually gunning for it. Can you believe that?" one guard said.

The five men jumped up and immediately started playing *rock-paper-scissors*. One after another, each soldier booed at their loss and stepped aside.

"What do you think you're doing? Those are innocent people down there. You can't just gun them down like murderers!" Lieutenant Rob Foster scowled and pointed a finger at them.

"Orders are orders," the man with the mustache calmly said. "Besides, we'll be doing them a favor."

*

"Victor, are you insane?" Ashley screamed in the passenger seat as the car sped out of control toward the horde of undead cannibals.

"It's our only chance…our *only* chance," Victor said, his voice shook with desperation. Wide eyes bulged on his terror-stricken face.

She reached up at the wheel trying to take control, but he was too strong for her. With the engine at full acceleration, the truck reached nearly 70 mph in the short distance. When the truck reached the first few zombies, it mowed them over with ease. Blood sprayed across the windshield, and the truck shook violently upon impact.

But as the mass of dead grew under the wheels, the truck stopped almost dead in its tracks. Not wearing their seatbelts, both Victor and Ashley flew forward—Ashley slamming into the dash. The fence bulged where the truck pinned a large number of ghouls. Automatic gunfire rattled—hot lead rained down.

Ashley was only out for a few seconds. When she came to, her head throbbed, and she was disorientated. She looked in the truck's bed. Kieta was gone! Frantic and shaken, Ashley scanned the surroundings, unable to focus because of the chaos around her. The windshield was busted, and Victor was knocked unconscious.

She looked in front and saw Kieta lying on the hood of the truck. Her eyes were open, glassy, and stared off into infinity. Her blood was everywhere. Zombies stood over her corpse and began feeding on her flesh. Bullets ripped through the sky and the ground around them. With the blood and bones shredding from pregnant woman's limbs, Ashley watched as the horde of ghouls reached deep into Kieta's swollen belly and gorged on her from the inside out.

Ashley looked away, instantly throwing up. Loud thuds echoed out around her in succession.

On each side of the truck, zombies pressed against the glass—pushing and pulling to get in. Several zombies tried climbing over the hood into the cab from the opening in the broken windshield. Ashley instantly reacted, bringing up her M-4, and started unloading into the pressing mob.

Ashley suddenly remembered Jenny in the back and jerked her head around to look, fearing the worse, and knowing that she had likely been thrown out of the bed like Kieta. She was wrong. Ashley glanced back just in time to see three zombies pull the girl from the back of the truck. She watched as they each grabbed a limb and ripped the girl apart alive. Jenny didn't even scream. Ashley watched as the last bit of life left the little girl's body and that same blank stare gripped her face. She was gone. There was blood everywhere.

She looked back to the front of the truck and shot more of the oncoming attackers. She screamed but couldn't hear her own voice.

Instantly, Victor woke to the bedlam and destruction around him. He yelled and panicked. Before he was able to reach for the steering wheel, a swarm of bullets cleaved through him from the guard tower. He shuddered as the volley of bullets pelted his body. Blood and flesh splattered inside the truck, coating Ashley with a thick spray of Victor's remains.

Had it not been for the sudden explosion that ruptured the hood of the truck right in front of her, she might have totally lost it. The engine sputtered as a shower of .50-cal rounds fell on the front of the truck. All hope was lost. She took in her surroundings one last time. The Chevy was completely consumed by the living dead. She couldn't see past them in any direction. They pushed and pulled at the large metal structure with her trapped inside. The little bit of truck frame she could see buried beneath rotting arms and hands was a total bloodbath.

"I'm not going to die like this!" She grimaced, throwing the empty M-4 out at the crowd at the front of the truck.

She grabbed the steering wheel of the truck, even though there was now gaping holes with billowing smoke coming out from under the hood. She kicked Victor's leg out of her way and pressed down on the gas with her left foot. Despite the oversize bullet holes and ungodly amount of damage, the truck managed to inch forward with sputtering steam billowing out from hood. The truck sounded like tin pots clattering together. The crowd of undead creatures around the truck shifted to the sides as the truck pushed onward through the hungry mob at a slow crawl. With a good dozen between the truck and the gate, the truck pressed forward, packing them in like a can of sardines between the fence and the sputtering grill.

The gunner behind the .50-cal realigned his aim and let a torrent of six-inch ammunition careen down on the passenger seat, the gunner swiveling left and right.

With only a few feet between the front bumper of the truck and the fence line, the truck stopped. Ashley was dead.

*

Up in the guard tower, Foster looked on in horror at the tragic and gruesome events. He felt sick and lightheaded. Beside him, the gunner stepped down from the .50 caliber, with a big fat grin across his face, as if to have just gotten his first lay. "Now that's what I'm talking about!" he said.

Suddenly, loud screeching sounds of flexing metal echoed out from below the tower. All six men standing atop the tower quieted and looked down.

The pressure between the truck and the several pinned in ghouls was pushing the chain link away from its post. From the ground up, the men watched as the fence line folded up in one place, the caged zombies falling in with it as it collapsed.

DESTRUCTION

1

The second the fence line was breached by the first zombie, Rob Foster had bolted down the staircase of the guard tower, leaving the five defending soldiers to their impending doom. With one man strapped to the .50-cal and the other four clinging to their rifles and handguns, they hurled curses at the fleeing officer.

The soldiers momentarily watched as Foster dashed past the first set of buildings, headed out onto the landing field. Wherever he was going, he was definitely in a hurry. The guy must have just flipped, they had said. Some people just are not cut out for a real war. Beyond that, they watched until he was clear out of sight, and then focused on the task at hand, staying alive and calling for support.

One of the five soldiers jumped on the horn, sounded the alarms, and radioed to the General with news of the break in. With reinforcements on their way, the men leaned over the high ledges, taking out as many undead as possible. This had gone on for what had seemed like a long time, and the cavalry still hadn't shown up.

Within moments of the fence giving way, over a dozen zombies fell into the military base's protected zone, having been pressed and pushed in by the hundreds that waited in the streets. Zombie after zombie fell into the opening on the fallen fence line, each one slowly making the hole grow, inch by inch. The wire lining on the fence gave more and more as it unraveled at the bottom.

Even with the .50-cal in full tilt and blasting out endless rounds of rapid fire, the two other soldiers with their M-4s set to full auto, and the fourth gunner popping singles from his pistol, they just kept coming. No amount of gunfire was going to stop a mob of this magnitude. It was an endless tidal wave of rot and pestilence in the form of maggot-filled decay. The stench smelled so wretched that, while in mid-succession, Corporal Swift literally blew chunks all over himself while running the .50-cal. He didn't let it stop him, however, as he relentlessly kept that massive gun going, watching as every single six-inch bullet ripped a gaping hole in the side of torsos and exploded moist, putrid heads. The rank decay, amazingly still, overpowered the smell of vomit sitting in the soldier's lap and running down his shirt. He just kept shooting. They all did.

The fifth guard on duty did little to hinder the incoming mob as they flowed into the base past the fence line like water through a strainer. He sat crouched down out of sight. Having already pissed his pants, the soldier wept uncontrollably. He had given up in the face of overwhelming odds.

The men in the guard tower could do nothing but watch as the zombies staggered past, farther into the military base.

"Fire in the hole!" one soldier yelled.

They all stopped firing for a second and watched the grenade land in the center of the massive horde of ghouls pressing forward on the outside of the fence line.

For a split second, the grenade's detonation had created at least an eight-foot hole in the mob. As quickly as the men had jumped to their feet to see, the blood and guts of that eight-foot radius quickly became swallowed up. The dead were on the march and nothing was going to stop them.

Corporal Swift squeezed the .50-cal's trigger; nothing happened. He leaped from his position behind the monstrous gun. "Gun's jammed! Get over here, Paterson. I need your help," he shouted, over the sounds of two M-4s.

Private Paterson looked like he was seasick on the deck of a boat.

Swift shouted, "I said get over here and give me a fucking hand, Paterson!" He struggled to eject a spent casing.

Paterson glanced between Swift, the machinegun, and the staircase leading down from the guard tower. He retrieved his 9mm from its holster and moved forward.

"About time, Paterson," the Corporal said.

Private Paterson dashed toward the steps and descending down them faster than Swift could react.

"That stupid prick," the Corporal said in a low voice, finally un-jamming the empty shell from the mechanism.

Near the bottom of the steps, Paterson froze. Two zombies had made their way up the first three steps. Easily a dozen more followed behind them. In a panic, Paterson slowly backpedaled up the steps. The gun in his hand shook. He slowly lifted the weapon while in reverse. His first shot was a miss. In a frenzy, he emptied the rest of the magazine into the ascending creatures. In a matter of moments, the gun clicked empty. Not a single zombie fell to the ground with a fatal hit. Bullets punctured arteries, lungs, and the like, sending small splats of blood out with each piercing blow. However, not a single shot went above the shoulder.

As the zombies took each slow staggering step up the stairway, Paterson fumbled with reloading the pistol, his breathing laced with excited gasps.

The first of several zombies climbing the steps was missing its lower jaw. Red, black, and gray mess covered the exposed mouth and neck. Its tongue hung out, wildly moving about. Its hair had once been long. The front of its head was scalped to the bone, leaving chunks of hair falling to its shoulders on each side.

The dead woman following close behind was only recognizable as a female because her top section was bare. With her face torn and chewed away, she slumped heavily over to one side. Having one arm freely swaying at the hip, her other arm reached out toward Paterson. The drooling moan that proceeded from her mouth hissed and bubbled with reddish-gray matter liquid pouring from her torn throat down her bare chest. Several ribs were bursting from her side. They looked cracked as they bounced about with each looming step she took toward the tower.

The other zombies that followed climbed the steps and crowded around at the bottom of the staircase pressing to get in on the action.

The guard tower was surrounded. More and more shuffled into view from farther out in the streets, from every direction.

"Shit!" The creatures were getting too close now, and Private Paterson was still struggling to slam the full magazine into the 9mm. In a raged lack of self-control, he threw the magazine at the oncoming mob as hard as he could. It flew through the air, crashing into the face of the first zombie. The zombie's jawless face caved in at the nose, spewing out dark fluids. Despite the new injury, the undead ghoul didn't waver. The creature kept coming, the others in tow.

Paterson calmly holstered the pistol and dashed up the final few steps, back into the guard tower. Corporal Swift and the other men had relentlessly kept at it. Paterson walked into practically the same setting as before. No one had moved positions, firing everything they had into the crowd of zombies below.

Blood and splattered remains lay in every direction. Undead bodies jerked and convulsed violently as bullets zipped through the air from above. As one zombie dropped, two more took their place.

Paterson watched as Swift sat behind the sights of the machinegun, laughing his head off. The other men had become similarly unhinged.

Paterson stepped up from behind one of the soldiers wielding an M-4 and removed their sidearm. The man didn't even seem to notice. He just steadily focused on the ground below, only stopping to reload, when needed.

With the fresh weapon, Paterson flipped around facing the staircase again. He could see the head of the first few zombies peeking up from the open pathway into the compromised sanctuary. He aimed the gun, waiting for the creatures to draw even closer before firing. He wasn't going to miss. This time, it was going to be all headshots. He wouldn't make that mistake again.

He fired a single shot from the pistol, its pop not even heard in the onslaught of fire around him. The hit was dead center to the brain. He hadn't missed and hadn't intended to.

Suddenly, pulling the gun to his head, he pulled the trigger. The shot sent skull fragments and pinkish red chunks into the air from the side of Paterson's head. Before the first bit of it splattered to the floor, his lifeless body fell back, toppling over the side of the tower railing. His dead body crashed onto the top of the fence before limply flipping over it and into the horde below. Instantly, his body disappeared under a swarm of undead creatures. Hunched over to gladly stop and feast, they feverishly tore him apart in seconds, devouring his remains.

Not one of the soldiers had let their fallen comrade distract them, or the mob of zombies filing in on them from behind, for that matter. With their focus solely on what gathered below, the dozen of more undead monsters that had made their way up the steps crept in, uninvited and unnoticed.

From behind, three zombies instantly came down on Swift and his men. Swift was still holding tight to the trigger of the .50 caliber machinegun, bullets wildly spraying out into the sky as he lost control. Still laughing uncontrollably unto death, the three zombies fell on him with open mouths. One of them landed its teeth into his exposed forearm, and another one bit into his throat—both pulling away chunks of the dying man's bleeding muscle and skin. The jawless ghoul hovered over him, sinking its top teeth deep into Swift's skull. The bone easily cracked open, caving in with the intense pressure. Blood poured out around the wound, sending it down the front of his face and onto his vomit-stained shirt. With eyes fixed open, the man was dead, and so were his fellow soldiers.

*

With the tower compromised, the dead feasted freely; others made their way farther and farther into the confines of the once-fortified military base.

In the distance, a dozen Humvee's rolled up, lining a defensive perimeter. Along with the loads of soldiers falling into line from each Humvee, every man and woman, soldier or not, filed out into the parking lot at the front of the military base. Men and women wielding various types of guns poured out of buildings in every direction to meet the line of Humvees. Within a matter of minutes, the very large lot overlooking the front entrance to the base was lined with several hundred soldiers, scientists, custodians, and cooks. Each person armed and ready to fight the horde of undead staggering toward them.

Having dealt with his fair share of battle, General Baker, along with two other commanding officers, quickly setup a human shield the length of a football field. They sat in the security of a lone Humvee set at the back of the line. Like the cowards they were, Baker barked out orders from an amplified speaker. With Baker in the passenger seat of the Humvee holding the microphone to his lips, he safely gave out orders to the line.

"Everyone prepare for battle! We're doing this *old school*, boys and girls. Musket style," he shouted, the static popping in his voice over the speaker. "Check your weapons. Safety off. First line fire until you run out, then fall to the back of the line leading in the next set of shooters. Do I make myself clear?"

A small spark of prattle echoed out amongst the men and women.

"I want a steady stream of fire at all times. Keep it focused, headshots! Repeat, headshots only."

The overwhelmingly large mob of zombies creeping forward steadily drew closer. From the line, their numbers seemed unending.

When the soldiers in the guard tower had called in the breach, General Baker took immediate action. Having been aware that this was an inevitable possibility, due to the amount of in and out traffic the extraction teams had been doing, Baker took it upon himself as leader to run several drills related to the potential scenario. With his mouth to the microphone and the full base at his command, it had paid off. He sat there for a second, taking in the accomplishment, mostly proud of great job and teamwork of those around him. He felt like a leader.

The final stand was at hand. Who would be the victor? Baker, for one, felt rather cocky about it.

*

From overhead, a lone helicopter flew across the swarm of countless dead entering the facility. Passing them from above, the passengers and pilot watched in horror as the base was overrun. Past the fence line and before the landing zone, the outlandishly large firing line of soldiers came into view. The dead were heading right toward them.

"Holy hell! This can't be good," Clay said holding onto the safety rail of the chopper as they passed overhead.

Gus just looked down in awe, speechless.

"What are we going to do, man?" Clay asked.

"Refuel and get the hell out is my vote!" Watts chimed in as he readied to land a little way off from the waging war at the entrance. His target, the landing field nearly center of the base its self.

2

Within the poorly lit set of holding cells, Gibbs and the others waited, quietly lost in their thoughts and hopes. It had been quite some time since the obnoxious group of soldiers had barged in, leaving the ragtag collection of civilians to their boundaries and bars.

Kent sat at the edge of the cell's bed toying with the broken glasses. Utterly beyond repair, he twisted and bent them in an attempt to fix the unfixable.

Eric wasn't doing so well. Seated on the cement floor, Eric was short of breath and felt as if he might be on the verge of passing out. He eased his head to the floor and laid down. The cold floor felt good against his otherwise burning skin.

Cynthia sat on the bed with her feet up and her knees to her chest.

With her face buried in her knees and her arms tightly wrapped around her legs, Gibbs was unsure if the red-headed lady was asleep or not. How anyone could fall asleep in that position was beyond her. Gibbs quietly paced back and forth in the little space still barefoot. Her shoes and jacket still lay neatly placed on the edge of the bed next to her cellmate.

Eric's condition was getting worse. The fungus growth had accelerated around his hand. Ghostly white skin crept from underneath the bandaged. Red specks had started to form around the wound.

Parasitoid spores, thought Gibbs.

Dark circles formed around his eyes, and he had complained of lightheadedness in the last hour. All she could do was sit back and watch.

From the look of things, everyone else in the makeshift warehouse was oblivious to the young man's rapidly growing condition.

She huffed a deep sigh, cutting a sharp turn making her way across the cell for the hundredth time. Biting hard on her thumbnail, the cell walls felt like they were closing in on her.

Billy was still dead asleep. George was on his feet. Holding onto the metal bars, George gazed off across the room at the building's entrance. His mind wandered between here and the *what if* of possibilities. Why had they been put in here in the first place? He had hoped to speak with the General by now, and his mind played out almost any and every possible scenario that could have happened. His mind was currently busy playing out one of those scenarios. Some of them ended with him and a group of soldiers searching the coastline for his boy. Others ended with his son bursting into the General's office and rushing in. The sweet embrace would cut the two men's conversation off in mid-sentence. The scenario he was currently fixed on, however, wasn't quite as hopeful. It was just him and his son standing in a room. Tyler was dead, but not. The decay-ridden teen shambled eagerly toward George, with his arms outstretched. This sweet embrace, however, would not be so sweet. The young man loomed over George as he crept closer, with eyes wide and teeth showing. It was terrifying, terrifying to have finally found his boy and know that it was too late. He had turned into one of those dreadful monsters. George just stood there defenseless and weak. He felt too weak and too ashamed to move. How could he have let this happen to his only child? He wept with both hands covering his face. He could look on his dead son no more. And if it hadn't been for—

"What's wrong, dude? Eric... Eric... Wake up." Kent positioned himself over Eric shoving the unconscious cellmate on the shoulder.

George instantly snapped out of his fantasy nightmare and turned to see what the commotion was about. In the cell next to him, Kent was hovering over Eric who lay passed out on the floor. Cynthia and Dr. Gibbs both stood holding onto bars looking in.

"He's not breathing," Kent said. "What the hell do I do?" Leaned over with one knee to the ground, he pressed his fingers to the base of Eric's neck. "I don't know if I'm doing this right! Shit, what's wrong with him?"

"He's turning," Gibbs said, sounding unsurprised.

"What? What the hell do you mean *he's turning*? I think he's dead, for Christ's sake!"

"You need to destroy the brain before he wakes up and attacks you, Kent. You have to destroy the brain," Gibbs said.

"Are you out of your fucking mind? He isn't one of them. I'm not just going to kill him," Kent said, his eyebrows arched toward his hairline.

"What happened?" George said.

"I don't know. I just looked over and he wasn't breathing. I think he's dead, man," Kent said.

"Well, do *something*," Cynthia said with desperation in her voice.

"Oh, and what am I supposed to do? I'm stuck in a holding cell for crying out loud!" Kent said.

Billy was awake now.

The ruckus stirred him from a deep sleep of candied dreams and cotton clouds. Startled from his peaceful slumber into the consistently recurring nightmare, Billy was still dazed as he sat up. His eyes tried focusing but had trouble. Between the racket and eye crust, Billy sat at the edge of his bed trying to figure out what was happening. As his eyes focused, he could see that everyone else was occupied with whatever was happening in the middle cell of the room. Billy looked over tilting his head to see around George and could see that Kent looked like he was helping Eric to his feet. He must have fallen over.

"Kent, look out!" George shouted.

Eric opened his eyes and sprung from the sitting position. His skin was pale and dry, his eyes glossed over and milky-white. His jaw dropped opened as if he were about to take a bite of air.

"Oh, shit," Kent said as he fell back on his bottom, landing atop his already broken glasses. His head smashed into the bars behind him. A little dazed, but not disoriented, Kent shot to his feet.

Eric slowly rose from the bed. Death had taken him. Something else had taken over his body and was now in control.

Eric was no longer *Eric*.

With both hands raised toward Kent as it ambled toward him, Kent leaped forward, shoving the zombie away from him with the heel of his shoe. The reanimated corpse fell backward, crashing into the toilet. It awkwardly flapped its limbs as it tried pulling itself up. Kent spastically looked around for a weapon, anything he could use to defend himself. There was nothing. The makeshift warehouse of cells was bare and empty. Frantically, trying to come up with a plan while blocking out the chaotic cries of the people around him, Kent watched Eric stagger to his feet again.

Kent's mind instantly flashed to the underground shelter and the legs that Eric had broken off the bed to use as a weapon. The zombie, with renewed balance, stepped forward. Kent caught eye contact with Cynthia and knew right away what needed to happen.

"Okay, here's the plan," Kent said as he struggled, pushing Eric's reanimated body away again. "You and the science chick get ready. I'm going to push him with his back against the cell wall. You two reach out and grab his arms and hold him there." Kent pushed the undead creature again. It staggered backward a few steps, but relentlessly pressed toward Kent.

"Yeah, but what are you—?"

Before Gibbs could spit it out, Kent grabbed the corpse by the shoulders, spun it to one side, and sent it crashing with its back against the metal bars. The two ladies reached out between the metal bars, grabbing hold of the dead teen's cold flesh. Cynthia had gotten a solid grip on Eric's upper arm by wedging her shoulder against the bars and throwing her arm out and around the zombie. Her other hand tightly gripped onto a loose portion of Eric's shirt.

Gibbs had grabbed the cold wrist of the zombie's arm with both hands. She held it firm and low at the hip. All she could think of was the infected bandages. With her hands only so far from the source of the infection, her hands were clasped around some of the red spots and puffy tissue. She started to panic.

As soon as Kent saw that the two women had a good hold on the attacking corpse, he instantly turned his back to them. Swiftly ripping off the bedding to the cell's bed frame, Kent hoped it would be just as easy as Eric had made it look back at the underground bunker.

The legs were bolted to the floor.

It was harder than it looked to keep a tight grip on Eric. With the zombie flailing its limbs, Cynthia had adjusted her grip twice already. The undead creature jerked violently against the bars trying to free its self. Its grunts and moans intensified. The more it was held against its will, with Kent so close in sight, the more irritated it became. It shook and yanked trying to get free.

The creature's right hand was suddenly freed and it flipped around, landing its disease-infested teeth into Cynthia's arm.

Gibbs had lost hold on the zombie's wrist, falling back onto the bed in her cell. Before she could leap back to her feet, it was too late. She looked up to see it.

Cynthia screamed. Its teeth fell down on her upper arm and went in deep. The pain felt slow and sharp, unbearable.

They watched in horror as Eric fell on her with his mouth wide open. The instant that its open mouth met with her flesh, Cynthia saw blood. Eric's teeth tore through the skin and meaty chunks of her muscle.

As zombie-Eric pulled away the massive chunk of flesh, Cynthia passed out from shock, falling to the floor inside her cell.

Gibbs sat frozen in place, playing back in her mind what went wrong. She looked down to see the blood spilling out on the floor around the red-headed woman. There was a lot of it and it just kept spreading.

The scream startled Kent from focus. He hadn't gotten the post free yet. With the legs bolted to the floor, it was a bit more difficult than last time. He jumped and turned around when Cynthia screamed.

Eric stood there before him, as if its undead mind was vacant of thought, blood dripped from its mouth as it chewed. With each bite more and more blood fell. The crimson spill stood out against his pale, cold skin.

"Eric…"

The undead ghoul tilted its neck, catching eye-to-eye contact with Kent. It stopped chewing and snarled. It opened its mouth wide, dropping a large chunk of flesh to the ground. Blood dripped heavily from its mouth, and its gaze went wide as it hissed.

"Oh shi—"

It leaped forward, falling on Kent, sending them both to the floor. Kent crashed onto the bed frame before wrestling the zombie to the ground.

Suddenly, the front door opened and the lights to the warehouse kicked on. The events that had unfolded in the last several minutes instantly became more apparent, no longer hidden in the shadows. There was blood everywhere. Cynthia still lay on the ground with large amounts of blood still flowing from her arm. Kent and his attacker wrestled on the floor. There was no way of telling if Kent had been bitten yet. There was just too much blood. One thing was for sure, he hadn't screamed out in pain, yet.

"Rob!" Gibbs shouted, pulled from her unconscious daze. She was unsure, at this point, if her mind was playing tricks on her or if he had actually just barged into the room.

Rob Foster had, indeed, just blow through the door and turned on the lights. Upon seeing the situation, he went straight for the desk drawers. "The keys—where are the keys?" Foster shouted, pulling each drawer out and rummaging through them.

Both Gibbs and George scanned the room with faces pressed against their cell bars but offered nothing.

Checking the last drawer and coming up empty handed, Forster was at a loss. The keys were nowhere to be found. He anxiously scanned the floor around the desk and the walls as well. Just like Gibbs and George, he had no clue.

The sounds of scuffling and wrestling had drastically changed to grunts and huffing. Kent lay still on his back. Straddling him at the knees, Eric's undead corpse hovered over him, feasting. The fight was over, and Kent lay motionless and blood covered. His eyes had frozen open, and terror remained on his face.

With Gibbs and George focused on what was taking place outside the cells, Billy watched in horror as Kent's dead eyes stared across to him. It was as if Kent was asking Billy to save him. Billy didn't want to look, but felt compelled, the image of Kent slowly being eaten, burning into the boy's mind forever.

Billy watched in disgust. The zombie reached down, sticking its hand near Kent's belly button. With the dead man's shirt already torn away, Billy watched as the creature's fingers pressed deeper and deeper into the want-to-be rock star's stomach. Slowly, the ghoul's ghastly fingers disappeared knuckle by knuckle. With the thick, wet sounds of ripping flesh and slopping organs, Eric's white, pale hand was suddenly sprayed with red up to the forearm. It suddenly came away with long, bloody organs. The streams of intestine and innards in Eric's grip came free as the creature lifted the putrid gunk to its festering mouth. Feasting on the remains of the fallen cellmate, the chomping and gnashing of body parts filled the small warehouse with a wet, horrifying sound.

Foster took a breath and looked around the room. With nothing to lose, he reached his hand under the desktop, below the drawer, and felt around. Metal against metal chimed briefly. His hand came back with keys on a ring.

3

As the chopper steadied on the ground, Gus and Clay stepped down from the platform to the earth. Clay nudged him on the shoulder and pointed.

When Gus looked up in the direction the young man had pointed, he immediately saw the concern. Wind whirled around them as Gus looked out, the three soldiers watched as a small group jogged in their direction from a small warehouse building in the distance.

With the engine off and the blades winding down, Clay was surprised to see Rob Foster in the lead. Dr. Gibbs was close behind. She was covered in blood. With them were two other people that Clay didn't recognize. An old man carrying a little boy laboring to keep pace with Foster.

"What happened?" Gus asked while readying his M-4 for battle.

"That doesn't matter right now. We need to leave!" Foster put his arm around Gibbs' shoulder.

"Can't right now. We need fuel. We saw a mass of zombies heading to the fuel pumps so I put us down here. There's a fuel storage drum in the hanger. We can swing by and pick up some juice," Gus said, slamming a fresh magazine into the rifle and racking the chamber.

Behind him, Clay was ahead of the game, pulling out the three five-gallon empty containers and passing one off to the pilot.

"The General has totally lost it," Foster said.

"Yeah, we figured that out. You aren't going to believe what we found out in Jacksonville. The General is—"

"Hey guys," the pilot said. "If we're going to get out of here in one piece, we need to move." He pointed in the direction they had come in. In the distance, past all the landing field's open space and between several buildings, a number of figures were piling up against a fence. The stagger in their step made it easy to tell that they were anything but friendlies. Their limp, swaying limbs and stiff postures marked them as the undead.

"Oh hell," Clay said with both hands tight around the containers, wishing he had a free hand for his sidearm. "I wonder how long that's gonna hold?"

"There's no way to know. That's a secondary fence, and it's not built as strong as the fence around the perimeter," Watts said. "Let's move now."

*

With Billy wrapped tight in George's arms, all six of them took off running for the hanger to fill the fuel containers for the helicopter. Out in the wide open of the landing field, George began to panic inside like he had never done before. He felt like the escape was going to go terribly wrong, and he couldn't do anything to stop it. He had watched Eric die and then turn, killing two other people *just like that*. What real chance did any of them have with the number of zombies heading their way?

His knees weakened as he thought of Tyler. The distance between him and the others slowly widened. He was running out of hope. What was the point of going on? Billy wasn't his to take care of. He had failed with Eric, and he had failed with his own son. There was no possible way he could bear the thought of messing things up for Billy. He slowed in mid-stride and looked down at the ground with Billy in his arms.

Gus said, "Come on, old timer. Don't quit on me now." He slowed his pace and waved George forward.

George looked deep into the massive man's eyes and instantly remembered the radio station, meeting Gus and the hope that he had felt. He looked past Gus. It wasn't that far to the hanger. Watts was already by the door and about to open it.

*

The hanger was a lot bigger on the inside than it had appeared. With its high arched ceiling and extended frame, the metal-aluminum warehouse held a few helicopters and a number of Humvees.

With the main drop doors closed, the small group had made their way in from one of the side doors.

"The fuel tank's all the way to the back," Watts called out.

The fuel tank was set next to a closed rear door, against a wall.

Once there, Watts, the pilot said, "There's a hand pump we can use. Clay, open that blue valve by the hose and put the nozzle in the first can."

Clay set his two containers by the fuel nozzle and quickly opened the valve.

Watts grabbed an eighteen-inch lever and pumped it back and forth. Fuel gushed into the container.

With Clay and the pilot on the platform steadily at work, Foster said to Gus, "Like I was saying, the General just lost it. He took Gibbs and the civilians you brought in and locked them away in the old holding cells we used to use back at the storage shed."

"That don't surprise me one bit," said Gus.

"What do you mean?"

"We got sent on the Jacksonville OP to go in and extract that Grech guy, and—"

"Wait, did you actually find Grech?" Gibbs said. She reached out and grabbed Gus' arm.

Gus continued, "Yeah, we found the old geezer, all right. The guy is definitely a nut-job for sure. Still, I trust him more than anyone else about the situation right now. Anyway, we get there right and you would never guess what we find."

"If you found him, then where the hell is he?" Gibbs asked.

"You going to let me tell my story or not, lady?" Gus grunted and swelled out his chest. "As I was saying. Sent there to get that science guy, right? We get there and find him. The old freak is hunkered down in lab monitoring the fucking world. Says the fungus crap, or plague thing, is spreading past the quarantine zone already. We sat there with the grease ball and watched some of what he swore up and down to be live footage of Atlanta."

"Outside of the dead zone," Gibbs said.

"Exactly. Grech has enough equipment down there to monitor the whole world, or so he says anyway," Gus said

"That means the blockades we had set up have failed," Foster said, staring off into space.

"And that isn't even the bad part," Gus said after a moment of silence. "Grech said the ones behind the whole thing is our very own government. He said they enlisted him and a team of scientists to work on the project for military gain."

"Oh, and you're just going to believe that horse shit?" Foster said.

"Yeah, actually I am. Like I said, the guy had the biggest sat-com system I've ever seen. He played back radio chatter between some of our people and who knows who else. That's how we found out General Baker has been kept in the dark about the real situation," Gus said.

"It's true," Clay said from the platform. Next to him, a five-gallon container was half-full and filling. The running fluid sloshed within the container.

Foster, George, and Gibbs looked back at Gus, as if questioning if he knew what he was talking about.

"Well, if Baker doesn't know what's going on, what does he believe and what is the truth?" Gibbs asked.

"That is what I was about to get to," Gus said. "Baker believes the airstrike comes in two days. He knows the base will be treated like any other infected area and will be bombed. But he plans on skipping out tomorrow. What he doesn't know is that the airstrike got pushed to sunup tomorrow. The government plans to kill everyone and leave no witnesses."

"That's ludicrous." Foster grimaced with disbelief.

"Foster, I know you don't want to believe this about Baker or our government. It's a hard pill to swallow. But it's true. We came back to warn everyone and to evacuate as many as we could. With the base overrun, looks like we're the only ones who'll have a chance," Gus said, his eyes widening.

Foster looked at the ground for a few dead moments. "How we coming, boy?" Foster said to Clay.

"Two down, one to go," Clay said.

"Grab one of those empties from over there. Let's take one extra one just for good measure," Gus ordered pointing at the stack of gasoline jugs in the corner.

*

Foster wasn't sure what to believe. One thing he knew, Baker had definitely become distant and was acting strange—stranger than normal. Then there was the incident with locking Gibbs away with the civilians.

After a moment when Foster hadn't spoken up, Gibbs said, "I believe you, Gus. What do we do?"

Gus looked up high to the large bay window overlooking the metal arch. The sun had gone down and it was getting dark, quickly. He glanced down at the watch on his wrist. "If what we heard is for real, I would guess we have something like ten hours or less before they start bombing. My vote is we make for Jacksonville again and get the hell underground with Grech. There's enough food and supplies to feed a small army down there."

Instantly, the reality of their situation crashed on Foster's shoulders. "Nukes."

"What?" Gibbs said.

"Nukes! Why else would Grech be held up underground with enough supplies to stay hidden away for so long? The bastard knew something like this was inevitable and prepared. He plans on holding out for a long fucking time, which tells me the bombers might be dropping nukes."

"The old geezer did mention something about having a few radiation suits on hand," Clay said. "But there's no way the President would allow nukes dropped on American soil. Radiation takes thousands of years to dissipate. Humans—all life would die."

"At this point, I don't know what our government is capable of. How do you know you can trust Grech?" Foster asked.

"We don't have any other choice other than to trust him. Besides, you got a better idea? I for one don't plan on moseying down to that battlefront to help out. I don't know how far the next safe zone is, and I'm not about to radio anyone to ask. We might be lied to or they might even send out a jet to prevent us from leaving the area once in the air," Gus said.

4

From the rooftop, he had watched as the war below raged on in a pure and violent fury of horror.

The massive line of soldiers let out an onslaught of relentless firepower. With over a hundred guns blasting in unison and a seemingly endless supply of ammunition for the various types of weaponry, the undead fell one after another. Shots pierced flesh and blew it to bits, cutting away tendons and rupturing ligaments, each met their end with the one shot that counted. Ears disappeared and necks busted, bleeding out with gaping holes. Teeth shattered as metal met bone flying through the air. Eyes ruptured in an explosive pop of pus, blood, grey matter, and meat. And still the dead inched forward, closing the gap between them and the poorly commanded band of soldiers. For every zombie that fell, five took its place, closing in inch by inch.

The war had been going on for what felt like well over half an hour. Little by little, they grew closer to the firing line, treading on fallen corpses as a stepping stool to reach their prey.

From the rooftop, he had also witnessed the unexpected. He watched as General L. S. Baker fled in secret. Once the firing started, which is what drew him to the roof to begin with, he watched as Baker and a few of his men quietly crept from one of the parked Humvees. With limited stealth and the torrent of endless gunfire covering his escape, Baker and his small posse of men skittered away unnoticed from the defending troops.

Baker and his group fled into a set of buildings not far from the commander's office. As he had sat on the rooftop watching this entire thing take place, he couldn't help but think that the General had simply left his cigars and scotch unattended and needed to get back to them before it was too late. The last thing the man needed on his hands was a guilty conscious. Leaving such nice commodities to waste away after the apocalypse unappreciated would have been the General's worst mistake. Baker couldn't have that, now could he?

In the end, he was glad to have made his way up there to witness these things. More important than the war waging and the General's lack of protocol, what made it all worth the while was seeing that chopper land. As it had flown overhead, his heart began to pound with a passion. He owed it to himself, and there was no denying him that. He watched as the three soldiers exited the helicopter. What was even more surprising was the bunch he witnessed running to the bird from the holding cells.

Through his binoculars, he witnessed it all.

He was somewhat surprised the group quickly broke for the hanger. Perhaps to get fuel? That was the most logical answer. But where to next?

Anywhere but here, he thought. *It has to be done. It has to be done.*

Looking back at the firefight below on the other side of the building, he couldn't blame them. It was only a matter of time before that line was overrun by the undead and devoured in a pool of relentless cannibalistic madness. He didn't even want to think of what would happen to him once that line did break and he was left helplessly trying to defend himself against hundreds and hundreds of the walking dead.

"I guess I better make it on that chopper if I want to have a chance," he had said from the rooftop of the barracks. "If anyone deserves retribution and to get out of this alive, it's me, but more so Megan *fucking* Linkouscie deserved it!"

It has to be done.

Luke Beal hurried his way to the ground and made it to the hanger. He followed the path Gus and his band of escapees took through the side door and figured to meet them any minute. The thought of running into Gus excited him, making him very happy he hadn't ended his life in that bathroom. Although he had come close, his finger on the trigger, Luke owed it to his lover to get even. Settle the score.

"Where the hell are you, Gus *the bus* Stanford?" Luke mumbled under his breath.

He leaned with his back to the wall, 9mm at the ready, safety off.

Gus was going to pay—pay with his life for what he did. He had killed his Megan in cold blood, and as a result, he was going to get what was coming to him. A bullet to the head, same as his true love had died, was the only proper justice that could be served. But not before taking him to the ground and having a few words of course. With sweat pouring down his brow, Luke stiffened his back, waiting for the moment. The anticipation grew within him, his heart beating faster and faster.

Thoughts of Megan flooded his mind. The images burned into his head with a fiery passion. Her tender kiss, sensual touch, that laugh, those eyes, it all just came crashing in. He quickly became lost in his dream of her.

They were sitting in the car at the edge of a dock watching the sea crash into the dock's edge. The birds and seagulls flew wildly around them. The wind smelled of salt, love, and the scent of her hair. Oh, her hair, it was like blueberries in the summer. His mind wandered to a meadow of wild berries ready to be plucked. He imagined the two of them dancing in the field of wild fruits picking and tasting the tart sensations of love and lust. Her hair blew freely in the wind. It would never do that again. She was gone and he was never going to get her back. He clenched the grip of his handgun cringing at the idea.

That man was going to pay!

It has to be done. It has to be done.

Suddenly, his mind was lost again in a dream-like state of past and hopeful futures never to come. Megan was holding their newborn child in her arms. She had just given birth and her cheeks swelled with pride while she held her baby in that hospital room. The baby was so beautiful and looked just like her mother. Her eyes and everything about her was exactly the same, innocent, pure, and thriving with life. Luke was holding her now. She was so small, so sweet.

Steps approached from the hanger. It was them. They were coming, and he was ready.

The voices rumbled in the distance, then became clearer. It was Gus, all right. His grip tightened on the pistol, his teeth clenched.

"—I'm telling you, the guy was nice, and I assure you he will accept us with open arms."

Someone else said something, but it was too hard to make out.

Another unfamiliar voice joined in with the other two. Luke cocked his head toward the door.

"Look, Foster, I know that this is hard for you. Yes, if the rest of the world is okay, then we're all in big trouble for abandoning ship, but who's to blame us? I don't want to try risking it out here.

I believe Gus and Clay. There is no one else. It's over. We need to think of ourselves and get somewhere that will give us the opportunity to start over. Regroup. And if we're wrong and this thing is contained, we will cross that bridge when we get there. We need to—"

"I get the point, George," Foster said. "I just don't like the idea of fleeing when there're people here that need our help."

"How the hell do you plan to help, Rob?" Gibbs said.

A moment of silence passed, and Luke knew that the instant was swiftly approaching. He readied, holding his breath, the sweat pouring out from his forehead down his head and onto his face. The perspiration of angst blotted itself along the underarm and chest of his shirt.

The doorknob jiggled. Luke leaned forward quietly on his toes, ready to spring at just the right moment.

The door swung open. Gus entered, the others following behind. Gus carried a five-gallon fuel container.

Luke brought up his pistol, his vision blurred from the sweat in his eyes, and he let the bullets fly.

The first shot went low. The next shot was a successful hit, puncturing Gus in the side. Two other shots were more focused and went higher, hitting the big man's collarbone and shoulder.

*

Wide-eyed with shock, Gus dropped the fuel at his side. The pain left him dizzy. Falling forward on one knee, he watched helplessly as Luke blocked the hallway with weapon drawn. He instantly knew what was happening and registered it for what it was. Luke's mind had snapped, much like a lot of others had done in the last few days. The last thing Gus heard before blacking out was the shouts and demands of Luke Beal waving his gun around. Gus fell face first to the floor, blood bucketing out from his wounds. A pool of crimson quickly formed around him as he lay there, unconsciously beginning to bleed out.

*

Luke stared for a moment at the big man lying on the floor. Justice was done. Just like that. Megan, though, was still gone.

He looked up in time to see Clay shoulder his rifle. Luke spun around and dove through a nearby office door.

A hail of fire rained down the hall.

Luke took refuge behind a desk, and the rifle's barrel poked in through the door. The contents of the room danced about in a wind of gunfire. Papers and office supplies popped and danced, the desk split and splintered.

Beside Clay, Watts and Rob Foster joined in with semi-automatic military issued handguns. They rained down terror on the room.

In the middle of the unwelcomed volley, Luke smiled in his victory. He got that son-of-a-bitch, *he did.*

It had to be done.

Luke reached his hand up over the desk and pointed the gun toward the door. He fired five shots without looking. The return fire ceased. Luke took the opportunity to make his last shot count. He jumped up for the briefest of moments and aimed before shooting the final shot. It blasted at head level, splitting a seam in the framework of the door. The shot missed Clay's head by only a millimeter.

And just like that, Luke was back down under his cover reloading as fast as he possibly could. Metal against metal sounded at the release of the empty magazine and a new one replaced it.

Instantly, Clay, Rob, and Watts unloaded a shower of gunfire at the desk. The desk ripped apart with the torrent of lead.

Again, Luke reached out taking shot after shot without looking, planning once more to take that final shot at the end. This time, he didn't plan to miss. He was better than that. He was a true marksman and there was no excuse for second shots.

*

Clay and the others jumped back clearing the doorway. They ducked low at each side of the door as the shots rang out. Clay glanced across at Rob and grimaced.

Foster said, "Do you—?" He stopped midsentence when Clay brought up a grenade in his hand.

Clay motioned for them to get Gus. When they left, he chucked the grenade into the room, right on top of the gunner's desk. Clay slammed the door closed and sped off.

The explosion was big, despite being behind a wall.

"Let's get Gus and get out of here!" Clay said and shouldered his rifle.

Gus felt like he weighed as much as a bus, Clay thought as he, Foster, and George dragged the unconscious, but still breathing man, down the hall.

"Shit," Foster complained as he stumbled forward.

"He's too heavy," George said.

Gibbs set Billy to the side and ran in to help. Together they struggled, but managed to get him moved. Gus' torso was covered in blood, and a huge trail of what he had already lost smeared the floor as they dragged him in.

"Who was that trying to kill us?" George asked.

"Didn't get a good look. Doesn't matter. That guy has got to be in a million bits by now," Clay said. "Guys, let's stop. We need to check on Gus." In his haste to escape, Clay had refused to consider his teammate might be dead. Now, with the chance to escape, they didn't need to carry out a dead man with them if that was the case.

Everyone looked down at the immobile Mr. Stanford. Silence filled the small space as they all just stared.

*

Foster knew who had fired on Gus Stanford. Gus had made himself very clear about Luke's behavior after losing Megan. This couldn't have been anything but revenge. There was no point in telling the others. He never saw reason to provide useless information, and right now, it was definitely useless. He was still beside himself and a little on the shocked side to see that Luke had actually taken it this far. It wasn't Gus' fault Megan got bit. She had to be shot—she was already dead.

Gathered closer and still trying to piece together what had just taken place, Dr. Gibbs reached up and checked for a pulse. He had one. "He's still alive," she said with a heave of surprise. "Flip him over!"

Between Clay, Rob, and George, they managed to get him on his back. "I think it's bad. We won't know until I can examine him. We need to get him to the med station. It'll have everything we need that might save him."

Watts raised his hand. "We're crunched for time. Our best chance to make it out of here is to leave now."

Gibbs said, "Leaving him is just like killing him. Do you want to be responsible for that?"

Watts looked down and bit his lip. "How do we get him to the med station? The guy must way a ton."

Foster said, "There're pull carts in the hanger. I'll go get one." He sped out the door and shortly returned with an oil-stained yellow cart with big air filled tires. "It's a little small, but he'll fit on it." He let the cart's handle drop as he came to a stop. "Help me get him on here."

The four of them managed to lift Gus high enough to lay him on the cart. Gus' feet hung off the end, but at least didn't touch the floor.

"You guys bring him to medical. I'm going to fuel up the bird and check things out. We've lost a lot of time," Watts said.

Foster said, "Clay and I can handle Gus. George, I want you to go with him. You'll need to carry the other two fuel containers."

George nodded.

The two men grabbed two fuel containers each and turned to leave the hallway.

George stopped and looked back.

Gibbs said, "Billy will be fine, George. He's with me. Just go! Get the chopper ready to fly and then meet us at medical. And for the love of God, don't leave without us," she said, turning narrowed eyes at Watts.

George nodded, and the two men headed out.

5

Foster set the cart's handle down as he opened the door to the outside. Nothing presented itself as an immediate threat—just as he had hoped. He couldn't see the lab from the door, but knew it wasn't too far away. "We're good to go."

One thing they did have on their side was the dark. Foster and the others quietly crept through the night shrouded in darkness. In the distance, the sound of waging war carried on. Firepower had diminished, and screams and cries of unrelenting agony floated in the mix.

Clay said, "The guns sound closer. The firing line is in retreat." He pushed the back of the cart while Foster pulled and steered.

Shots rose from the roof of a nearby building.

"We're almost there," Foster said. "It's the next building over—we just have to cross the parking lot."

With renewed vigor, Foster and Clay had the cart rolling faster.

Gibbs and Billy kept silent as they followed.

Foster looked back at Clay and saw the chopper was a little ways off to their left. Two figures left the rear of the chopper and jogged their way. They closed the distance by the time Foster and crew made it to the lab entrance.

"The bird's filled. We're ready," Watts said and heaved for breath.

George rested his hands on his thighs and fought to catch air.

"We need to get to medical. He's lost enough blood. Let's move," Foster said.

Watts opened the door, and the race was on down the hall.

Gus was in a bad way. Blood trailed behind the cart, evident now in the hall's light. Though he had been unconscious since they left the hanger, he opened his eyes and let out a ferocious cough.

"You do realize there are other people here that can fly a helicopter, right?" Watts said.

"He's right," Clay agreed. "We can't just leave the bird unattended. Someone might highjack it from us."

Foster slowed to a halt and looked around. Looking down at Gus then back up at Gibbs, his blank stare told everyone he didn't know what to do.

Before he could say anything, Gibbs said, "No. I refuse to leave him here, Rob. I can save him. I know I can. It will just take some time."

"What kind of time?"

"I'm not leaving him Rob, and that's that," she said.

Foster thought a moment, and said to Watts, "Go back to the bird. Can you drop it on the roof of the building?"

"Yeah, sure thing!"

"You'll wait for us, won't you?" Foster asked.

A moment of silence passed between them, Foster locking gazes with Watts. "Can I count on you?"

"Yes… yes you can count on me. What is it with you people not trusting me? I'm a soldier, for Christ's sake."

"You cheat at poker," Clay said.

"Well, fuck me," Watts said and raised his upper lip. "This is life and death, man. It ain't the same."

"Okay, go. And don't let anyone take our bird for anything." Foster nodded to Watts.

He turned and headed back out the lab.

"Do you think he's going to wait for us?" George asked.

"I sure as hell hope so," Foster said.

Foster and Clay had Gus rolling again, and after a few turns down the hall, they came to the med center and dashed into the first operating room.

"Put him over there. Get the light," Gibbs said as she ran to the sink and started washing her hands.

George turned on the light. Looking around the white room, he realized that it was just him and Billy now. Cynthia was gone, Seth too, Eric had turned, and Kent—it was awful what happened to him. George stood there thinking of everyone and everything he had lost in such a short period of time. His mind raced with the incident in the bus on the way to the base and how that poor girl died after Willy jumped her unexpectedly. And Tyler, what had happened to Tyler? What was going to happen to them now? He had a bad feeling in his gut, and it was telling him the worst wasn't quite over yet.

"Give us a hand!" Foster called out.

George snapped out of it, stepping over to help get Gus up on the operating table. On the count of three, the three men heaved the nearly three-hundred-pound man onto the metal table in the center of the room.

"I need you to cut his shirt off and loosen his belt straps," Gibbs said as she frantically gathered supplies. "As long as his lung isn't punctured and he didn't take a vital hit, he'll be fine. We just need to stop the bleeding and remove any fragments."

After removing the shirt and loosening the belt like Gibbs had asked, Foster stood back taking in the room for the first time. He hadn't noticed it at first because it was dark and Gus was bleeding out pretty bad, but the tile floor had a thick trail leading to the door that couldn't have been that of the man currently laid up on the table. This blood was dried and clotted. It looked as if it had been in that spot for at least a few hours by now. Looking up and following the darker trail of blood that led past the backside of the table, Foster's eyes fell upon Professor Taft. The zombie had eaten both forearms and had broken free of his bonds. Foster instantly retrieved his 9mm from its holster and aimed it at the zombie's head.

Clay started, "No, don't. The noise might draw attent—"

Foster pulled the trigger.

Taking the round in the side of the head, Taft's rot infested remains went limp. The bullet exited the opposite end, embedding itself into the wall, spraying it with blood and gray sludge. Taft was no more.

"You were saying?" Foster said.

"Nothing."

Gibbs stood over Gus now, laying out several surgical instruments at her side. Already wearing a paper face mask and surgical gloves, she leaned over the big man, taking a closer look at his wound. "We're going to start by removing the easy ones first. None of the hits were critical. Hopefully, they aren't too deep either."

"How long is this going to take?" Foster asked. "Is there anything we can do to help?"

"I'm going to move a quick as I can and not kill him," Gibbs said.

"I need the two of you to lather up and rinse off. Gloves are in the box next to the sink, and masks are in the cabinet above that. I'm going to clean the entry wounds and then we are going to begin," Gibbs said.

As Foster and Clay stood over the unconscious Gus, they watched as the first of several small incisions cut away at parts of the big man's shoulder. Gus' breathing increased, suggesting that he felt every inch of pain that Gibbs inflicted with her surgical instruments.

6

General Baker leaned back in his leather chair with both legs kicked up on his expensive desk. Baker enjoyed the finer things in life. With a cigar in hand and smoke trailing from his mouth, Baker then brought the fresh glass of scotch to his lips. He had downed several already, and reflected for a moment on memories of the good old days. The pictures on the wall stole him from the present and brought him back in time, away from the undead cannibals threatening to overrun the base.

The two other commanding officers that had joined him lay dead on the floor. Baker drew his pistol and killed them both after they entered his office. He wasn't in the mood to play any more games. The two men didn't even see it coming. The first soldier took a shot to the head right between the eyes, and before he fell to the ground leaving the other officer to react, he too fell to the same fate.

Baker took a deep breath and pulled from his reverie. He rose from his chair and sauntered to the window, the scotch still in hand. "Won't be long now." He'd be safe in the building until tomorrow when a chopper would arrive and take him away.

The bulk of the horde had gotten past the firing line and at this point was just about everywhere on the base. Every man for himself. Soldiers ran in every direction. Zombies were everywhere. Dozens of ghouls poured into the hanger.

Men and women lay helplessly entangled in the massively growing crowd of undead. Baker couldn't hear the violence from the safety and seclusion of his office, but he imagined it. Watched as his soldiers fell victim to agony. He imagined their final pleas for help but didn't let that weaken his command. Orders were orders. Whether everyone died from the undead or from bombs, in the end, the results were the same.

The handset radio on his desk popped with static and then Jesse Watts' voice. The chopper pilot confirmed he had landed the bird on the roof. First Class Lieutenant Rob Foster answered back.

7

"Roger that, over."

"Wrapping things up now. It might be a little slow going getting Gus up to the roof. Be ready to meet us at the staircase when I call. Over."

Foster handed back the radio handset to Clay. He was happy Watts didn't leave without them. "Looks like we're good to go."

Gibbs was wrapping things up, and Gus was actually conscious. Everyone was surprised by this, considering what the man's body had endured. He was definitely in no condition to be walking across the building, let alone up a flight of steps to the roof. Luckily, the bullets hadn't found any major organs or veins as Gibbs had feared from first glance. Still, he had lost enough blood to make him weak. He was pale and his eyes were dark. With roughly thirty fresh stitches, it was nothing less of a miracle that the man was even as alert as he was.

Sitting up now, Gus held one hand to his shoulder and the other to his side. "How… how did I—?"

"Save your strength," Gibbs said and patted his back. "You've been shot, several times. Can you stand?"

Gus tried to inch his way off the table. "Ohhh… I'm not too sure."

"We need to move, Gus. There's no time," Foster said.

"Just give him a minute," Gibbs said.

Gus reached down for his hip, the sidearm missing. "I… I feel like Hell warmed over."

"When we get out of here, you can rest. You'll recover just fine. We almost lost you there," Gibbs smiled turning from the sink. "Here, take these. This should help the pain a bit."

Gus took the pills and shoved them into his mouth. He grimaced as the pills went down dry.

"I need you to try and stand on your feet again," Gibbs said.

Gus reluctantly inched forward sliding slowly from the table to the white tile floor. Legs loose and wobbly, he managed to find his footing.

His shoulder and a portion of his chest were bandaged up hindering mobility. Two small splotches of blood had soaked through the bandages. His lower torso was covered in taped bandages and soaked blood.

Clay stepped up with Gus' shirt in hand, motioning for the brute to lift both arms in the air. It was no easy feat, but he did it nonetheless.

Foster reached for the door. "You guys ready?" No one protested, so he opened the door.

The hallway was clear and quiet. With Foster in the lead, pistol drawn and at the ready, the others followed.

Gibbs led Billy by the hand.

In the rear, Gus staggered along slowly shuffling his feet one after the other. George and Clay were to either side under each arm, supporting as much of Gus' weight as they could. Gus moved slowly and so far had only taken a few steps from the doorway out into the hall.

Foster became aware and kept pace of their slowest soldier.

They pressed forward down the hall toward the corner leading toward the front entrance's doors. The elevator leading to the top floor was near the main entrance.

Foster stopped dead in his tracks next to the bathrooms, not far from their goal "Shh…" he said turning to face everyone with his hand in the air. "Did you hear that?"

Everyone froze.

"What?" Gibbs whispered.

"I thought I heard something," Foster said.

A shadow bounded off of the floor ahead of them. Someone or something was moving up the hall. It edged around the corner.

The zombie crept into view heading straight for Foster and the others. With arms stretched out, the young lab assistant still dressed in his white lab coat and khaki pants shambled into view. He was covered in blood from an open wound on his neck and both outstretched arms. With teeth wide and eyes fogged over in a grayish milky-white mist, the reanimated Stately Christopher inched forward moaning uncontrollably.

The group took Foster's lead backing up a few slow steady steps as it inched closer.

"Shoot him already!" Clay said.

As Foster raised his weapon and sighted the creature for a solid headshot, the door to the bathroom flung open.

Before anyone could react, a short and heavy creature spilled out, falling on Gus and the two men holding him to his feet. Gus fell backward from the unexpected impact. Gus' fall was broken by Clay, who got buried in the mess of bodies at the bottom. The impact happened so quick that it jarred his M-4 free. It bounced along the floor, skidding away from him as he fell on his back, Gus on top of him.

Gibbs yelled, "Benton!"

George screamed as the overpowering weight of the dead man crushed him, pinning him to the floor. George's head slammed against the tile upon impact.

Foster froze for a moment trading glances between the zombie digging its teeth into George's chest and the one blocking their path ahead.

Clay still pinned, struggled under Gus' weight to break free.

Gus was trying to roll on his side, clearly in pain.

Gibbs wrapped her arms around Billy—trying to shield him with her body.

Benton lay on top of George, devouring a large chunk of the man's now open chest. Initially sinking its teeth into shirt and skin, the zombie quickly worked to expose several ribs. Ripping past skin with its germ infested jaw, the reanimated Benton gulped down a meaty chunk of flesh. Blood covered the fat creature's lips and hands as it smacked down on the fresh morsels of red and white blood-soaked meat.

George lay still, a quick growing puddle of blood forming around his body on the floor. The creature reared its head once more pulling up another chunk. George had taken his last breath.

Clay was finally free, jumping to his feet with the M-4 in hand. He squeezed off several rounds into the fat corpse's back as it feasted on George. Holes popped splashing blood and goo over the white coated back. One bullet found the head and blew blood and grey matter against the bathroom door.

Foster sent one single shot from his pistol into the creeping ghoul that stood before him blocking their path. The shot hit dead center between the eyes. The creature fell limp to the floor.

"Fuck, me…" Clay said throwing the rifle around his shoulder and doing what he could to help Gus to his feet.

Gibbs stepped up and tried to help.

Billy's head hung low, gazing at George.

"Billy, don't look. George is gone now. We need to leave. Follow Rob down the hall. I'm helping Gus. Be a little man and lead the way for us," Gibbs said.

Billy pulled back a blank stare and then turned toward the hall, running toward Foster.

Foster inched steadily toward the hallway corner to peek around. "Let's move, it's clear." He turned around the corner, weapon at the ready. This time in a dash, he left the group behind, checking for surprises of any kind. With quiet but brisk steps, Foster opened every door along the way to find each of them empty.

As the others finally rounded the corner, they slowly inched forward eventually meeting Foster at the elevator.

Foster pulled out the radio, and said, "Watts, we're coming up." He pushed a button and the crew found sanctuary inside the elevator. Another push of a button sent them headed to the top.

When the doors opened, Watts was waiting for them, the stairs leading to the roof right behind him.

"Uh... George... I guess he didn't make it," Watts said.

"No, but we still have time. Lead the way. I'm going to help with Gus," Foster said.

"You up for this, big man?" Clay asked as Foster traded places with Gibbs.

Gus simply nodded.

Gus made a steady climb up the steps. Well ahead of them and already at the top, Watts watched as Gibbs and Billy went through first. The light breeze and sound from the winding helicopter propellers outside reverberated down the stairwell.

Gibbs followed Billy toward the chopper. Watts waited for the three to pass through the door onto the roof before he bolted for the chopper.

As Watts put his hand on the chopper's door, a voice called from behind:

"Leaving so soon?" General Baker said, his pistol pointed at Foster. "I trusted you, Lieutenant. How could you have betrayed me with treason?" the General shouted.

Below them, all around the building, chaos was in full swing. Zombies gave chase as soldiers ran, fired, hid, or got eaten alive. The base was overrun.

Foster and Clay maneuvered Gus around to face Baker.

"How could you?" Baker shouted.

Foster momentarily locked gazes with Clay, who was gesturing with closed lips and wide eyes for him to speak the hell up.

From the helicopter entrance, Gibbs had her arms locked around Billy as they looked on in disbelief.

"I see you rescued my detainees, Lieutenant. Now why would you go and do something like that? You do realize that she is the cause of all of this? She let them in. She knew that one of those kids was infected, and she let them roam free on our base unattended. It's because of her, Foster."

Foster looked back at Gibbs.

"That's right," the General continued. "Your precious little girlfriend is a traitor, a spy. Now look at what has happened!" The General motioned with his weapon to the carnage that surrounded them.

From the rooftop, the ground showed a wasteland of disease and festering decay. With the courtyard in plain view from up top, Baker motioned below. Zombies feasted rampantly.

Foster said, "No offense, sir. But, fuck you!"

Clay shook his head, and said, "Well, it looks like my two years are finally up."

Foster continued, "And the higher ups, sir? Are they aware of what you've done here?" He stepped away from Gus, giving a furtive wink to Clay.

Clay stiffened, and slowly moved his left arm supporting Gus toward his rifle.

"Me?" the General said. "I'm just taking orders." He fired the gun.

A single shot rang out. Foster's hand instantly went to his left shoulder.

Clay brought up his rifle and pulled the trigger—nothing happened. In frantic effort, he pulled back on the ejector and sent a bullet casing flying.

Baker turned his gun in Clay's direction and hastily fired while running for the sanctuary of the door leading down from the roof.

"Clay!" Foster shouted while Gus teetered in place.

The soldier dropped to his knees. His rifle fell from his hands. Blood pumped from a hole in his chest.

The General fired from roof's doorway. The bullet whizzed past Foster's ear.

Clay turned his eyes to the heavens for a moment, and then removed a grenade from his belt. "We don't have time for this shit." Still on his knees, he pulled the grenade's pin. His left hand drew back…and then Clay went limp, the grenade bounced twice on the roof and stopped.

Billy's eyes widened and instantly broke free of Gibbs' grasp.

"Billy!" Gibbs screamed and nearly fell face first as she lunged for him only to grab empty air.

The young boy ended his short sprint by dropping to his knees and scooping up the grenade. His arm came back amidst cries of surprised horror. The grenade launched from his small hand and flew directly toward the roof's door. Lying flat, Billy covered his head with his hands.

Baker cursed at the top of his lungs, and then the grenade rocketed past the doorway into the stairwell with him, and went off.

The shockwave knocked Gus to his ass.

Gibbs rushed away from the chopper. "Billy!" she called and ran to his side. "You could have been killed."

Clay was on his back, laboriously breathing.

"Clay…" Foster said, surprised that the soldier was still alive with a bullet hitting so close to Clay's heart.

"That's a nice toss you got there, boy. You'll be a pitcher someday," Clay said slowly and smiled. His smile melted as his teeth gritted together. And in one long, shallow breath, the soldier gave up the ghost and went limp.

"You saved us, Billy," Gus said.

"Heck, I used to play army with my friends after school. We'd through the plastic grenade back at each other all the time," Billy said.

"Rob, help me with Gus!" Gibbs cried out as she grabbed him by the hand.

Foster looked up, somewhat dazed by the situation. He looked at his shoulder and saw the General's bullet had only grazed him. Foster ran to support the big guy as he struggled to stand. With some effort, they managed to get Gus in the chopper.

Once everyone was securely in place, Watts powered up the engines to full.

As the rooftop slowly drifted from the bird, a wave of zombies poured out of the doorway, with outstretched arms and wide mouths, their eyes white and riddled with the cloud of death. But by then, the bird was well out of the reach of their festering, gnarled fingers.

8

The Tallahassee Military Base was no different than any other place within the so-called quarantine zone. It was a wasteland of rot and festering bile. Countless bodies lay tattered and feasted upon. Those not entirely devoured eventually rose to become one with the never-ending horde of lingering undead creatures. With throats torn out, limbs gnawed off, and the putrid filth of decay spread across the base in every building and on every square inch of its grounds, the dead owned the once militarized fortress.

As the helicopter glided across the dark night sky, no one said a word. Their only hope was to make it toward Jacksonville and the Cordyceps Unilateralis Research building.

If what Grech Vonhinkly had said about the clean sweep was true, then the group en route was cutting it close, too close. Sunup was only a few hours away and the trip would leave them landing soon after daybreak.

Foster looked over at Gibbs and rested his hand on her shoulder.

She turned and looked longingly back, placing her hand on top of his.

*

Back on the base hidden away in the Laboratory Research Facility that had *LRF* stenciled in large block letters over its doors lay several bodies. Two of the bodies belonged to the people that had worked on the base as lab assistants. The other belonged to a very dead Mr. Wellington. With the final bit of life drained from his body, the fungus began to take over. Starting from the infected area on the dead man's chest, it quickly spread through the heart and into the blood stream, taking over and quickly devouring any non-vital soft tissues. His body began to rot and rapidly decay as the parasitoid began eating things away from the inside. As it steadily reached the brain, the fungus released its over 48-million-year-old spores rupturing into a rapidly duplicating parasite.

Slowly, his limbs jerked and twitched with reanimated vigor. The once-dead man abruptly opened his lifeless and glazed eyes and began to rise. The hallway was familiar to him. His senses were tingling anew as he stood. As he took his first shambling step forward past the overweight thing that lay next to him, like a distant memory, he reached down with a jerking motion and the lack of coordination. Just as soon as he retrieved the crumpled note in his pants pocket and remembering his son, the thought passed. The thriving hunger for flesh instantly overtook him, pushing out all other thoughts. As his arms lifted in the air, the note fell from his grip. It softly landed in a pool of still-drying blood. The small paper slowly soaked away, fading from Mr. Wellington's thoughts forever.

EPILOGUE

Entry # 352
This will be my final data entry.
I don't see what the point is in all of this anymore. We are stuck like animals in cages, and I've had enough. We can't be the only ones left. I refuse to believe that.
It's time. You knew that this day was coming. I really do hope you don't take it the wrong way. You have been like parents to me. I would be wrong to deny you, any of you as my family. I am thankful for what you have all done.
Someone has to find the truth about what life is like outside this building, and it might as well be me. Don't bother trying to come after me. It would do you no good.
Sincerely,
Billy Woods

And with that, he placed the handwritten note on the center of his desk and stood. Having packed beforehand, he quietly slipped away before anyone awoke. The only sound he made was that of the elevator. It stretched and groaned from over ten years of neglect as the underground Jacksonville facility's elevator doors slid open.

A new day was dawning, and Billy set out to be its master.

THE END

Afterword by P. A. Douglas

This preferred edition of *The End* was a long time coming. Its first publication in 2011 was met with a price. Having originally been written out at nearly 110,000 words, the first release of this book was chopped up and dissected by the publisher in such a way that I felt it was no longer truly considered my work. When it finally went to print, it was a meager 70,000 words, losing a large portion of the story and characters. After several other fiction releases and years of honing the craft as a writer, I decided it was time to give this novel the true justice is deserved as my first official publication. This re-release of The End is the original extended revised version. Dane and I poured a lot into bringing this book back to life, and we hope that you enjoy it as much as we do.
Stay scared,

P. A. Douglas
www.beardcakes.com

 SEVERED**PRESS**

f facebook.com/severedpress

twitter.com/severedpress

CHECK OUT OTHER GREAT ZOMBIE NOVELS

900 MILES
by S. Johnathan Davis

John is a killer, but that wasn't his day job before the Apocalypse.

In a harrowing 900 mile race against time to get to his wife just as the dead begin to rise, John, a business man trapped in New York, soon learns that the zombies are the least of his worries, as he sees first-hand the horror of what man is capable of with no rules, no consequences and death at every turn.

Teaming up with an ex-army pilot named Kyle, they escape New York only to stumble across a man who says that he has the key to a rumored underground stronghold called Avalon..... Will they find safety? Will they make it to Johns wife before it's too late?

Get ready to follow John and Kyle in this fast paced thriller that mixes zombie horror with gladiator style arena action!

WHITE FLAG OF THE DEAD
by Joseph Talluto

Millions died when the Enillo Virus swept the earth. Millions more were lost when the victims of the plague refused to stay dead, instead rising to slaughter and feed on those left alive. For survivors like John Talon and his son Jake, they are faced with a choice: Do they submit to the dead, raising the white flag of surrender? Or do they find the will to fight, to try and hang on to the last shreds or humanity?

CHECK OUT OTHER GREAT ZOMBIE NOVELS

VACCINATION
by Phillip Tomasso

What if the H7N9 vaccination wasn't just a preventative measure against swine flu?

It seemed like the flu came out of nowhere and yet, in no time at all the government manufactured a vaccination. Were lab workers diligent, or could the virus itself have been man-made? Chase McKinney works as a dispatcher at 9-1-1. Taking emergency calls, it becomes immediately obvious that the entire city is infected with the walking dead. His first goal is to reach and save his two children.

Could the walls built by the U.S.A. to keep out illegal aliens, and the fact the Mexican government could not afford to vaccinate their citizens against the flu, make the southern border the only plausible destination for safety?

ZOMBIE, INC
by Chris Dougherty

"WELCOME! To Zombie, Inc. The United Five State Republic's leading manufacturer of zombie defense systems! In business since 2027, Zombie, Inc. puts YOU first. YOUR safety is our MAIN GOAL! Our many home defense options - from Ze Fence® to Ze Popper® to Ze Shed® - fit every need and every budget. Use Scan Code "TELL ME MORE!" for your FREE, in-home*, no obligation consultation! *Schedule your appointment with the confidence that you will NEVER HAVE TO LEAVE YOUR HOME! It isn't safe out there and we know it better than most! Our sales staff is FULLY TRAINED to handle any and all adversarial encounters with the living and the undead". Twenty-five years after the deadly plague, the United Five State Republic's most successful company, Zombie, Inc., is in trouble. Will a simple case of dwindling supply and lessening demand be the end of them or will Zombie, Inc. find a way, however unpalatable, to survive?